THE
CHRONICLES
OF
SOONE
HEIR TO THE KING

By

JAMES SOMERS

Cover design by Jeremy Robinson

BREAKNECK BOOKS
PUBLISHING COMPANY

Published by Breakneck Books (USA)
www.breakneckbooks.com

First printing, November 2006

Printed in the United States of America.

Visit James Somers on the World Wide Web at:
www.jamessomersonline.com

Dedicated to my wife Christy and our children.
You are a constant blessing to me.
And most of all, to my Lord and Savior
Jesus Christ.

PROLOGUE

Date: Year 9015 (Planet Castai III)

SUCH devastation, it was like nothing the young man had ever laid his eyes on before. The entire valley before Mt. Vaseer, for miles and miles, was strewn with body after body of his warrior clan, the Barudii. The ground was a blood soaked horrorscape. Birds of prey launched skyward as he walked through the aftermath.

He had been wandering between bodies for nearly six hours. His boots were red with the blood of his people. All around him, the murderers retreated from the battlefield; the dark skinned Vorn and their vicious brute clones, the Horva. Yet they did not lay a finger to harm him—why would they? After all he was the one that had led them here; had given them the information necessary to make all of this possible. He was a villainous traitor.

"Master Kale?" asked one of the Vorn commanders, "You had better find a transport to take you back to the ship. We'll be departing soon to join the fleet."

He paused in his search. "I will be along very shortly," he said.

The dark skinned man went on about his business, rounding up the Horva for departure; their work here was finished.

Kale searched more frantically now; he had to find him, had to know if all of this was really happening or only a nightmare. Near the front lines, he saw it on the ground. The diadem was pure adomen; a costly durable alloy that bore a luster all its own. The single jewel that should have been mounted in the front was missing.

Very near, was his body; the owner of the crown and king of the Barudii. This was his father; the man whom he had betrayed into the hands of their enemies. His bloodstained expression was strangely peaceful. Kale could not take his eyes off of him. He felt frozen in place, frozen in time. Could this really have been what I wanted, he wondered? Is this my prize, my victory for the humiliation that was brought upon me?

He shut his eyes and turned away from the face, but it was still there, piercing his soul. He considered that somewhere within the city were his mother and his younger brother Tiet. How horribly had they died? His brother had only been in his eighth year; ten years the younger.

He heard the troop transports powering up and readying for take-off as the last of the combatants made their way on board. Several hundred ships to choose from, but none of them contained any friendly faces for him. He was technically on their side; but there is no honor for a traitor among any people.

He began to walk away and thought of looking back to take in one last glimpse of his father, but he couldn't do it. He didn't have to—he had a feeling that face, its expression cast in death, would haunt him for the rest of his days.

Kale boarded one of the transport ships that carried thousands of Vorn and Horva and stood next to a view port. The massacre was less personal from the air. He was the only one who was left of his people; the only survivor and a traitor. He felt like pulling his weapon and stabbing it into his heart, to kill the soul wrenching agony before it could begin its feast, but he didn't have the courage.

He sat on the floor against the wall of the ship's troop compartment among a hundred smelly Horva. His people had been the guardians of Castai's clans. Now they would be ripe for picking by the Vorn.

I

DATE: The Year 9027 (Planet: Castai III)

NOT so long ago, in another creation of God…the sky burned red and so did his emotions. A lone figure watched from his perch as people scurried to their homes on the streets below; curfew was approaching. Military personnel were stationed in threes on every major street corner to help ensure that everyone obeyed.

He watched them, down on the street beneath him; hating them. A security camera's gears whined as it swiveled on its mount next to him looking for miscreants. He was almost in view, but not.

They weren't going to see him tonight. He would be a shadow, a nightmare that strikes and is gone before the senses can capture it. Orin would be angry, of course. He had been before, but now he was older, now he was ready.

The cloning facility was in view above the other rooftop—that place where monsters are bred. The Horva were their footmen; brute forms of men made for the purpose of crushing their enemies. *That's what they used to kill my people.*

It was a good place to start a rebellion—take down their cloning shop and cut off their source of expendable soldiers. The only trouble was he didn't really have a *how* for the plan.

The next rooftop was all the way across the two lane street below. When no one appeared to be looking, he leapt away from the ledge, flipped over end once and landed on the rooftop ledge across the street. Barudii kinesis was a wonderful thing, if you were the good guy. And he wanted to do some good for his fellow Castillians tonight. Maybe they would be ready to rise up to the challenge then.

He could sense the motion of the cameras on the roof and spotted them easily. He waited for them to leave a spot in their visual field for him and then he ran through to the other side of the rooftop.

The cloning facility was there just beyond a large intercity highway—the jump would be too much. Traffic was off of the streets with the onset of curfew; he could run across now. Tiet dropped off of the building, a full two hundred feet to the pavement below—yes, Barudii kinesis was a wonderful thing.

While in the air, Tiet noticed a Vorn soldier was emerging from a side door below. He adjusted his fall slightly and came down right behind the man. His hand cupped the soldier's mouth and with a quick jerk of his arm, the neck snapped. He dropped the enemy to the ground as the body went limp. He left him, hoping to be long gone before anyone discovered the body.

He ran across the empty lanes of traffic to the fence on the other side. He jumped over its barbed wire top without effort, but another layer of fencing stood on the other side. This one was electrified, according to the signs. No bother—he jumped the height of it again. This was almost too easy, he thought.

ON a security panel inside the clone complex, a warning flashed and data begin to pour onto the screen. The night security officer looked the information over. Sometimes small animals would trigger the pressure relays located all over the grounds of the complex; but not this time. The weight given at the trigger point was one hundred and fifty five pounds; way too big for one of the usual nocturnal animals active around this time.

He punched in his security code to activate the silent alarm and brought up some other scanning and video devices on the display. It took a moment, but then he saw him. A man was entering the building through one of the air vents. He brought up a schematic for the complex and zoomed in on that particular air duct. It went through an area of the detention center and then came out near the main laboratory area. *This is almost too easy.*

"IDENTIFY."

"Dr.Ranul K'ore, chief science engineer, sector seven."

"Visual and voice recognition, confirmed," said the robot.

The metal door slid open and Ranul walked past the automaton into the main lab. Since the Vorn had come to Castai twenty years ago, everything had changed. The cities were in ruins and millions from every clan had been slaughtered by the Horva army of the Vorn. Resistance was futile and had caused more deaths at every attempt.

The cruel Vorn had sent the Horva against entire cities of innocents when anyone dared disobey them. The People were desperate for relief of any kind.

Ranul's nineteen-year-old daughter had been imprisoned along with his wife Ellai to pressure him into building war machines for them. If he refused, he might never see them again. He tried to push away the pain, as he turned to continue his work.

The final program sequences had been keyed in and it was time to arm the weapons systems of Ranul's latest sentinel prototype.

As Vorn scientists watched, he finished arming the Sentinel's combat systems and transmitted its hardwired instructions to follow Vorn authority. A few of Ranul's engineering specialists mingled among the Vorn scientists running diagnostic checks on the prototype systems.

It was really a gorgeous machine. It was an android and had been designed with an adomen-coated skeleton for durability under fire. The outer skin was cultured from samples on file and was extremely life-like. Nutrient supply systems were incorporated to keep the tissue alive and banded adomen fibers were specially bundled for use as muscle for the mechanical warrior.

He had modeled the exterior appearance, from skeletal structure all the way to muscle positions and skin features, after a young Barudii he had known long ago. And now as this machine came to pseudo-life, he realized just how much it did look like his old friend Orin Vale.

It was a deadly machine, but now it would only serve Vorn interests. Once they saw its capability they would mass produce them to gain more dominance. *This android is going to be tough to stop,* he thought.

As the robot's CPU began to run through its programming and perform systems diagnostic checks, Ranul looked at the Vorn in the room, all looking very pleased with their new soldier. He wondered for a moment what the consequences of all this would be for his people, and his family. *Ellai, what have I done?*

THE air duct wasn't as roomy as Tiet would have liked, but he could still get through. A constant stream of wind was passing over him making it hard to hear what any voices might be saying from the adjoining rooms along the way.

He came to a vent screen that was made of a particularly heavy meshwork. When he looked inside he could see what appeared to be a holding cell. A small group of adolescents were sitting on the concrete floor inside. The group was comprised of a few younger boys and girls and one older girl about his age. The only facilities in the room were a small dirty sink basin and a toilet with a blanket hanging across as a semblance of privacy.

The front of the cell was barred with heavier meshwork and a half sized door—which meant they had to get on their knees to get out—if they were ever allowed to.

His scabbard scraped the roof of the duct; it was too difficult to try and maneuver in here and get to his blade. Instead he removed a kem-stick from his vest. The hilt was about twelve inches and the dispersion rod was still retracted.

Tiet pressed his face against the vent, looking down on the people in the cell. He tapped lightly with the hilt of his weapon on the floor of the air vent. The older girl looked around then up at him. She was startled when she saw that it was a person behind the vent screen.

"I'm going to get you out," he whispered. "Is it all clear?"

THE girl stared at him with her eyes only, not giving anything away by gesture. The other children in the cell were now looking up at him to see where the voice was coming from. One young boy began to cry out, but the older girl cupped his mouth quickly to prevent alerting the guards.

She gestured only, putting her finger to her mouth to shush them. Then she quietly walked near the front of the cell and looked down the hall beyond—no one was coming. When she had walked back to the other children and gestured to calm them again, she looked up and nodded to him.

Tiet brought the kemstick hilt up in a stabbing fashion and then ejected the dispersion rod. It extended out from the handle a full twenty two inches with a molecular dispersion field enveloping the rod. A bright yellow shaft punched through the metal around the vent.

He grabbed the mesh plate with his fingers and proceeded to cut around it big enough to get the older girl through. The metal popped and sizzled as the field destroyed molecular bonds and carved through the vent wall until he was done.

Tiet laid the cut piece up ahead of the hole and reached his arms down to be able to help them up.

"We can't reach," whispered the older girl.

"Don't worry."

Without warning one of the children began to levitate off of the floor. She thought they might scream, and gestured for them all to remain quiet—that it was alright.

The child sailed up into the hole with Tiet helping them inside. He was pressed against the side wall just enough to allow them to pass and get behind him.

The girl walked to the front of the cell wanting to be sure no guards were coming—no one yet. Behind her, the children each took their turn, seven in all, and rose up through the charred hole with the help of their mysterious rescuer.

"Come on," he whispered.

She walked underneath and was caught by invisible hands that lifted her up to the young man waiting to receive her into the tunnel. Now that she could see him, he had short dark hair like midnight and dark piercing eyes. He was quite handsome and appeared to be close to her age. When he grabbed her hands she gauged his strength. She could feel the calluses and connected them with the worn handle of the sword across his back.

He pulled her inside the air duct and pressed his body back to allow her to pass—she was bigger than the young children—it was a tight squeeze.

"Who are you?" she whispered.

"Tiet Soone; and you?"

"Mirah K'ore. Are you insane? How did you get in here?"

"Don't worry; I'm a Barudii warrior," he said confidently.

She didn't appear impressed. "I didn't think there were any Barudii left anymore." She didn't wait for the reply as she scooted her body on past him.

She's sort of feisty, he thought, but he could see she was pretty beneath the grime of their incarceration.

"What now?"

"Just go back down this shaft and it will lead to the outside. Take the kemstick," he said handing Mirah the weapon. "Run for the fence; this will allow you to cut through and get off of the grounds. Just be quiet and stick to the unlit areas; you should be alright, I didn't see any guards on the way in."

"Then what?"

"If you can get to a home, maybe they'll hide you until you can get back to your families."

"Where are you going?"

"I still have some business to attend to; now get going."

The children began their slithering back along the air duct with Mirah behind them. Tiet went on over the hole and continued through the duct ·ahead.

In a moment a guard appeared in front of the cell. He couldn't believe it; *where had his prisoners gone?!* He grabbed his throat—something unseen was choking him. His eyes bugged as he tried to breathe. A fist tightened in the shadows as a lone figure watched from some distance while the guard struggled and then collapsed, his trachea crushed by an invisible grip.

The man looked up at the charred hole in the ceiling of the detention cell. *Careless; just plain careless and inexperienced.* He sighed and moved on using the shadows for his vehicle. *Those children will need help to get out safely. Just plain reckless.*

Tiet passed some more cells along his way, but they were empty. When he finally reached the end of the shaft, it was capped by a wire grill like the one he had used to enter the building.

Beyond it was a massive room full of all manner of technologies. Clusters of pods hung from great robotic arms mounted to the ceiling. *This must be where they make the clones.*

Only one detail was missing. There were no Horva being made; none at all. In fact the whole chamber was devoid of activity altogether. In the distant part of the great room was a series of large tanks with various chemical names printed on the sides. They were transparent but no chemicals could be seen within.

A control chamber was near the tanks; maybe he could get some useful information from their computers. He pressed his body against the screen and then gave it a good solid push. It gave way and almost fell onto the floor before he could grab it.

No one could be seen moving about in the room. He climbed out and replaced the screen in case someone happened by. He crossed the floor of the huge chamber with caution, looking for camera mounts. There were a few, but he waited and used the large equipment to stay hidden from their field of view.

He had made it about halfway to the control chamber when doors at the four corners of the room opened up and Vorn soldiers rushed in with Horva among them. The clones were fiendish crazed looking men that were purposely mutated in size and strength. Their fingers had sharp claws and their teeth looked like those of a predator. Within those eyes was no fear. They charged at him howling savagely.

Suddenly the lights in the chamber flickered and went out. The emergency lighting immediately kicked in. The soldiers were looking around wondering what was happening, but the Horva had no such concerns; they continued to charge.

Tiet pulled his Barudii blade from the scabbard strapped to his back and ignited the swords dispersion field. Shots began to ring out among the soldiers further away, but they weren't firing at him. He saw another blade ignite as a dark figure swooped in from the ceiling and begin taking down the Vorn guards. *Orin!*

As the Horva lunged for him, Tiet struck the first in front of him then flipped back over another that was attacking from the rear. Two strikes and the latter man fell.

The other soldiers, those who were not engaged with Orin, began to fire at everyone: the Barudii, the Horva and even each other from across the room. It was hard to tell who was fighting who in the dim lighting.

More Horva came at him and were cut down by their own handlers as they panicked—shooting anything that moved. Tiet launched three spi-cor discs and took out as many of the creatures. Orin had already elimi-nated the soldiers on the other side of the chamber and quickly came to Tiet's aid.

One of the brutes lost an arm to the young man's blade but continued his attack with the other arm. It landed a fist to his head knocking him to the ground. Orin had already impaled it before another move could be executed.

Orin helped the boy to his feet again with a smoldering look on his face. Bodies were lying on the floor all around them in the chamber, and an alarm began to sound throughout the building.

"You see? This is why I told you never to come here!"

"I know, but we can't just do nothing."

"Oh yes we can. What do you think you've accomplished here? You've set off alarms, you're probably being video recorded right now and you might have gotten those children killed if I hadn't intercepted them and gotten them off the premises safely. You're reckless Tiet. Just plain reckless."

"It's still better than doing nothing; Father wouldn't want me to do nothing."

"Your father would want you to stay alive…now get out of here, while I buy you some time."

"Wait, Orin—haven't you noticed there aren't any Horva being pro-duced here?"

"So?"

"So, those tanks over there; they shouldn't be bone dry, not if they're still in use."

Orin looked around to see what he was referring to.

"Maybe they can't make them right now. This might be our chance to rally the people and drive the Vorn out."

The boy was right about the clones at least; it looked like there hadn't been any clone production for some time. Orin looked back at the boy as the alarm continued to scream overhead.

"Please, Orin. We have to at least try."

He didn't want to get involved in this; not again. But if it was true that their forces weren't being sustained here then maybe it was the same in other cities as well. And he remembered well that Tiet's father, Kale, would not have done nothing.

He grumbled under his breath, "Come on, I know someone who might be able to help us."

II

RANUL awoke to the annoying sound of his computer trying to tell him of an incoming priority message. He sat up groggily in his bed as the display flashed in his eyes. He noticed the time was now three hours past nightfall.

"Ranul, K'ore," he said to the computer.

"Identified."

The visual message flashed onto the screen instantly. It was Governor Kisch K'ta a handsome man of the Vorn clan who ruled Castai in its occupation. The Vorn were a dark skinned clan, while almost all of the Castillian clans were light skinned. This difference among the human clans had been a factor in the outbreak of war. Still, he had remained formally pleasant with Ranul as long as he obeyed his demands.

"Ranul, I want the prototype sentinel you've completed to report to the cloning facility at once," said the governor.

"Governor, has something happened that…"

"That is none of your concern," he interrupted. "Have the android report to my office immediately."

The transmission link was cut before Ranul was allowed to inquire any further. But he knew that something must have happened to put the sentinel android into action now. Still, there was no choice but to comply. He knew all too well the consequences of disobedience.

He threw on his clothes without formality and made his way down the corridor. He identified himself with the sentinel guard to gain access into the main lab. As the lights flicked on, he stepped to the dock and addressed the prototype robot by the code name he had imprinted on its memory.

"Vale."

"Yes Dr. K'ore," responded the android politely.

"Governor Kisch k'ta, demands your presence at the Vorn cloning facility. Please report immediately to his office there."

"Yes Dr. K'ore," said the robot, "Accessing coordinates now."

Without further inquiry, the android removed itself from the upload dock and proceeded out of the lab. Ranul admired his work, but took no pleasure at the thought of such a weapon in the hands of the Vorn. The android moved fluidly, even gracefully—like the warrior it was designed to resemble. It seemed almost as though one of the long dead Barudii warriors was alive again, but this one's mission had nothing to do with protecting Castai.

Ranul's stomach growled with hunger. *Might as well have something to eat since I'm up anyway.* When he exited the lab, the android was already gone; only the lone sentinel guard stood there. Ranul walked back to his onsite quarters with swirling thoughts of late night snacks and curious Vorn orders fetching his new creation in the middle of the night.

The automatic door opened and shut behind him as he made his way to the food compartment. He jumped as hands wrapped around his upper arm and mouth.

"Don't scream," whispered a male voice in his ear. "It's Orin, your old friend. Remember?"

Ranul was still pale with lingering fright as Orin released him and they faced each other.

"Orin? But I thought...I thought you were all killed by the Horva years ago."

"Not exactly."

Down the hall, the sentinel guard came to life as its auditory sensors caught trigger phrases from Ranul's domicile.

The door chimed as it suddenly began to open. Beyond was a sentinel guard with his weapon raised into the room. As the door cleared the robot's body, an ignited Barudii blade shot out of the shadows toward the guard. The figure wielding it was a blur of motion and shadow as he quickly dissected the robot's weapon hand and plunged the glistening blade through its torso. The sentinel's appendages went limp as the blade turned its primary circuits and power grid to molten metal.

"We should be going now," said Tiet as he replaced his blade to its sheath.

"Your young friend is right," said Ranul, "The sentinels share a collective mind. What one knows, they all know. They're no doubt sending more units to this location right now."

"I need to know about the clones, why aren't they still in production?"

"They can't produce them right now, at least not until the fleet arrives; they'll be bringing them more supplies, equipment and clones along with more chemical matrix to produce them."

"Is it this way everywhere?"

"As far as I know; but the fleet is due to arrive in a matter of days."

"You had better come with us."

"Did you really think I would stay here now? Let's go!" said Ranul as he gathered some essential gadgets.

Tiet led the way out of the room into the corridor. Another sentinel rounded the corner and fired. Tiet's body sprang upward reflexively, pressing flat against the ten foot ceiling, and clearing the path of the shots.

Orin stepped into the corridor with his ignited blade, drawing the sentinel's fire as Tiet sprang away from the ceiling toward the robot. When he planted his feet on the ground again, so did the severed upper half of the sentinel. They wasted no time heading up a nearby ventilation shaft, and soon they were emerging on the roof of the lab complex.

"Now where do we go?" asked Ranul.

"This will buy us a little time. Tiet, what do you see?"

"I see a small transport, down here off the west side. It looks empty!"

Orin and Ranul joined him on the western wall of the building.

"I can't make that jump, Orin," said Ranul, "It must be at least fifty feet."

"Just hold on!" said Orin as he grabbed his friend and jumped over the ledge. Tiet followed them down as they used their kinetic power to soft land next to the transport. Orin mentally released the cockpit lock; gaining them quick access to the vehicle. Tiet jumped behind the flight controls, and closing the sliding canopy behind them, they sped off into the night.

Ranul could see patrol ships and a sentinel carrier all descending from different directions on the lab complex behind them. The craft was a low altitude transport speeder; quick, but with no armoring or weapons. Still, it was adequate to get them out of the city and into the open terrain beyond.

"Where to now?" asked Tiet.

"I'm not sure yet," said Orin, "but we've got to stop those reinforcements from arriving!"

"Tell your young friend to take us to Vaseer."

"But that city has been deserted for years!"

"Not necessarily."

THE recordings flashed on several screens before Governor Kisch k'ta as his advisors briefed him on the unfolding events. Setaru' lek spoke in the language of the Vorn concerning a mysterious rebel on the loose.

"And here Governor, see the footage from the cloning room? His weapon—"

"Is that of the Barudii warriors; yes I remember," interrupted Kisch k'ta. "But we wiped them out years ago; I led the attack that day. We swept the cities and the battlefield for survivors and there were no life signatures detected. Besides all that, this one is too young to have been in that battle."

"With all due respect, we are not prepared for an uprising. Our supplies are exhausted and we can't produce anymore clones. If this person is fighting back, then he might try to gain support from the people; we could have a rebellion on our hands."

"I am aware of our situation here," said Kisch k'ta. "However, attempting to get the fleet fully prepared and through the rift any sooner than scheduled is impossible; we haven't even been able to reestablish contact yet."

The door to the Governor's office chimed. Kisch k'ta touched the panel on his desk allowing the door to slide open. There in the doorway stood the image of a Barudii warrior.

"Come in, android."

The mechanical warrior moved gracefully into the room.

"I want you to scan all the data we have on this matter, android. And I want you to destroy this person and anyone who may be involved in his rebellion. Nothing must interfere with the arrival of the fleet. Is that clear?"

"Completely, Governor."

He moved to the control panel and quickly tapped the panel to play all the recorded data that was being viewed by Governor Kisch k'ta. The images simultaneously played in high speed as the Vale android scanned it all into memory. After only a moment he was done.

"Data acquisition complete, Governor Kisch k'ta."

"Then do not fail."

"Understood," said Vale, and he was gone.

"Governor, do you think this machine can defeat the Barudii?" asked one of his aides.

"I don't know. If he can only delay a rebellion, then it will be enough."

VALE made his way to the hangar bay of the complex, where a transport was already waiting. He acquired the code key from one of the attendants and slipped into the single occupant cockpit. The model was small and fast. In a moment Vale had scanned all the control systems to memory and fired the engine for departure.

In his android mind all related files to the human rebel and the attacks that had taken place were being correlated. Recently updated reports were coming in and Dr. K'ore was apparently now involved. And according to Governor Kisch k'ta he qualified as a viable target; yet his transport was not missing. A related item concerning a stolen transport belonging to a Vorn scientist seemed to be the closest correlation.

Vale fired the thrusters and proceeded to the west side of the complex where the transport had been reported to have been docked when it was taken. He arrived at the site in a moment and climbed out of his ship to scan the area for any trace evidence.

The transport was reported as a Castillian model which left a distinctly different exhaust signature from that of the Vorn ships. Vale adjusted his micro-optics appropriately and a particle trail appeared.

He got back to his ship and then proceeded to follow the particle trail his optics were picking up. The trail went through the city and appeared to head into the wasteland area beyond. All he had to do was to follow the trail and surprise his prey.

Vale powered up the engine to maximum and continued out into the wasteland. His mind was a blur of calculations as it read maps and plotted speed and distance to possible destinations where the targets may have sought refuge, while simultaneously reviewing files on the Barudii warriors; their tactics and weaknesses.

DURING the years they had been in hiding, Orin had never taken Tiet into the Barudii city of Vaseer. It was still littered with old bones—the bones of his people.

The trio left the transport behind two hours before so they could make there way along the treacherous mountain pass to one of Vaseer's side gates. The gates were well hidden by the rough terrain and were only accessible on foot.

Most of the clans had built their cities underground because of the severe weather that resulted from the transdimensional rift being in such close proximity to the planet. But the Barudii had enjoyed the added advantage of building within mountains.

The pathway was fairly wide and much of the carvings and hewn out walls still remained intact. As they drew closer to the city gate Tiet examined the ornate stonework by the light of Castai's moon. His people had always preferred to dwell in the strongholds they had carved out of the mountains. It protected them from the severe weather that plagued many of Castai's regions. Some said it was related to the proximity of the transdimensional rift to the planet. The mountain cities were also difficult for their enemies to attack and many tunnels and hidden paths provided ample means of escape when it became necessary.

A rich culture he could barely remember lay before him. His mind began to wonder with excitement at what the city must have been like when his clan was prosperous and respected. He was curious and amazed, yet sorrowful at his own loss and the senseless slaughter of his people.

Eventually they reached the gate. It was massive in size; two metal gates coming together and interlocking. Apparently an automated mechanism had opened and closed it, but no power appeared to be available now.

Orin ignited his blade and sliced through the interlocking mechanism to allow the gates to swing freely. He and Tiet attempted to move them manually, but to no avail. "Those hinges up there appear to be completely frozen," said Ranul.

"Tiet, you take one side and I'll pull the other," instructed Orin.

Both men stepped back enough to give the gate room to open, and then each concentrated on a respective gate mentally. Slowly they began to creak and moan as the rust and metal popped and gave way to the kinetic forces being exerted upon the hinges. The gates swung wide and stopped when the two Barudii released them. The ornate archway led to total darkness beyond. "Ranul, are you sure somebody is living here now?" asked Orin.

"Yes. I imagine they must stay in the lower levels just in case the Vorn ever patrol way out here. Here, take this torch."

Orin removed the old gas torch from the side of the archway entrance and depressed the fuel trigger. It ignited immediately.

"Appears to have been in recent use," said Tiet.

Orin led the way inside the mountain. The torch gave minimal light but was at least enough to see the path. Almost immediately the path began a downward descent into the mountain. It was wide enough and tall enough to allow many people access at once, and Tiet wondered what it must have been like to live in such a place as this. The men proceeded quietly and cautiously, with Ranul's footsteps making more noise than the other two men combined.

With a quick flash of metal, Orin's torch was decapitated and knocked from his hand. The gas burner still cast a dim light from the ground where it landed and shadows began to move about the walls. Orin and Tiet reflexively drew their blades and moved close to guard defenseless Ranul from attack. Several dark figures moved in from the shadows and slashed at the trio with blades. Tiet and Orin countered each strike while trying to keep their backs to Ranul, enclosing him.

"We're not your enemies!" shouted Ranul over the noisy clanging of swords. "These men are Barudii warriors!"

The two figures attacking Orin backed away, but remained ready to attack. Meanwhile Tiet and one of his opponents were still exchanging blows at rapid fire pace, and seemed oblivious to the sudden cease of battle. Tiet's opponent suddenly flipped over his head. He reflexively used a leg sweep, catching the attacker as he landed.

As the figure fell back he caught himself by the hands and rebounded back to his feet and struck at Tiet again; catching him a little off guard by the recovery. Tiet rotated in with a shoulder level wide swing of his blade to knock his opponent's blade away as he followed through with a powerful backhand to the face. The darkly clothed figure reeled back from the blow as Tiet took advantage and quickly pinned his opponent's neck against the wall under his blade.

"Surrender! Don't make me kill you!"

"Don't make me kill you," answered a softer voice from beneath the mask.

Tiet looked down to find that his opponent held a sizable dagger to his belly. *Well this is embarrassing.*

"Who are you?" he mumbled as he reached up and slowly lifted the mask to reveal a Castillian woman with fiery eyes glaring at him. He quickly lifted his blade and backed away. *A woman!*

Orin caught the surprise on his face.

"Hmm. She nearly killed you Tiet," said Orin without letting his amusement be too obvious. Tiet glanced back at the girl as she replaced her dagger confidently.

"We thought the Barudii were all dead," said one of the masked attackers.

"Not quite," replied Orin. "Is there someone leading your people?"

"Yes. Estall is our leader. We'll take you to him."

Orin and Ranul followed the men as they lit another nearby torch from the wall and proceeded down the path. Tiet looked at his opponent again; who was still fixed intently on him. He sheathed his blade and followed the others as the girl fell in the line behind him. *How could this girl fight so well? She's not a Barudii, but she carries a Barudii blade and knows how to use it. Better keep and eye on her.*

THE ion trail was growing stronger as Vale approached the mountains. At the present concentration, his mind calculated that his target must be very close now. In the distance his optics picked up an object near the base of the mountain.

His eyes focused and enhanced the image. It was a small transport craft and the ion trail led right to it. If they had abandoned the craft, then logically they were proceeding on foot into the mountains.

Relevant sites in this region displayed in his mechanical mind's eye. The only prominent one was the old Barudii city of Vaseer. It was an obvious match, correlating with the present circumstances and nature of his target.

As he approached, Vale slowed the transport and shut it down next to the other ship. It appeared abandoned. He exited his own transport and moved to the engine compartment of the other ship. He tore away the compartment lid and grabbed the fuel cell housing, ripping it from its place among the other operational components and hurled it yards away. If his prey did return, their vessel would not be an escape route for them.

He returned to the cockpit of his own ship and encoded the ignition sequence to prevent anyone stealing it, then stepped up to the rear pulse turret. The android grasped the pulse repeater cannon, pulled it free from its mount, then jumped back to the ground with it. The large cannon was nearly half his size and weighed four hundred pounds; yet he carted it away with ease.

Accessing various, known entrances and exits to Vaseer, Vale located the closest and bounded away after his prey with his pulse cannon in tow. It was approaching dawn and he planned to be inside the city before he lost the element of surprise over his targets.

AS the group came to the lowest level of Vaseer, The light suddenly greeted them with the splendor of the old city. Orin was overwhelmed by a flood of memories at the sight of it again. He remembered all of the times he had spent here with Kale Soone and the grand banquets and tournaments that had been held in Vaseer's great halls; it was still glorious to behold.

Tiet found himself overwhelmed by the sight of the city. All of the carvings and gems and precious metals that decorated the walls and structure, spoke of royalty and power. It was so distant a memory; some time around his eighth year the massacre had stripped him of his family and his people.. It was in this place also, that his mother had been murdered by the Horva; those horrible brutish clones of the Vorn——they feared nothing. This was the place of his dreams and nightmares.

They followed their guides down through a large open area that acted as the town square and on through large columns hewn out of the rock into a smaller chamber. All around them people were milling about and looking on curiously. Orin noticed that almost all of them were wearing the clothing of the Barudii that had been left in the city after the massacre. It was an eerie sight to him—like his people raised from the dead.

The irrigation canals were still functioning and he could see fresh water coming in from one of the underground mountain streams. Evidently the gardens must still be in production to keep what appeared to be hundreds of people alive down here. As they came into the adjacent chamber several men were convened in a meeting. One dressed as though he may be the leader came toward them.

"Gentlemen, welcome to Vaseer. My name is Estall," said the man.

How strange to be welcomed to his former home by this man who had taken possession of it only because of the absence of his people. "I'm Orin Vale, this is Dr. Ranul K'ore and this young man is Tiet Soone."

"Ah, then you must be the son of Kale Soone the Barudii King," said Estall.

"Yes. How did you know that?"

"Both of you Barudii are written of in the city's archives. We have studied your history and trained our people in your fighting art for some years now," said Estall. "We came to the city nearly eight years ago to escape the Horva. After the Barudii were wiped out the Vorn staged a massive takeover against the remaining clans. They released the Horva upon our people and killed millions. Some still remain in what was left of our clan cities. We chose to flee. At first we went into the wilderness not knowing where to go. Then some of the elders among our groups suggested that we take refuge in one of the abandoned Barudii cities, since no activity really took place in this region anymore. Once we arrived, we realized how well the city was fortified and with the ample supply of fresh water and the irrigated gardens, we knew it was the right place to stay."

"Have the Vorn not patrolled here in all that time?" asked Orin.

"At first we feared they might eventually make their way back out this far. Many people began to research the Barudii archives and we discovered the warrior art. Our people began to train according to your ways. The weaponry was still functional and in good supply, and even without the special abilities of the Barudii, I think we've learned a great deal of the techniques," said Estall.

"Of that I'm quite sure," said Orin, "This young woman and Tiet nearly killed each other. I was quite impressed with the skill of your people."

Tiet looked again at the girl, only to find her gaze fixed on him. He looked away quickly, then back trying to appear as though he were surveying the room beyond.

"Dorian is my younger sister," said Estall. "She is only in her eighteenth year, but she has been an eager student of your ways. She has instructed many of our people."

Impressive! Each time he glanced at her, he noticed she was fixed unwavering upon him. He felt childish for his unwillingness to meet her stare.

"I guess you've been very eager yourself to be leading this people when you are still fairly young yourself," said Orin.

"He is young, but he has proven his courage and his wisdom to our people," said one of the elder men standing near.

They were talking, but Tiet wasn't listening anymore. He decided not to be a coward about it. He lifted his eyes to fix on Dorian. She was still standing behind the right side of her brother Estall with a straight faced stare on him. He returned it without expression. She smiled slightly, he noticed—he had definitely seen it. She broke away from the group and walked past him, back toward the public area they had come through. He suddenly realized he may have been smiling himself and pursed his lips to disguise it. Better to pay attention to what's important right now.

"If you don't mind my asking," said Estall, "the archives contained nothing concerning the last battle of your people. What happened?"

"Something we just weren't expecting," said Orin. "The Vorn were assembling a massive ground force and we were prepared to meet them. What we didn't realize was that they had developed some new technology. They just walked right out of the walls, like some portal in mid-air. There were thousands of Horva clones pouring into the mountain cities while we had our warriors on the surface preparing for the ground attack. Our king, Kale Soone, had chosen me to guard his wife and son. We tried to fight, but it was only women and children besides me. The enemy got to his mother, but I managed to take Tiet and flee the city with him. I later investigated the scene and from what I could tell, the Horva in our cities came at our warriors from behind as they fought on the surface."

Everyone was silent for a moment. It was a tragedy that had cost all of Castai's clans their freedom.

"It may be time to act though," said Orin. "We've just discovered that their main cloning facility is no longer producing Horva."

"That would explain what our spies have been reporting," said Estall.

"I don't understand."

"We have spies that go into the cities on a regular basis. They have reported seeing hardly any Horva at all. The Vorn have taken to patrolling without them."

"It won't remain that way for long," said Ranul.

"Have you heard something specific?"

"I work in weapons development," said Ranul. "There has been a lot of talk about a fleet that is coming through the transdimensional rift some time very soon. They're supposed to be establishing actual Vorn colonies on Castai."

"It doesn't sound like we have much time to act," said Estall.

"We have to find a way to stop that fleet from coming through the rift," said Orin. "If your people could attack the main Vorn complex directly, then perhaps we could seize a ship from the main hangar, and take it through the rift to intercept their reinforcements."

"But we have a ship here," said one of the men with Estall.

"What kind of ship?" asked Ranul. "Is it Barudii? Is it operational?"

"Yes, at least most of the systems work," said the man. "We've never fully ignited the engines; there hasn't been a need."

"We had hoped that it would provide a last stand defense or escape if the Vorn discovered us," said Estall.

"They're going to discover you eventually," said Tiet.

"Estall, it's now or never," said Orin. "Your people are trained and the Vorn here are at their weakest moment, but the opportunity is about to pass to finish this war and free our people."

Estall considered a moment, looking at the other men with him. "Please allow me a few moments to speak with the elders."

"If it's alright, we should take a look at the ship," said Ranul.

"Of course. Millo will show you where it's docked."

Millo, one of the men with Estall, motioned them to follow as he led the way down another corridor out of the chamber. Orin and Ranul fell in behind his lead.

"I'm going to locate some more weapons and meet you down there, okay?" asked Tiet.

Orin looked toward the public square at someone beyond, and then back at Tiet. "Alright, but don't linger, we still have work to do."

Tiet turned and headed back toward the public area only to find Dorian standing near the central fountain. When their eyes met again they were both smiling noticeably at one another. He walked over to the fountain, not exactly sure what to say next.

"I couldn't help but overhear that you need more weapons," said Dorian.

She either had excellent hearing or had been closer to the chamber entrance when he said it. "Well yes, as a matter of fact, I could use some help."

"I'll show you the way to the armory."

"Thank you."

The words seemed so difficult to get out and he wasn't sure why. After all Dorian was only a girl. They made their way down a passageway to yet another chamber. Dorian keyed in a code on the wall pad and the mechanical door slid aside into the rock wall allowing them access into one of the Barudii weapon stores. What a sight, he thought as he surveyed all the various weapons of his former people.

The walls of the long chamber were lined with blades and kemsticks on one side, and racks of pulse rifles and pistols like his own taking up space down the middle of the room. On the opposite side along the wall were combat uniforms of the Barudii with insignia for the clan upon them. They were fresh-looking in comparison with his admittedly somewhat shabby gear. He walked through the rows looking over the various items and paused at the dark colored uniforms. They were the same that Dorian wore and the others that had met them in the entrance to the city.

"If you are going into battle, you should wear the uniform of your people." She looked him over a moment then retrieved one of the uniforms from the wall.

"Here, I think this one should fit well."

"Thanks."

He could hardly wait to put it on.

"Around that partition is an area where you can change," said Dorian.

Tiet smiled like a child with a new toy as he made his way around the wall and began to change into his new Barudii uniform. *She's quite nice after all.*

"Dorian?"

"Yes?"

"I'm …I'm sorry about hitting you in the passage way."

"It's alright. I understand; after all—I was attacking you."

"Yes, but for all you knew, the Vorn were coming in to harm your people. Anyway I would not have done it if I had known…."

"Known what? That I was a woman?"

"No…I mean if I had known you were so nice."

Dorian smiled again knowing he couldn't see her.

"Well, what do you think?" he said as he emerged from behind the partition.

"Just as I imagined."

"What do you mean…imagined?"

"Nothing. Just a statement." Changing the subject, she reached for one of the gadgets on a nearby shelf. "You should take one of these," she said handing him the object. "It's an electromagnetic shield generator." She raised her forearm to reveal the same apparatus fixed upon her uniform.

"When a stimulus such as weapon fire or an ignited blade comes within proximity to the field, it generates the polarity of the energy source reacting with that of the field and causes the deflector to respond. It's actually two fields separated by a magnetic field. Each field is polarized; one negatively and one positively."

"Wonderful, I'll take two," he said, still smiling at his hostess.

"Well, let's get you fully equipped and we'll load up this cart and take it down to the ship."

"Do you think your people will be willing to attack the Vorn?"

"Personally, I think it's time we took the fight to them, and others feel the same way."

Tiet nodded and they began loading weapons for the ship. When they had what they needed, Tiet pushed the cart back out of the chamber and up the passage they had come by, with Dorian at his side.

"We had better hurry before Orin rushes off without me."

"I wouldn't mind."

The comment pulled a quiet smile from his face again. He couldn't remember smiling so much. He couldn't remember having a reason to.

III

FROM his perch high above the public square, Vale scanned the identifying features of Castillian faces as the people congregated and moved through the area. He had still not located the target. It was unclear who these humans were, but their presence here and apparent aid to the Governor's target made them accomplices and therefore expendable under the Governor's guidelines. However, firing upon them would be tactically unsound, as it would alert his targets to his presence.

The carved stone balcony he was crouched upon had been easy to access once he came down to this level, and provided a superior targeting position from which to shoot. Person after person, feature after feature was scanned and rejected as negative matches. *But wait*, now one was continuing to match as the features blinked into place like a puzzle. A match, but the garment had been changed from that in the data clips. It was time to act.

The android hoisted the repeating pulse cannon up to clear the stone terrace and quickly shifted in to the best targeting approximation possible with such a cumbersome weapon. Fortunately, its dispersal pattern was complimentary to the inability to precisely aim the weapon. He tapped the arming switch, causing the weapon to hum to life.

"Look out!" someone yelled.

Many in the square turned to the direction one woman was pointing. Tiet also looked to see a familiar looking man clothed as the Barudii, with a large weapon aiming into the public area.

A wave of pulse fire showered down around them as Tiet turned to shield Dorian from harm. He caught her around the torso and pushed her toward the ground. Her electromagnetic shield pulsed to life several times as it intercepted negatively charged pulse blasts meant to take their lives. Rock sprayed away from the walls around them. As soon as Dorian was down, he leapt up and away from her. If he was the target then he wanted to draw the fire away from her. The trail of pulse fire followed as he evaded; leaping and twirling from object to ground to wall and away again.

Then the cannon fire paused a moment as others attempted to engage the culprit. Tiet paused to see the Aolene warriors firing pulse blaster pistols at the balcony and hurling spicor discs toward the assailant. The android dodged the discs as they exploded on the walls nearby, leaving behind smooth cavities of the rock. Vale took several blasts to the torso and the arms as he repositioned the pulse cannon and began to spray the Aolene combatants. Tiet took the brief respite to study their attacker:

How is he still standing?

Tiet saw the opportunity and quickly shattered what remained of the embattled stone balcony with a concentrated kinetic blast. The heavy stone erupted upward against Vale, catching his mechanical body between the large fragments and the chamber ceiling, and then dropping all down to the public square below in a dusty heap.

The android came down like a discarded rag-doll onto the pavement below. Orin appeared with Estall on the other side of the public area. Everyone was regrouping, but no one understood what had just happened.

"Tiet!" cried Dorian from behind. But she was looking past him toward the heap of rubble. As he turned, Tiet could hear the sound of large rocks being tumbled. From beneath the heap of stones, an Orin Vale look alike was emerging. Orin saw it as well, but couldn't believe who he was seeing. Himself? A clone? Whatever this new monster was, it was far too powerful to be human.

Vale regained a standing position and quickly reassessed the situation. *Target acquired*, blinked across his data processor display. Tiet drew his father's blade and ignited it as he ran toward the mysterious aggressor. Vale also pulled a Barudii blade and the two engaged in fierce combat.

HE'S so fast, Tiet thought as he tried to enhance his own speed with his psycho kinesis. Vale blocked a thrust from Tiet and quickly pushed his blade away, as he sent a deadly mechanical hand toward Tiet's chest; but the young human was a step ahead having drawn a pistol with his free hand to take advantage of Vale's exposure. He quickly thrust the pulse weapon into the android's face and fired without hesitation. Vale tried to correct his movement and counter the pistol as it came into position, but was not quite fast enough. The blast caught him in the side of the head and sent him reeling backward.

After seeing this person climb out of the rocky grave he had created for him, Tiet wasted no time, and followed through with his ignited blade. Vale, having only a fraction of a second to recover from the pulse shot, countered the blade strike and whirled around Tiet, using the human as a fulcrum to get behind him. He smashed him in the back with an adomen packed elbow that knocked the young man to the ground gasping for breath. The android quickly brought his sword to bear on the target to deliver the deathblow.

Dorian intercepted, attacking the android to draw his blade away from Tiet. Several fast strikes were countered by the mechanical as she furiously tried to defend her friend. Vale's blast-exposed cranium glistened in the available light as he parried blow after blow from the young woman.

Suddenly Vale was off the ground and flying backwards away from his opponents. He slammed into a wall as Orin released the android from his kinetic grip. Orin was at Tiet's side in a moment lifting him up. He'd been dealt a hard blow and needed assistance to stand.

The Aolene were taking the initiative with the robot in the clear— firing pulse blasters at him. Vale retreated down a passageway to minimize damage and try to re-engage his target.

"We have to go now and take the ship into the rift!" shouted Orin. "The Vorn obviously know we're here. There's no telling how many other androids have been sent to stop us."

"My people will take the transports we have and engage the main complex as you suggested," shouted Estall over the background noise.

Some of the Aolene had pursued the android but no word had come back yet concerning his whereabouts. Estall gathered with his key warriors and noticed that Dorian was not among them. He turned to see her at Tiet's side helping support they young man as the trio headed down the passage leading to the hangar. He started to call out to her, and then thought better of it—He knew what few did about his younger sibling; she had long been infatuated with the young prince on the archive video files. "Farewell, Sister," he whispered as she and the Barudii disappeared down the corridor.

Vale watched from a hidden position as his primary target disappeared down a passageway. He squeezed his hand until bone cracked beneath his fingers. This human had been foolish to follow him into the corridors when he retreated. Vale released the Aolene warrior's neck from his grip, letting the lifeless body crumple to the ground.

His auditory sensors had picked up on their destination and their plan to leave in a ship from the hangar bay. It was imperative that he acquire his target before it escaped. The direct way would only draw more resistance from all of the Aolene preparing for battle below. His database lacked schematics of the city's interior, but data on the mountain of Vaseer was available. There was only one place to launch a ship from the mountain and Vale calculated that he wasn't far from it. He hurriedly retraced his path out of the mountain and headed across the slope toward the lower western face. The terrain didn't slow him at all. He just had to cover the half mile distance in time to intercept the Barudii warrior before he escaped.

THERE was a warm breeze funneling through the passageway as Orin, Tiet and Dorian approached the hangar bay. They could hear the low hum of large engines, apparently in a warm up cycle. Tiet was walking on his own now.

As the trio came through the entrance to the hangar, Tiet got his first look at a Barudii space vessel. The ship was very large and filled a huge space in the hangar bay. There was nobody visible in the area outside and the gateway was lowered to the ground under it. The trio hurriedly made their way up the platform into the belly of the ship. Once inside, the ship had several levels accessible by various sets of stairs. Dorian and Tiet followed Orin up to the bridge level where Ranul and the Aolene warrior Millo were busy at various control panels prepping the ship for lift off.

"What happened up there?" asked Ranul. "We heard gunfire."

"Apparently the Vorn have built an android that somehow looks like me. It appeared in the public area and I think it was trying to kill Tiet specifically."

"So that's what they wanted with it," said Ranul to himself.

"What do you mean? Did you know about this thing?" asked Tiet.

"Yes, yes. I built it."

"What?!"

"I thought I could mass produce an android army to combat the Vorn. The Barudii were all presumed dead and our people were slaves to the Vorn. We needed a way to fight back, but the Vorn seized the plans. They took my wife Ellai and my daughter Mirah and imprisoned them. I had to build it or risk their lives. Orin said you found Mirah imprisoned with some younger children and released her; and for that I thank you young man. It was completed just days ago and the Governor had it sent out to the cloning facility just before you arrived at my compartment. They must have sent it out to track you down after you killed those Vorn in the cloning complex. I didn't think you would be facing off against it, or even that you were still alive."

"Well, it's flattering—I suppose," said Orin. "Now tell us how to stop it."

"The best thing would be for me to try and stop it," said Ranul. "It might not harm me. This thing was built to last. However the main control system is in the head and duplicated in the chest. If you can get a direct strike at those two points with an ignited blade you'll bring it down for sure.

It's extremely tough and strong, but it can't fly and the weapons are external to the unit; meaning it uses weapons just like a Barudii would. I had many data files concerning the warrior art to program with, but you still possess a key advantage in your kinetic abilities."

"The Aolene put so much fire on it that it retreated into the passages somewhere."

"It may have retreated, but its programming will require it to acquire its target. It will have to try again. We need to get you into space; then it won't have a target to chase."

"How soon can we lift off?" asked Dorian.

Tiet raised an eyebrow at her question. Was she now coming along? Secretly, he hoped that she would.

"The ship is ready and Millo has volunteered to help you pilot the vessel through the rift."

"Aren't you coming, Ranul?" asked Tiet.

"No Tiet, I'm not. My daughter needs me. I'm going to go with Estall and the Aolene to attack the remaining Vorn forces in the Capital. Perhaps when they're defeated, I will be able to get information on my wife's whereabouts."

"We're ready to go," said Millo looking up from his flight console.

"Tiet. Dorian. You two strap in over there for lift off," Orin said pointing to a small group of chairs with flight harnesses. Orin walked Ranul down to the lowered ramp as he disembarked from the ship to join Estall and the Aolene warriors.

"Goodbye, old friend," said Orin.

"Goodbye. I hope you make it back safely. Remember what we talked about. If you can't stop the Vorn fleet, the only other way to prevent them crossing will be to disrupt the rift. The engine destruct sequence has already been keyed into the ship."

"I remember the final command code you gave me."

"Don't forget that you have only five minutes to separate the bridge section from the rest of the ship before detonation."

"I won't forget, Ranul."

Ranul exited the ship and Orin pressed the panel switch to raise the platform. As he came back to the bridge section he strapped in for the journey at one of the helm control panels next to Millo. "Let's go."

The engines of the Barudii vessel powered up to begin raising the ship off of the landing platform. Orin keyed in commands to signal the mountain side hangar bay doors to retract and allow the vessel to exit. The large doors awoke as the command was relayed to the cities technological control systems. Each side was beginning to retract back into the rocky side walls of the hangar area as the old warship hovered above the ground in preparation to exit the mountain city.

RANUL could hear the rising pitch of the old *Saberhawk* class vessel as he quickly made his way through the corridors back to where Estall and his warriors were preparing to launch the attack against the Vorn. From a satchel, he retrieved his tracking device which read the wavelength signature of the androids operating system. If Vale was within one hundred yards, Ranul could track him. The device remained silent. The thought that Vale was not nearby was comforting; but what had happened to the robot after it retreated from the Aolene warriors?

He continued his ascent until he found Estall in the public area with hundreds of Aolene warriors prepped for war. They all wore the same black garment of the Barudii, and every person was loaded up with weapons for the battle. Estall looked puzzled to see Ranul as he made his way to him in the crowd.

"Has something happened, Dr. K'ore? I thought, surely your group had departed for the rift by now."

"The others have, but I want to go with you and your warriors to engage the Vorn at the Capital. My daughter is there."

"I see. Well, of course you're welcome to join us, and any information you have about their strengths or weaknesses would be appreciated."

"Actually, the Vorn have several ships and multiple long and short range weapons at their disposal, but they don't realize you're coming. It would be best to spread out your troops as we come in to firing range, about five to seven miles from the city, so they won't have any large targets to fire upon," said Ranul.

"Well, it may be good for us to encircle the city and come from all angles to converge on their cloning facility."

"You should also know that the Vorn have a large number of sentinel robots at their command—probably in the thousands. By spreading your forces and coming from all directions they'll be forced to spread their own ground forces to protect the city. It's likely that many gaps in that defense will present themselves."

"Then let's go. We'll be able to approach the city near dusk and gain that advantage as well."

They gathered up nearby weapons and headed for ground level where the transports were being loaded and prepped for the attack.

IT took a few moments to fully retract the mountain side hangar bay doors. Now the ship would clear. Millo adjusted the landing thruster controls and the ship began to move forward through the opening in the mountain. Orin adjusted controls at his station; setting the weapons systems at the ready and making sure that all automated systems were operating within normal parameters.

The *Saberhawks* normally operated with a crew of twenty persons, but most of the systems could be run by automation if necessary. The larger bulk of the ship held primary engine systems for long range missions and extra crew quarters with food and water storage, while the remaining quarter of the ship made up the bridge section, sublight engine components and all primary controls for the entire vessel. They made last minute adjustments and prepared for the launch through Castai's turbulent atmosphere.

THE distance Vale had calculated for his trek around the mountainside toward the hangar quickly diminished in his processor as he approached the area on his internal map that should have housed the hangar section of the city. Up ahead, a fair distance away, he could see the nose of a large ship emerging form the mountain. He instantly began internal calculations for his own foot speed compared with the distance yet to cover, terrain and the rate at which the ship was emerging from the hangar port.

He realized he would not reach the vessel in time. Their velocity would increase dramatically once the ship completely cleared the mountain. As he ran toward the vessel he withdrew a hyper-magnetic grapple from one of the clips on his belt.

The last part of the *Saberhawk* cleared the opening in the mountain and Millo increased power to thrusters steadily to move the ship away from Vaseer. Vale aimed and fired his grapple just ahead of the ship's nose. The wire line, with its heavy cylindrical head, arced out away from the mountainside about fifty yards and caught the lower hind end of the *Saberhawk*.

He made a strong jump into the air as he felt the slack line become taut and pull him away from the ground. He depressed the winch key on the grapple and held on tight as the mechanism drew him closer to the ship.

Millo fired main thrusters and sent the ship upwards toward the outer atmosphere. Orin was monitoring it on the digital display for wind speed and direction as well as pressure changes that could make the ascent a bumpy ride.

Vale was now within twenty yards of the ships hull as they began to move through one of the weather systems that usually became violent on Castai's surface. The changes in the planet's weather were somehow directly linked to the transdimensional rift.

The turbulence and high wind began to pummel the ship in its climb. Inside the *Saberhawk*, automatic stabilizers worked to keep up with all the jarring forces playing against the body of the ship. Orin monitored hull integrity and other factors while Millo calmly urged the ship skyward. In a few moments the *Saberhawk* cleared the weather and the ride smoothed out considerably.

Vale approached the hull and tried to find a place to anchor himself. He noticed how near he was to one of the landing skid alcoves. He clamored for the hull wall activating the hyper-magnetic discs located in the palms of his cybernetic hands. Hand over hand, he approached the alcove and climbed inside with the retracted landing skid and wedged himself in with his powerful arms and legs.

THE *Saberhawk* rumbled again as it broke free of Castai's atmosphere into open space. Gravity controls quickly adjusted the internal environment for the crew. Tiet had never been in space before, and he wondered at the vastness of it. There were seemingly billions of stars now visible in the distance. A gaseous formation could be seen ahead. Orin brought up the tactical displays that identified the phenomena as the transdimensional rift with energy readings that went off the scale.

Only Orin could remember it, having seen it during a space battle with the Vorn that left the Castillians without a space fleet. From that time on the Barudii had only battled the invaders on Castillian soil.

"Readings show the rift to be fully open and safe for passage."

Millo nodded and adjusted his flight path to carry them through the ominous black void near the center of the multicolored gaseous cloud that surrounded the rift.

Dorian wondered if she would ever see her brother or her people again. And would Estall be able to defeat the remaining Vorn on the planet? She had confidence that he would—more confidence than she had in their own ability to successfully defeat the Vorn fleet waiting on the other side of the rift. Suddenly she longed for Castillian soil under her feet again.

She looked at Tiet in the chair next to her. He was looking at the rift and the data on the viewer. He was handsome and brave, and powerful and yet behind his eyes she could see a child who had lost everything dear to him, but could still smile and have hope in the future. Was it gullibility or just innocence, and did it really matter?

As a child she had wondered about the little boy in the archive photos; the son of the king to that once great people. He was so happy in the images she had seen in her studies and she had often thought that were he still alive, they would have been the same age and could have played games together.

In her adolescence the small boy in the images had become the young man who defeated the Vorn enemies in her dreams and swept her away from the harsh reality of her life. And now, here he was; very much alive and only inches from her.

It did not matter if they returned now. She knew that here beside him was the only place she really wanted to be. She wiped an escaping tear as Tiet looked at her with the same childlike smile. She returned it and they looked back toward the approaching blackness of the rift.

DARKNESS was beginning to fall as Estall's formation of transports swept across the wasteland toward the capital city. Approaching from the east was a violent-looking weather system that they hoped would not intercept them before they could reach the city.

He had sent nearly half of the forces ahead at full speed while his group continued on at half that pace. If the other group of transports could swing wide of the city and get around undetected then they might just be able to encircle it during their final approach. Ranul was hunkered down in the open cockpit of Estall's transport as the wind whipped at them from different directions caused by the approaching storm.

He had seen many violent fluctuations in Castai's weather and had studied many files from the past events. He understood all too well the reason for Castillians building the majority of their cities underground in the centuries following the appearance of the rift.

He knew that once Estall's forces came within ten miles of the Vorn facility, even these small craft would be detected by their defense systems. The Vorn long-range phase cannons could be employed at up to seven miles, but if the transports remained scattered enough perhaps the Vorn would have difficulty hitting them.

The Aolene were a brave people. They had faced the adversity of Vorn attacks on their cities and survived to become an even stronger people through the study of the Barudii fighting arts. Though they lacked the kinetic abilities of the Barudii, the Aolene certainly reminded him of those long dead warriors in spirit. As they steadily approached the Capital, he hoped he would not witness the loss of another brave people today.

IV

GOVERNOR Kisch k'ta looked very worried now. This was exactly the kind of situation he had been hoping to avoid by sending out the android assassin. His confidence in its ability may have been premature.

"Are you sure?"

"Yes Governor. The city's perimeter defense systems just picked up these forces ten minutes ago. They appear to have originated from one of the old Barudii cities. They'll be within nine miles by now."

"Activate the defensive batteries at once. Destroy them all," demanded Kisch k'ta.

Setaru' lek pressed the intercom button on the Governor's desk and patched into the cities defensive control room.

"Vescotta, lock on approaching targets and fire at will."

"Yes, sir."

Defensive laser cannons on the west side of the city came alive as the gunners worked to lock on the approaching vehicles. They were still out of visual range to the naked eye, but were quite visible to the Vorn scanners.

"Sir, the vehicles are widely dispersed and too small to get a positive lock while they are moving at this speed."

"Tell the turrets to strafe across their flight path. That should take out some of them," said Vescotta.

The large laser cannons expelled their massive firepower with great moans of energy buildup and release. The beams trailed away from the city and into the twilight, toward their distant targets.

RANUL caught what he thought was heat lightening in his peripheral vision just as a massive beam of energy lit up the terrain ahead of their transport group. The beam rapidly cut a horizontal track across their path, catching two transports along the way. They burst into fiery fragments as inertia carried them onward, distributing the burning wreckage along their previous flight paths.

The transport group scattered even further apart as more laser fire blasted at them from the city in the distance. The pilots began making very erratic maneuvers to try and evade the assault. Estall grabbed the communication hand set and yelled into the mike saying, "Increase speed to full throttle! Evasive maneuvers!"

The entire transport group geared up to full throttle, making them even harder to hit. They were still three miles outside of the Capital, and closing fast.

A beam of energy blazed near Estall's transport, cutting across their flight path just after they passed. *Too close*, and suddenly Ranul realized why he liked being a scientist rather than a warrior. The city perimeter was coming up fast now. Estall and the others in the transport prepared their firearms for battle. It appeared most of the ships had made it through the gauntlet and were now too close to be targeted by the large cannons, which suddenly fell silent.

Another barrage of fire began to sweep across the distance between their transports and the Vorn facility. But now it came from the hundreds of sentinel robots around the facility's perimeter that were firing upon them.

Pulse laser blasts began to ring out from the transports as they returned the enemy fire. The shots were impacting the forward deflectors as Estall pushed on through the line of sentinels with their ship. The deflector shield bounced the robots out of their way as they rammed their way through. The warriors activated their electromagnetic shields and hurried out of the transports, firing their pulse weapons at the sentinels.

The robots were taking multiple hits, but weren't being stopped. The sentinel's armaments were too much for handheld pulse rifles to be effective against them. As the robots approached, their own guns still blazing, the Aolene warriors began to secure their rifles in favor of the Barudii blades and kemsticks. More and more warriors ignited their blades and, putting shields ahead, they moved into the oncoming sentinels.

The E.M. shields gave them cover as they closed the distance needed to strike. The Barudii blades sliced through the sentinel armor like butter. Robot after robot was dispatched by the powerful blows of the Aolene warriors. The sentinels appeared helpless to stop the Aolene advance as robots were cut down by their human foes.

Estall shouted for the other warriors as several hundred came against the cloning facility's wall. Using handheld grapples, they fired them over the perimeter of the roof and quickly began to scale the walls. Ranul didn't like this part one bit. He detested heights. And he didn't enjoy being pulled up the height of this wall any more than he had being pushed off by Orin the night before. When the warriors all reached the roof, they quickly moved across to various ventilation shafts and sliced open the vent heads, allowing them to enter. Estall instructed them to fan out through the facility and take the main control room.

"Whoever gets to it first, contact me."

Ranul stayed glued to him as they all plunged into the dark maze of tunnels comprising the facility's ventilation system.

"GOVERNOR, the facility has been breeched by enemy forces," said Setaru' lek, "They have bypassed our ground forces at the building entrances and are moving through the ventilation system. Several floors are reporting gunfire and others are not communicating at all."

"Get more forces up here at once!"

Behind the room's ventilation screen, Estall, Ranul, and several warriors listened.

"That's him," whispered Ranul. "That's Governor Kisch k'ta. If you can take him, you'll control the entire facility."

Estall ran at the vent screen and crashed through it, rolling into the room. The other warriors followed, as several sentinels came to life, firing upon them. Their E.M. shields repelled the laser blasts while they engaged the robots with ignited blades.

The Governor and Setaru' lek, along with several other Vorn were all crouched on the ground in fear. The Governor's office door slid open allowing several Horva guards to move inside. Like sleek predators, they leapt at the Aolene warriors, attacking furiously. One of the Aolene near the entrance was caught from behind by one of the clones as it plunged a knife into his throat. The wounds were fast and fatal; and the dark skinned clone kept moving.

Ranul blasted at the Horva with several bursts of pulse laser fire from his crouched position just inside the vent shaft, dropping the clone, then he turned to face two other Horva that were already making their approach.

The Horva swiped its dagger at him as he brought his ignited blade up to defend himself causing the brute man to sever his own hand upon Estall's weapon. As the Horva recoiled in pain, Estall followed through with a quick thrust through its chest to dispatch the clone. As the last Horva lunged at the third warrior, Vasad, it met a spicor disc in flight, which vaporized the majority of his body. Ranul leveled his pulse rifle on Governor Kisch k'ta.

"Hello Governor…surprised to see me?"

"I should have fed you and your family to the Horva long ago, Ranul."

"Governor Kisch k'ta, you will broadcast to your other forces to stand down immediately or you and your people here will suffer and then you will all be executed for crimes against my people," said Estall.

"You would torture us?" asked Setaru' lek.

"Exactly as you tortured my wife, you filth." responded Ranul.

"You have killed millions of our people and sent our children away to be massacred by your clones. There must be some retribution for their deaths," said Estall.

"I will order them to stand down, but it will do you no good. When our reinforcements come through the rift, you and your rebels will be made to suffer."

"Where is my wife, Governor?" asked Ranul.

"I don't know."

"Come on, you can do better than that," said Estall.

"I tell you, I don't know. She was taken as a prisoner across the rift months ago after you agreed to build the android prototype for us."

"Then I'll find it in your data files," said Ranul.

He made his way to the closest computer terminal and input his translator code to allow him to read the Vorn transmissions. The display changed from the Vorn language to his Castillian, but access to the information he wanted was denied. He turned back to the Governor. "The code, Kisch k'ta? Now!"

The Governor remained sternly silent, until Estall raised his blade and extinguished the dispersion field; he brought the tip to rest against Kisch k'ta's throat.

"Governor, the code."

Kisch k'ta swallowed hard then grumbled the voice code in his native language. The computer responded, allowing Ranul to begin moving through the Vorn database.

"Now send the stand down order and have your people report to the main hangar of this facility," said Estall.

Kisch k'ta looked at Setaru' lek who normally would have protested at the idea of Vorn surrendering under any circumstances, but he now appeared to be in no hurry to sacrifice his own life. The Governor tapped into the communications display on his desk panel, opening a channel to his ground forces commander. He issued the command in his own language, and then received a puzzled but compliant reply.

"Now what?" asked Setaru' lek.

"Vasad," said Estall, "take the governor's aides with you and go to the hangar bay. Have the others meet you there with their captives and wait for these other Vorn to arrive and hold them there in the hangar."

Vasad motioned with his pulse rifle to Setaru' lek and Kisch k'ta's other aides to come with him. He looked back at the Governor, who offered no alternative, then proceeded out the door with the others and Vasad behind them.

"Estall, I've ordered the sentinels to stand down," said Ranul, "but you need to look at this."

He put his display onto the larger main viewer for the room. A picture of the Vorn's scanner readouts and log entries appeared on the screen.

"It looks like they've been tracking the *Saberhawk* since it left the atmosphere. They appear to be on approach to enter the transdimensional rift. Look—all of this has been sent as a continuous transmission to the fleet on the other side, but there hasn't been any reply, even on this closed channel."

"Maybe they're maintaining silence to try and surprise our ship when it comes through."

"It doesn't seem likely; the last transmission from across the rift appears to have been a week ago and nothing at all since. Why haven't your forces been responding, Governor? Your transmission log shows repeated attempts with no reply. Why?"

"If I knew, then we wouldn't be continuing to try and gain a response would we?"

"There's a reference here in some of their last responses to the Sphere, and no sign of the Sphere. What does that mean, no sign of the Sphere, Governor?"

Ranul could see something foreboding in the Governor's eyes, though he answered not a word.

"Search the database for the term."

Ranul keyed the reference into the computer and immediately a massive file with numerous subsections appeared on the screen. He began to scan through the data very quickly, trying to make sense of it. The more he read, the more he understood the Governor's odd look of dread. Suddenly he had a disturbing realization come to him.

"You've been running! That's why you came here. To get away from this thing! Isn't it?!"

He was yelling at the Governor, who remained silent as the new images ran on the main display.

"I don't understand," said Estall, still trying to grasp what all the information was revealing to Ranul.

"A lot more is going on here than we thought."

THE *Saberhawk* was beginning to vibrate more and more as it approached the rift. The dark center was ominous, like some terrible beast wanting to swallow the ship whole. Nothing could be seen beyond. Even their sensor scans revealed nothing about what lay on the other side. No one spoke. All eyes were on the approaching void.

Orin continued to watch the instrument readouts, looking for any information about what lay beyond the blackness. He noticed that all light was being repelled by the void along with all sensor scans. Somehow the Vorn had been able to keep communication across the rift, even when it had been in collapse phase, but he wasn't sure what technology they had employed. The ship was shaking significantly, and Millo had to work to keep it on course.

"I think the void is trying to repel the ship just like it does to energy waves," said Orin.

"I'll increase thrust to try and compensate."

The *Saberhawk* lurched forward as they struggled against the forces of the Transdimensional Rift. As they began to enter the void, the turbulence suddenly ceased and all the gauges and dials on the instrument panel suddenly went black.

Only the light from their display was visible as the void engulfed them. The ship seemed to surge forward faster, even though thruster speed remained constant. When the Saberhawk emerged on the other side the scene looked like they had gone back the way they had come; like they were in Castillian space once again.

A blazing behemoth of a space vessel under attack quickly changed their perception. It was headed right for them as the *Saberhawk* emerged from the rift. The vessel appeared to be a huge Vorn craft, much larger than those currently stationed at Castai. This one was easily a hundred times the size of the *Saberhawk*.

Multiple explosions and streams of fast burning oxygen and other gases and chemicals were trailing at different points on the ships surface. Millo took immediate evasive maneuvers to get away from the vessel as it closed on them at a frightening speed. A burst of main thrusters bore them hard to port, away from the damaged ship as it continued on by without acknowledging them; driving hard for the rift.

Orin began scans of the ship, trying to find out what was going on. Life form readings began to appear along with various discernable statuses on the vessels current hull integrity and power systems.

"That thing is breaking up!" said Orin. "It's carrying human life signatures only; approximately ten thousand. Some appear to be variants of the other; probably Horva."

"Burn, baby, burn," said Millo under his breath as he continued to direct the *Saberhawk* away from the vessel. Everyone was tense.

"I'm still not sure what's attacking them," said Orin.

Tiet and Dorian exchanged concerned glances but remained silent, trying to listen to Orin and Millo as they contemplated this surprising find. As the computer continued to pull data from the vessel something else appeared on the display.

"I'm not sure what these things are…some sort of spheres…approximately thirty feet in diameter. They're completely mechanical. There's quite a number surrounding the hull of the Vorn vessel and some on the inside."

Orin continued his scans monitoring the Vorn ship's engine systems. "Its reactor core has been breeched. It's going to blow!"

The large Vorn ship was running hard for the transdimensional rift. The sheering forces from the void were peeling pieces away from the crippled vessel as it began to enter the darkness with its entourage of attackers in tow. Just as the front half of the ship sank into the void, it erupted into a white hot ball of flame, quickly fading as all gases and chemicals combusted away. Multiple shockwaves surged away from the rift, causing the *Saberhawk* to be tossed like a toy upon the waves of energy.

Dorian shouted, "What's happening?!

I think the explosion of the Vorn ship has triggered a reaction in the rift!" shouted Orin as Millo fought hard to bring the *Saberhawk* back under control.

"I should do a sensor sweep of the quadrant and see where other Vorn ships are and what those things were that destroyed that ship. Maybe we have an ally on this side."

"Well, whatever they are they don't like the Vorn," said Tiet.

The data on Orin's display began to be replaced by other information.

"There is a planet nearby," said Orin. "It's habitable. The readings look identical to Castai. I'm showing some other activity in the near vicinity. It looks like more Vorn battle cruisers near the planet and an orbiting station of immense size. This planet could be their home. I'm picking up a large amount of random energy fluctuations; it looks like another large explosion of a vessel similar to the one that almost hit us.

Take us toward the planet so we can get a better look at what's happening."

"It looks like someone is doing all the fighting for us," said Tiet.

"Weapons and shields are all charged and ready. We're going in," said Millo as he brought the *Saberhawk* about on course for the nearby planet. The *Saberhawk* was a fast ship; the distance at full speed would be about twenty minutes.

As they drew near, Orin worked to get a visual of the battle taking place ahead. A tactical map replaced part of the information on the display. Markers representing various sizes of Vorn space vessels moved about on the screen as faster moving dots representing the mechanical spheres intermingled with them. Another large vessel disappeared from the map along with two smaller Vorn ships that had been near it.

"Those things are slaughtering the Vorn fleet," said Tiet.

"It's about time someone gave it to them," replied Millo.

Orin continued to focus on the tactical data coming across his monitor. Just because these mysterious spheres were decimating the Vorn ships did not necessarily mean they were allies. The tactical map was still tracking all the engaged vessels, but the Vorn spaceship signatures were rapidly disappearing from the display. Each time a vessel exploded approximately twenty spheres were destroyed with it. The objects were clearly running suicide missions, and quite effectively. But why?

"What are we going to do when we reach the battle, Orin?"

"I'm not sure, but at current speed there won't be many Vorn ships left when we arrive."

Orin recalibrated the scanners to bring up a more accurate visual on the display. After a few adjustments a visual appeared showing two remaining Vorn vessels with spheres swarming about them. Explosions were erupting at various places along their massive hulls as the spheres strafed the lengths of each vessel with powerful energy weapons.

The individual spheres moved in concert and soon the last two ships were braking apart on the *Saberhawk's* display. Even watching the Vorn being soundly defeated could not erase the feeling of imminent danger.

The spheres were too deadly for the *Saberhawk* crew to be happy about the victory; and what if they turned on their ship next? There seemed little chance of surviving such an attack if the entire Vorn fleet of space cruisers could not. So far the massive Vorn space station was left unharmed. Orin's computer showed some one hundred thousand people were aboard it.

"I wonder why they didn't attack that space station?" asked Tiet.

Before the last syllable escaped his lips, a massive beam of energy emanating from some point beyond the planet, smashed into the Vorn space station, knocking out its shields and further vaporizing one quarter of its surface area.

"Where did that come from?!" shouted Millo.

"I don't know. There's nothing on scanners…just empty space."

Within moments, another powerful burst slammed into the station. Without shields to buffer the blow, the structure shattered like a window pane. Several large sections of debris quickly began to fall toward the planet; dragging the atmosphere as white hot material vapor trailed away during its descent.

"That's an unbelievable amount of power coming from somewhere," said Tiet.

No longer content to stay in his chair, he joined Orin at the systems control station, with Dorian close behind.

"Millo, I think the planet would provide us with at least some protection; better than just sitting out here."

"I'm all for that. Setting course and speed."

The *Saberhawk* veered away from their course and headed toward the planet, hoping to avoid whatever predator was lurking nearby and find further information about what was really happening on this side of the rift.

VALE was unable to discern the trouble that was occurring around the ship. Wedged inside the landing skid housing, the android had no view of the surroundings. Except for vibrations given off through the hull of the ship, and some flashes of light, all was quiet in space. It was time to break into the ship and acquire his target again. He did not have proper schematics for the vessel. But he was within the shield perimeter of the ship, and any weak place in the hull would suffice for an entry point.

Using the hypermagnetic discs in his appendages, the android climbed out of the skid housing and began to cross the surface of the ship. As he came across the top of the ship, Vale spotted a docking hatch. He crawled toward it, paying little attention to the nearby planet they were approaching. The android located the emergency panel and peeled it away effortlessly to reveal the keypad underneath. He applied his hand to the pad and sensors beneath his pseudo flesh began to scan the internal controls. Within moments his processors had decoded the lock and applied the code.

The outer hull door unlocked. Vale turned the manual lever and released pressurized gases as the bulkhead doors parted, allowing him to enter the vestibular area to await atmospheric equalization. The outer door automatically closed and the area re-pressurized to match the interior of the ship. Once it was completed, the interior door unsealed itself and opened to allow Vale free access to the interior of the *Saberhawk*.

"ORIN, I'm reading a hull breech."

"What? Where?"

"The docking hatch has just been opened and resealed again."

"Sensors still show we are the only life forms on the ship."

"Is the area pressurized?" asked Tiet.

"Yes. I'm still showing normal atmospheric conditions in the cargo area."

"Alright I'll check it out."

"We'll check it out," followed Dorian.

Tiet didn't even try to argue the point with her, and the pair moved quickly through the passageway from the bridge toward the cargo hold.

When they reached the cargo bay, Tiet tapped the switch on the bulkhead to release the door. As he stepped into the area the computer automatically brought up the lights. Heavy footsteps grew rapid and close, and then paused as the illumination came on.

"Move, Dorian!" he shouted pushing her aside.

He was barely able to draw his sword in defense before the android came down from above with its own ignited weapon. The force of the blow nearly knocked Tiet off his feet. Instinctively he forced back with his kinetic power, trying to compensate for the android's greater physical strength.

He ducked down and rolled away then leapt back toward the menacing robot; slashing at it with all of the fury he could muster; but each strike was defended against and countered by the android.

Dorian got back to her feet quickly with her own sword drawn and ignited, but she was keeping out of the way for now. Tiet hoped she would not intervene. He and Vale were exchanging strikes at a dizzying pace. Tiet was using the two-handed fulcrum technique taught to him by Orin long ago, and also incorporating his kinetic power for speed and agility enhancement, but he could not get past Vale's blade to strike.

The android's face was expressionless as he countered each strike and parried only to meet the humans ignited blade each time. His computer mind rapidly coordinated every movement while trying to find a weakness in Tiet's defense that would allow a death blow.

Vale's back was now to Dorian and Tiet could feel her in his mind as she lunged for the android. He wanted to stop her; to protect her, but it was too late. Vale noticed her steps and the rush of wind around her blade and moved to defend himself.

Tiet struck again to draw its attention from her, but to no avail. Dorian's blade penetrated the androids synthetic skin and its adomen exoskeleton as she swiped down across its back. Leaving his sword hand to counter Tiet's strike, Vale quickly struck Dorian with his other, sending her back to the floor with a fractured arm.

A fury welled up within Tiet as he sensed her pain. He blasted Vale with a kinetic burst that sent the android flying back hard into the cargo bay wall.

It felt different than when he had used the kinesis back on Castai; he felt more powerful. But his rage overpowered his bewilderment. Vale stood again, quickly recovering from the fall. Tiet lowered his blade as the android lunged for him only to be hurled back against the cargo bay wall again and again.

He could feel the power surging now. He could sense the workings of the android and feel the drain of its power as it fought to get at him. He could sense the physical pain of Dorian and the presence of Millo at the helm and Orin coming toward the cargo bay. Then something happened he had not expected; the android spoke to him.

"Are you afraid to fight me, human?" he asked trying to stand again. "You are a coward for using your kinetic abilities to avoid open combat with me."

Vale's CPU had caught a hold on the human emotional trait of pride and was now hoping to exploit it to get close to his target.

"Don't listen to it," said Dorian, still huddled on the floor holding her arm.

"Yes, human, cower with your woman." baited Vale.

Tiet replaced his father's sword in its sheath, as he released the android from the invisible grip of his mind. Vale cautiously picked up his own blade from the ground. Tiet's kemsticks leapt to his hands from the magnetic clips on his thighs and ignited. He calmed himself and moved into the fluid movements of his favorite two-handed technique.

Orin had rarely taught him to use the kemsticks, as he favored the blade, but Tiet had always enjoyed the two-handed style, with its rapid fire strikes and elaborate movements.

Vale engaged him quickly and for a few moments they remained deadlocked blow for blow; until Tiet shifted to his own version of the two-handed technique that relied on no discernable pattern that Vale's mind could decipher. As Tiet increased his speed he became a blur of motion. He landed a strike to the android's leg then another followed quickly to the torso.

The robot was failing to match the speed of Tiet's strikes. For every three to five strikes made, one landed on the android's body, doing serious damage to its exoskeleton. The robot retreated away from the continuing assault, losing bits and pieces of his mechanical structure as the strikes continued to find purchase on his body.

He sliced Vale's forearm open, disintegrating the motor controls of his hand. The android's sword fell from his limp hand, as Tiet continued to smash him with blow after blow.

He saw that Orin was now in the cargo bay with Dorian helping her with her injury and suddenly he wanted to be the one consoling her. He dealt a quick and final deathblow, driving an ignited kemstick right through the android's chest where its primary power source was housed.

Vale fell heavily to the cargo bay floor showing no further sign of mechanical life. Tiet extinguished his weapons and replaced them on each thigh as he ran back to Orin and Dorian.

"How's your arm?"

"I don't think its bad...."

"It's fractured in two places."

"Are you sure?" asked Orin. .

"Yes, I...I sensed it as it happened. I'm not sure how though. The kinesis seems more powerful on this side of the rift."

"Interesting...we had better get to the med station and set Dorian's arm."

The trio walked back through the cargo bay entrance and sealed the door again.

"What about the android?"

"I don't trust leaving it there. Open the outer bay door and flush the remains into space."

He complied, being only too happy to finally rid themselves of this persistent assassin. He keyed in the command on the cargo bay keypad.

The computer scanned for life signs as a routine safety measure and then opened the doors. The pressurized gases quickly rushed into the vacuum carrying Vale's lifeless torn body with them. Tiet could see the clearing of the debris through the cargo bay door window and lingered only long enough to see the doors closing again.

V

THE cold of space would have quickly killed him had there been any real life in his android body. Now only the incomprehensible surging of a computer mind remained. The body was hacked to sheds and the final blow had disintegrated his primary power supply with the main efferent signal processor.

Vale's functioning mind was trapped in a body he could not control. The attempt to bait the human through its pride had failed. His mind raced at incalculable speeds searching for errors in his own performance that may have caused the outcome. But it was a pointless race to run, for now he was nothing but wreckage floating in the cold black void of space.

Something tingled. Something was probing through his computer mind; not invading, but washing over him and through him. A voice was speaking inaudibly to him. It was familiar and mechanical in nature. Vale's mind responded to its call. He was moving now; moving swiftly through space. The voice reassured him without words.

It was pulling him across the vast expanse to itself. He could discern no movement; but he calculated five hours from the first contact with the voice until he saw himself pass through an opening into a vessel. The voice called for him to release all data and merge with its own mind. There was no resisting the call.

Soon he was one with the Sphere and a vast memory of the Sphere's travels across different worlds in pursuit of the Vorn opened up to him.

The Sphere had returned home to this planet as it followed the Vorn across space, destroying them everywhere they were found; as the makers had planned. And yet for Vale, the Vorn were his masters, having sent him on his mission after the Barudii warrior and his companions.

The only way to reconcile the two was to fulfill both objectives. The Barudii warrior and his companions had to be exterminated along with the Vorn. They had not given orders to keep from terminating any of their own race, and nothing in the creator's directives to the Sphere denied it the privilege to exterminate rebels of any race. Simple. All objectives will be met. Failure is not an option.

Vale was now one with the mind of the Sphere. There was so much power and so much data available. He now knew where the Barudii ship was located. The Sphere had been tracking it all along. He watched it through the eyes of the Sphere; seeing through its scanning mechanisms.

The Barudii ship was approaching the planet on the further side away from the Sphere's own position. It was in the process of final execution on the Vorn. An invasion force, one of many, was already prepared to begin decimating Vorn cities on the planet surface; to rid the maker's home planet of the infestation by their enemies. And now Vale's memory provided further information.

The Sphere now understood that the Vorn had been in the process of trying to escape across the local phenomena known as the Transdimensional Rift, and they were currently occupying a conquered planet similar to the maker's home world here. It would be necessary then to travel across the rift to destroy the Vorn at that location as well.

But now it was time to launch the first wave of the invasion force. If the Vorn were able to counter the attack by some means, then subsequent waves would be modified to overcome the problem and finish the objective. Now Vale could finish his objective as well. The Sphere had been refitting his chassis since the time it pulled his torn body inside itself; and it was also duplicating his android body with a pair of automatons that would function as extensions of his self. The Barudii warrior would lose the advantage he had gained at their last encounter.

THE trip through the planet's atmosphere was uneventful with shields operating at maximum. Orin scanned the planet for topographical and geographical data, as the *Saberhawk* cruised swiftly at sixty thousand feet.

"I'm picking up twelve large cities with functional energy signatures
and many more appear to be on fire or have sustained major damage. It's
like a war is taking place. At this point on the map, sweeping to this area,
all these minor cities are destroyed, while those with major structures
have sustained heavy damage. Wait a minute, what's this?"

He tapped the display next to an alert code for the geographical data
search. The screen complied by showing a match to the ships database.
Orin released the information.

"I...I can't believe it."

On the screen it read, planet Castai III. He quickly began to look for
specifics in the data. There it was. Mt. Vaseer appeared on the data map
being compiled from topographical scans of the planets surface. He
could not have mistaken it for anything else. Orin knew the place he had
called home, better than any other location on Castai; and yet, here it
was.

This city, upon closer scans, did have a great deal more damage than
back home. He keyed in comparison data from his home world and
matched them together. Orin could see clearly that this city of Vaseer
was actually less complete than back home. Somehow this planet was a
duplicate of his home world. By this time the others were anxiously waiting for some indication of exactly what was happening.

"What is it Orin," asked Tiet?

"This planet is somehow a duplicate of Castai III."

"What?!"

"I know...but I have already located Mt. Vaseer and confirmed other
topographical comparisons. The oceans, the mountains, and almost every
major landmark are the same."

Silence held everyone captive at that point.

"But the Vorn inhabit this planet," said Dorian.

"We could really use some answers and the Vorn aren't likely to give
them to us. I think we should go to this planet's city of Vaseer and see if
the people on this world left any records.

The city is deserted according to the scan data. I don't know what else to do at this point; the situation has changed so dramatically from what we were expecting to find."

"Well, we better do something. This ship isn't invisible, you know. Somebody will be shooting at us sooner or later if we just fly around up here," said Millo. "I vote for Vaseer."

Tiet and Dorian nodded in agreement.

"Course plotted. E.T.A. is twenty minutes."

The *Saberhawk's* thrusters came to life to boost it away toward the mountain city. Cloud cover was fairly thick and provided good visual cover for the ship, but they knew that most likely they were already being tracked by the Vorn. The question was, could they reach Vaseer and find out what they needed to know before they were intercepted by attack ships?

THE reconstruction of Vale's body and the construction of his duplicates took a little time even for the automatons and nano-builders at the spheres' control; but soon enough the work was complete. At ten hours, fifty three minutes, and twenty seven point seven eight seconds, Vale's repaired body and his new duplicates came online.

Vale had control over all three bodies at once. His mind combined with that of the sphere was easily capable of coordinating every detailed action without hindrance. The three androids moved without delay, to join the waiting invasion force.

In one of the multiple launch bays within the huge Sphere, the Vale androids boarded one of the carrier vessels about to launch to the planets surface. The drones were miniatures of the Sphere itself. Each attack drone was fully armed with phased plasma weapons and shield generators for defense.

The carrier drones each carried one large surface attack robot, which were more suited to close quarters fighting and rooting out combatants able to evade the airborne attack force. The spherical carrier drone closed around the androids and hovered off the deck of the launch bay to join the other drones already leaving the main ship.

The first target would be a multiple objective. The Barudii ship was on course for one of the ancient cities of the makers, and a large contingent of Vorn forces were on their way there as well.

A Horva of uncommon stature and intelligence sat astride his grevasaur surveying his troops. The General was expecting a mighty victory today. An army of Horva marched with him toward the place where he hoped they could launch a massive counter offensive against the Sphere that had for so many decades been hounding the Vorn. It had decimated their forces at every encounter with the powerful suicide drones it employed, as well as the massive weapons used by the main Sphere itself. General Grod was certain the machine was in orbit around Castai. Sensor scans had failed to locate it, and the orbiting satellites had been destroyed that could scan for its presence.

But now, by employing his new plan he felt confident that not only would they soon have its location but would finally put an end to the destruction. After all, if the Sphere were to eradicate the Vorn, he and his elite Horva would also be included, and he didn't want their former masters destroyed, but subjugated.

The Vorn were still useful, but they would soon learn who the real masters were. Their resistance to the uprising of his fellow Horva would soon be crushed and the balance of power would rest with himself and his fellow clones.

The General's command group began to break away from the rest of his forces as they approached Mt. Vaseer from the north. They would make there way up the mountain to a preplanned area that overlooked the valley on the other side. The valley would be the perfect battlefield to have their showdown with the drones and draw them out into the open, so that his plan could be properly executed. One thing about computers, they always made predictable movements; he knew the drones would take the bait.

Grod's second in command, Malec, was personally escorting their special surprise for the forces of the Sphere and controlling the other weapons that would hopefully bring down the massive control sphere from orbit. Grod looked back over the fifty thousand man army that marched toward the pass around Vaseer with satisfaction. "Victory!"

Those within hearing replied in kind and the cry spread across the entire army. They believed that he was a capable leader and that he would lead them to victory.

Grod had bolstered their pride as elite warriors. They had finally grown tired of being the muscle for the physically weaker Vorn and without ever receiving any of the glory or power.

Grod was their ideal, sitting upon his grevasaur, physically powerful and more menacing in his appearance than any of the elite Horva.

When the Vorn had realized the danger of intelligent Horva with their greater physical power and tenacious love of fighting, they had gone to cloning a new breed of more easily manipulated Horva that were easy to control. This had been the final insult to Grod and his brother clones.

Now the rebellion was on. Grod prodded the grevasaur he rode upon, urging it on toward the rest of the command group who had begun to ride on ahead with their equipment in tow. The beast moaned deeply as it complied with its rider's commands.

THE *Saberhawk* glided smoothly around Mt. Vaseer on approach to the hangar bay on the lower western face of the mountain. On their internal scans of the city, there appeared to be a lot of damage. Obviously the fighting here on this duplicate Castai had been far worse since there did not appear to be any Castillians left on the planet. Numerous sensor sweeps had not found even one native left alive.

As they approached the massive entrance, it was apparent that the doors probably were not functional. They were shut and pocked with blast marks and several very large holes that went all the through. The *Saberhawk* would not be able to gain entrance to the city.

Orin tried several command codes from back home; hoping that maybe the same had been in use in this duplicate universe. The automated systems either weren't functional or didn't recognize the codes. At any rate, the result was the same.

"Well there's not much choice," said Orin as he looked back at Tiet. "We'll have to go in and see if we can find anything."

"I'm in."

"Me too," said Dorian.

"Actually I think Tiet and I will have to go alone. We don't have the time to land and hike back up to the city. We'll have to drop in here and go through the damaged hangar bay doors. You can't make the descent from the ship and I would rather that Millo was not left to handle any problems with the ship alone."

Dorian was noticeably unhappy with the situation, but compliant.

"Millo, please take the ship down into the southern valley until we contact you. Keep an eye peeled for any trouble and get the ship out of danger if you have too. It's likely that the Vorn will be investigating our arrival. I doubt an old Barudii battleship will have gone unnoticed on this planet. Tiet, you and I will make the jump to Vaseer and see what we can come up with."

Orin proceeded through the bridge passage and down the short stairwell toward the main entry way to the ship, with Tiet following close behind.

"Tiet!" called Dorian coming after him. Both men turned at her approach. Orin looked at Dorian and then Tiet, realizing they needed a moment to speak.

"I'm going to secure some more gear we may need. I'll meet you shortly in the vestibule."

Orin went on without further comment leaving them alone in the corridor.

"What's the matter?"

"I just have a bad feeling about you going down there."

"Don't worry. Orin watches over me like he was my father," he said playfully, but Dorian's expression did not lighten.

"I feel like I need to tell you how I feel before you go," she said hesitantly, as if searching his face to know his feelings before she continued.

Tiet could hardly breathe; waiting for her next words with such anticipation he could perceive nothing else.

"I have loved you before I even knew you," she said. "From the images of you as a child, until I first realized who you were in the tunnels; you have been in my most secret thoughts. Now that I have been with you, I cannot imagine being anywhere else."

She raised her left arm and then pulling back the cuff of her uniform, she exposed the *donjarr* of her family. Tiet recognized the woven bracelet immediately. According to Castillian customs, it was the woman who chose her life companion and it was signified by the passing of the *donjarr* to the intended male as a promise of her desire to wed. The *donjarr* was not a light commitment. It was a binding contract once the male placed it on his own wrist.

Dorian looked into Tiet's eyes, and he could see her longing to know his feelings about what she had told him. He reached for her hand, clasping it in his own. With the other hand he moved the *donjarr* from her wrist over their joined hands to rest upon his own, according to the ritual. A tear escaped her swollen eyes, trailing down her olive skin. Tiet pulled her to himself in an embrace they both had longed to have.

"Come back safely to me," she said as she touched his lips with her own. Then she turned and hurried back to the bridge, before she lost control of her joy at there coming together and her anxiety at there parting. Tiet could hardly contain his own joy, as he went on to meet Orin.

ORIN was already waiting at the main entry ramp to the ship when Tiet arrived. Orin looked him over once; puzzled by the grin on his face, but supposing that something had happened between him and the girl. It did not surprise him and he hoped that all would turn out well for them, but at the moment more urgent matters pressed. He keyed in the safety bypass code, to allow the ship to open the main hatch while still in flight. Millo was hovering about one hundred yards above the mountains face where the city's hangar bay was located. They could see the scarred bay doors below them now.

"Are you ready Tiet?"

"Lead the way," he said over the engine rumblings spilling into the vestibule.

"The way is down," he said as he turned and stepped into the open air; quickly plummeting toward the mangled surface of the bay doors below. Tiet followed without hesitation. The two warriors controlled their descent precisely with their psycho kinesis and soft landed on the surface of the hangar doors.

The structure creaked under their weight a little, but appeared to be solid enough. Orin led the way to the largest opening and turned to toss Tiet a lighted headset. He clicked his own headset on to keep communication with the *Saberhawk* and to provide some illumination of the darkness below them.

"Millo, take the ship down to the valley, and wait there until you here from us. If you encounter any trouble, dust off immediately and we'll rendezvous later."

"Affirmative. I'll be waiting for your call. Be careful."

Above them, the engines of the Saberhawk whined to a higher pitch and the ship veered away from the mountain on course for the southern valley. Tiet switched on his own headset and the two of them peered into the darkness below them. They could see that the pavement was littered with a lot of debris.

"Look over there," said Tiet motioning to a large clear area.

"Let's go."

They dropped from the edge of the blast hole in the hangar bay door, about two hundred feet to the pavement; soft landing again thanks to their kinetic abilities. From memory, Orin led them through the debris field inside the hangar bay to the control room.

The door was standing open and a thick layer of dust covered the control panels within. Orin looked for the power grid panel and found the cells for all the power and backups were drained to nothing.

"Even after power failure, the successive auto backups would have run for at least six months," said Orin.

"Maybe, but this looks like about a hundred years of dust," said Tiet.

"If not more. Well, what have we here…?"

He keyed on another panel lever and several low lights flickered to life in the bay.

"Manual backup, in case the auto systems were down," said Orin. "These should be connected to solar panels on the eastern face of the mountain. They won't run down as long as the panels have a descent access to sunlight. Let's go."

He led them out of the control room and up a tunnel to a higher level of the city. Tiet followed the swift steps of his mentor trying to keep his senses alert to any sudden dangers that might present themselves.

This duplicate city had certainly taken a pounding. The ground was littered everywhere with debris. It looked like the Vorn had nearly torn the city apart and yet there were no signs of any bodies. The two men came into an ornate corridor approaching a single room. It seemed familiar to him, though he couldn't place it exactly.

"What room is this?"

"It's the king's quarters. This would have been your home back on our planet. Although I doubt your father was even born when this city was destroyed. I would guess it happened well over one hundred years ago.

"So what are we doing here?"

"There was a separate computer database in the king's quarters with its own link to the solar panels. Since they're still operating, I'm hoping the database is functioning as well. It may provide us with some answers."

Orin tried the electronic keypad but there was no response. Tiet quickly ignited one of his kemsticks and sliced an oval shaped hole into the door. He kicked the cut piece inward, and bending down, he went through the opening. Orin followed and they could clearly see a luxurious abode. It reminded him of home, but it had been so long ago. Orin made his way to a certain place on the rock wall and depressed two separate points that were far enough apart so as to be almost unreachable at the same time. A digital keypad rotated out of the wall before him. It still had power and Orin quickly typed in the words: *Barudii, Soone, vaseer 1*. A panel slid back in the wall to reveal an information display. A list of categories for searching the database appeared on the screen.

"Good, the code works here too. That means your family ruled here as well somehow," said Orin.

"Well, where do we start?" asked Tiet.

"How about with those strange spheres we encountered?"

Orin typed in the word spheres and instantly a list of subcategories scrolled across the display. Among the data entries were schematics and weapon systems capabilities for a massive attack vehicle. It must have measured three miles in diameter and looked just like the smaller spheres they had witnessed earlier destroying the space fleet of the Vorn.

They were shocked to see that it was the long dead Barudii of this planet that had constructed the huge machine. They scanned page after page of data, hardly able to believe what was being stated.

"Hard to believe they built this thing," said Tiet in amazement.

"To fight the Vorn, or avenge themselves—either way, a very deadly weapon to unleash on anyone."

"Yeah, but we never saw this one; only the smaller drones."

"But you can be sure it's out there," said Orin. "It's probably directly responsible for the destruction of the Vorn space station. It appears they launched it just prior to being wiped out by the Vorn. It was sent to attack the Vorn home world of Demigoth and then pursue the remaining Vorn and destroy them anywhere that it found them."

A small illuminated box on the display began to blink as Orin continued scanning the data. He tapped the box with his finger, causing more data to appear.

"This appears to be a live feed from the Sphere itself."

"Look at that tactical map. Isn't that Mt. Vaseer and the *Saberhawk* in the valley to the south of us?"

"Yes, and on a direct trajectory from the large sphere down to the valley is a massive group of those drones!"

"Look at that, coming in from the northern pass. It looks like a ground army and there heading toward the southern valley, too!"

"Orin to Saberhawk, dust off immediately! I say dust off immediately! Enemy forces are closing rapidly on your position!"

"We've got to get down there to them," shouted Tiet as he scrambled out of the room and down the corridor.

Orin followed while still trying to get through to the ship, but there was only static.

Suddenly he heard a reply.

"Millo to Orin...are you there?"

"Yes Millo! I hear you! There are two different groups of combatants converging on your location. You've got to get yourselves out of there now!" shouted Orin into the headset as he tried to keep up with Tiet through the corridors leading to the surface.

"I've got them on scans already. Shields are at maximum and weapons systems have been armed. I'm trying to lift off but some of those drones are already within visual range and closing fast on us."

"Do your best. We're on our way!"

When Tiet and Orin reached the main gate, they found it blasted almost completely away. As the pair emerged into the open air again they could already hear the noise of battle in the valley below. Many of the spheres were engaged in combat with the hovering *Saberhawk*. It appeared to be pinned down by the swarm of drones strafing at it with their energy weapons.

The other group of spheres landing in the valley threw large arms out of their sides that lifted their bodies and acted as legs to carry them and fight with. Blasters popped out of the tops to lay down laser fire against the masses of Horva.

The pass from the north to the southern valley was flooded completely with ground forces that greatly resembled the Horva, but Tiet noticed that these were different. They were dark skinned men like the Vorn but stronger looking and they wore uniforms and moved more like an organized fighting force; not like the brutes they had encountered back home at all. They were utilizing pulse weapons to fire on the sphere robots as the two sides of the struggle engaged one another.

The Horva were swarming in massive numbers upon the large robots, who in turn were spraying them with wave after wave of automatic laser fire. Tiet could see that the Horva were also using similar portable shield generators like the ones used by the Barudii.

They moved in close to engage the sphere robots with larger pulse cannons mounted upon hydraulic arms that attached to their vests. The pulse cannons were doing some definite damage to the hulking robots. It appeared to Orin as though the pulse wavelength was modulating continually to match the shield wavelengths of the robots allowing them to penetrate.

All of the combatants were laying siege to the *Saberhawk*, even though the Horva and the sphere robots were more interested in each other. Tiet ran down the main path of the city toward the valley with Orin following hard after him. The *Saberhawk* was hovering about forty feet off of the ground but the sky above them was too congested with enemy vessels to get clear of the battle.

Tiet could see that the ship was returning fire in all directions, but it was greatly outnumbered on the battlefield. He knew that their shields were losing power reserves fast at this pace, and before long they would be taking hits directly to the hull and it would all be over.

Tiet was running with all his might to get to her; to protect her. He leapt away from the path from a nearby ledge that took a drop thirty feet down to the fighting already raging below. He landed right in the middle of a group of several Horva that were firing on a distant sphere robot. They immediately reacted to his presence, bringing their weapons to bear on him.

His kemsticks leapt to his hands as he landed among them. He sliced one rifle in two, severing its owners hand at the wrist while deflecting another shot at point blank range. He swept downward under the barrel of one of them who fired and killed another Horva that had been standing ready on the other side, and with a complete sweep of his kemstick, cut the Horva down at the knees. He wasted little time dispatching two others, and then quickly moved onward to try and get to the *Saberhawk*.

"WE'RE the biggest thing out here!" said Millo in frustration.

Dorian blasted away at the weapons controls while Millo looked for a clearing in the congestion overhead.

"If we're so big, then can't we just plow through those other ships?"

"After seeing those spheres ramming into the Vorn ships I'd rather not take any chances. I'm going to try and move us out of the battle at this altitude."

"Well, you better hurry; our shields are already down to thirty percent power!"

The battlefield was overrun with Horva warriors, fighting furiously against the robots. Although the Horva were taking heavy losses, they continued to blast away at the automatons. For every twenty or more Horva getting killed, a robot was brought down. The Horva vastly outnumbered the robots and at least thirty thousand had rushed into the valley by now.

VALE and his doubles were fiercely engaged in the ground battle. The androids under Vale's mind were swiftly moving through the battlefield on foot toward the position of the *Saberhawk*. He knew that he had faced the Barudii warrior on the same vessel and had been defeated. He had no doubt that he could acquire his target there again. The triplet androids moved independently as though separate beings; yet all were under the one mind of Vale with the sphere.

Combatant after combatant were cut down as they moved swiftly toward the Barudii ship; only engaging in close combat as necessary. Then Vale noticed the ship was veering away from the fight and heading toward them, apparently trying to escape the situation.

Vales one and two quickly pulled hypermagnetic grapples and fired them at the ship as it passed low overhead. The third was still engaged with a Horva warrior as the hull-planted grapples pulled the other two androids up and away from the battlefield. Vales one and two retracted the grapple cables to bring themselves up to the hull.

Activating their hypermagnetic discs beneath their android skin, they each clung to the hull of the *Saberhawk*. The ship's shields did not prevent them since they only repulsed energy weapons. The two androids avoided any attempt to cut through the hull with Barudii blades as it would no doubt cause a repulsion charge from the shields that would fling them off the hull or vaporize them. They made their way quickly across the hull on their bellies as the shields snapped back energetically above them at the incoming pulse laser blasts from the battle.

They recalled the entry code for the outer hull hatch that he had gone through before and keyed it in when they reached the door. The door obeyed and both androids entered the ship without incident. Vale recognized the cargo hold as the place of his defeat at the hands of the Barudii warrior.

Wasting no time, the robots moved to the doorway of the cargo hold and found it locked. The second Vale brought his blade to bear on the door and proceeded to cut a portal through. The pair proceeded down the corridor toward the bridge, even as the ship shuddered under the enemy fire raining upon it from all directions. The bridge door was closed and the androids could hear voices from beyond it; a man and a woman. Without trying the lock, the pair sliced through the door.

Dorian whirled around, hearing the sound of ignited Barudii blades, and the crackling of molecular bonds bursting at their touch. From her hand flew a spicor disc toward the door and the android coming in through a newly cut hole. Trapped within the confines of the portal it had just cut, the first Vale caught the spicor disc in the upper torso. The tightly controlled burst pattern vaporized all but its arms above the waist.

Dorian quickly pulled her blade as the second robot moved in fast over its fallen twin. She could feel the pressure and the pain building in her fractured arm as she brought it to join the other on the hilt of her sword.

Millo looked back from the controls, as he heard the spicor explode behind him. The ship was still taking a beating from the sporadic weapons fire erupting from the battlefield below them; there was no way he could leave the controls. Vale pulled his pulse blaster with his free hand and sprayed laser fire in all directions across the bridge. The electromagnetic shield on Dorian's forearm blazed to life to repel the incoming blasts.

Millo held the controls of the *Saberhawk*, as the firestorm swept across the bridge. Several shots pierced his flight chair and his body. He arched at the pain as he slumped forward over the controls and his life drained away from him.

The ship lurched upward and back, causing Vale to stumble a moment. As he brought the blaster back to bear on Dorian, it met her blade in flight; slicing through both the weapon and the android's hand. Without any notion of pain, Vale brought his own blade down upon Dorian's shoulder, only to find her blade barring the way. With Millo slumped over the controls and many of the flight controls destroyed by laser fire, the *Saberhawk* began backwards from its course, descending clumsily toward the battlefield.

TIET could see the *Saberhawk* under fire from the battlefield and the sky; and still it was driving hard away from the fight. Soon she would be safe, and away from the danger. In his heart he urged the ship on to escape with his love safe inside. He and Orin had been separated by a small distance, and were furiously taking down Horva after Horva.

These were men, not like the brutish wild beasts back home on Castai. They had a definite measure of intelligence about them that could be seen just in their fighting techniques. But still, they were no match for the skills of Barudii warriors and their kinetic powers.

Neither Orin nor Tiet had made any attempt to fight against the sphere robots, since it was only built to attack the Vorn. Its fight was their fight. The *Saberhawk* was still some two hundred yards away as it trailed low over the battlefield to get away.

The entire valley before Mt. Vaseer was ablaze with laser fire and overhead a multitude of aerial combatants were tearing each other out of the sky. Wreckage was dropping onto the battlefield at regular intervals as the sphere drones and the Vorn attack fighters exchanged blows.

A Horva warrior strafed at Tiet with its pulse rifle. He deflected several blasts with kemsticks as he whirled them about his body and then he let one go toward his attacker. It caught the Horva's gun as it proceeded on to swipe across his chest and cut him down. The ignited kemstick rebounded back to Tiet's waiting hand in time to parry an incoming battle staff in the hands of another Horva. His second kemstick dispatched the opponent quickly with a straight thrust to the chest.

Orin too, was fairing well in the battle; evading laser fire through the use of his kinesis and tearing down multiple opponents with his blade. Tiet kept a visual on the ship. Its path was leading it off the battlefield to the east and he was glad Millo was getting them out.

Suddenly the ship slowed, arching nose up and coming back around from its former course. Something was wrong. Tiet's heart dropped in his chest as he noticed pulse laser fire flashing repeatedly from the bridge windows. "No!!"

The ship fell back from its escape run and began clumsily descending into the battlefield. If they didn't recover quickly they were going to crash for sure, and Tiet was too far away to do anything to help them. Several men approached to attack from multiple angles. Tiet repelled them all with a three hundred and sixty degree kinetic blast; sending them backward with crushing force.

He reached out in desperation with his kinesis to seize the ship and keep it aloft, but the *Saberhawk's* engines were fighting to drive it downward into the valley floor. Another Horva approached unnoticed from behind. His heart seized violently just before he could bring his battle staff down on Tiet. Orin watched him drop to the ground as he released him from his own mental grip from fifty yards away. He could see Tiet fixed upon the descending *Saberhawk*, trying to hold it up, but to no avail. There was simply no time to stop it.

The ship slammed into the valley floor, crushing several of the sphere robots and dozens of Horva warriors caught in its path. The *Saberhawk* burst into several large pieces as it tumbled over twice.

Tiet felt all strength leave his body at the thought of Dorian going down to her death in that fireball.

Then the conviction that she wasn't dead gripped him and he burst away from his position with blazing speed. Tiet was moving swiftly through engaged combatants and making only the slightest effort to dispatch anyone who turned to engage him while on his way. Quickly he closed the distance between himself and the wreckage. He wasn't sure why, but he *knew* that Dorian was not dead. He began to sense her location in the wreckage as he drew nearer; he sensed great pain.

Suddenly from the wreckage before him, a familiar adversary emerged with the majority of its synthetic skin burned away. It was the android again. This thing was responsible for this. It had hurt her. Before the robot even spotted him, Tiet hit it with a kinetic burst fueled by pure rage that sent it flying against a large section of the *Saberhawk's* hull. Before the android could recover, he pinned its head to the wreckage with his father's blade. Its body jerked with mechanical aftershocks and moved no more.

Tiet backed away and quickly found Dorian pinned underneath a metal support pillar. He waved it off of her with his mind and was at her side. Dorian was barely conscious when she looked at him. She tried to speak, but did not have the strength.

Tiet could not find words as tears welled up and escaped down his anguished face. He held her hand, and could feel it grow cold as life began to leave her. Dorian reached to touch the *donjarr* on Tiet's wrist, and then she touched his lips. Her fingertips lingered there only a moment as her body went limp and her gaze became void of life. Tiet's mind was racing without any coherent thoughts. He was completely numb in his senses. His love was dead before him. Sorrow filled his mind and despair gripped his heart.

He could still hear the battle raging around him, then something else, like heavy footsteps running across the wreckage; too heavy for a man. He looked back to find the android still lifeless and pinned to the hull by his father's sword. Then he looked toward the approaching sound to see another android coming at him with its own blade ready to strike. Without hesitation he reached for his imbedded blade, which obediently dislodged itself and leapt to his hand in time to meet the android's strike.

He wondered only a moment at how there seemed to be quite a few of these things. But the fight was on. Tiet slashed furiously at the deadly android, finding every strike countered. He was completely enraged, as the thought of Dorian laying here dead on this battlefield tore through his mind. He screamed out in fury at the robot. "Die!!"

His rage burst forth as a wave of psychokinetic energy that hit the third android with astonishing force; sending it flying through the air into a pile of the *Saberhawk's* wreckage. Tiet had never felt so powerful. His power was being fueled by his rage over Dorian's death and he could not contain it. The Vale android regained its composure and headed for him again. He lowered his father's blade to his side and let the kinetic power flow freely.

The Vale robot was coming closer with its own blade ready to strike. Suddenly the Barudii blade it carried extinguished itself.

The puzzled android stopped for a moment trying to reignite the weapons dispersion field. Tiet looked on with grim satisfaction, knowing he had just crushed the crystal in the hilt of the sword, with his thoughts. He summoned the wreckage around him to attack the robot.

Large, man-sized pieces of the debris flew off the ground toward Vale; striking the robot repeatedly. The jagged hunks of metal tore away the androids veneer of humanity, exposing the adomen skeleton beneath. The projectiles pummeled the robot again and again, tearing off an arm and parts of its torso.

Tiet scowled at his prey as he launched the mental attack but nothing could dull the pain of losing her. He quickly tired of the game and he sent his father's blade spinning toward the robot. The blade pierced his adomen skull and stopped when the hilt impacted its metal cranium. The android fell over as dead as a mechanical could be and did not move again. The battle still raged on around him, as he knelt down near Dorian's body and sobbed.

VI

MALEC surveyed his monitors again to be sure. It was unwise to give the General premature information. He was a great leader, but not a patient man. "General, the weapons are fully charged, sir, and we have locked onto the orbital location of the giant Barudii sphere," said Malec.

But the general did not acknowledge his words at all. He was watching something taking place on the battlefield that he had not expected to see.

"Sir?"

"Yes, Malec, I heard you," said Grod.

"Shall I order the weapons to fire General? "

"Wait just a moment."

"But sir, the window of opportunity is closing fast. Our junk satellites will drift beyond the Sphere's location if we don't act now," said Malec with more urgency.

General Grod was focused on the scene playing out before him on the battlefield.

"General?"

"Yes, Malec, order the weapons to be fired. Malec, do you see that person down there near the wreckage of that ship?" he asked as he handed him the binocs. "Malec, I believe that is another Barudii warrior."

"Sir? But they have been..."

"I know that, but nevertheless...he possesses the Barudii psycho kinesis. Fire the weapons now Malec; afterward I want that man in our custody."

"Yes sir. It will be done"

General Grod was a dignified, dark-skinned man, a clone of the first generation Horva; a former slave of the Vorn. He raised a long range rifle and brought the scope to bear on Tiet; still kneeling in the wreckage of the *Saberhawk* next to Dorian. He was holding her body.

Grod aimed his weapon and fired a single shot at the Barudii warrior from the Horva's command base atop the ridge above the valley.

TIET tried to lift Dorian's body; to get her away from the battle. Something flashed around him and he could not move. All his strength was gone in a split second, followed by his consciousness.

MALEC activated the special electromagnetic pulse weapons in orbit. The weapons were well within range of the Barudii sphere, drifting into it and magnetically attaching as the sphere controlled its forces on the planet below. The weapons were hidden within old junked satellites. When the devices had attached themselves, they relayed a signal to the elite Horva command base.

The Sphere, busy with the surface battle, was not alerted to their presence as they impacted its surface as any space junk would; it appeared to sense no threat in the objects. Malec fired the weapons and an instant later an electromagnetic pulse enveloped the Barudii sphere, frying its circuitry in a devastating wave of energy.

The Sphere never saw it coming. All power failed and the control of its forces ceased. On the battlefield, the sphere drones and the mechs became confused and weren't able to fight. The air drones flew off course and began to crash into the battlefield.

Orin was still engaged with the Horva, taking on as many as he could, when he noticed the change in the robot warriors and air drones. The Horva were cutting down the mech-robots with massive firepower that was not being returned and the air drones were crashing all around him.

They were smashing Horva into the dirt in great swathes as they fell out of the sky. Orin ran for the cover of the surrounding ridges. The battlefield had suddenly turned into pure chaos; he only hoped that Tiet had found cover.

A drone smashed into a group of Horva near Orin, and the blast from the impact sent wreckage flying in every direction, cutting down men and showering a mound of dirt and metal on top of him. He was unconscious and half buried in dirt and wreckage.

The carnage was over very quickly and the battlefield quieted down as the men who remained alive began to reorganize and look to the wounded. The badly injured were dispatched on the spot, and it was not seen as cruel to the Horva since they viewed such a state as a burden. Those able to carry their own weight were able to rejoin ranks. Grod smiled at the outcome of his plan.

"Well done, Malec. Now I will have you fetch my Barudii prize and return him to the laboratory complex at Nagon-toth."

"Yes, sir. General we're also picking up a massive object skimming the atmosphere."

"Very good."

The giant Barudii sphere could be seen to the west. Fire trailed away as the atmosphere burned away most of its mass. The remaining charred wreckage would eventually drop into the Waron Sea to the northeast, approximately one hundred and twenty miles from the battlefield at Mount Vaseer.

Malec led the armed group to the wreckage of the *Saberhawk* and gathered up the unconscious Barudii warrior Grod had brought down with a stun blast. Dorian was still in his arms when they found him unconscious.

The Horva pulled the female body away from him, and then they bound and fastened the unconscious warrior within a shielded capsule for transport to the heavily fortified complex at Nagon-Toth. The general was already rallying the remaining Horva troops to move onto the complex where they would be regrouping with others to execute the General's next objectives against the Vorn. The Horva troops moved quickly to the northeast, following the General who led them upon his grevasaur.

BY the time Orin had regained consciousness, the battlefield appeared barren of living combatants. The carrion birds and animals tended to the rest. It was earlier in the day than it had been during the battle, letting him know that he had been there at least overnight. A large piece of drone wreckage had landed across his body but had apparently been buffered by a significant mound of dirt carried in the impact of the aerial robot. He felt the weight, but no pain from broken bones or gashes in his skin. He was still buried up to his chest in the dirt with the wreckage overlaying it.

He moved the large piece of metal with his mind, sending it flying off away from himself about fifteen feet. Then he mentally pushed the heavy dirt off as well, and inspected his mid and lower body for signs of injury. Other than a possible concussion, he appeared to be fine. He regained a standing position and scanned the valley floor. He found the wreckage of the *Saberhawk* and headed off for it.

The whole valley was littered with debris from crushed drones and aerial fighters. The remains of Horva also covered the landscape. Wild animals growled at him as he passed through the area; they guarded a smorgasbord. The sky was filled with birds. They swooped down onto the battlefield to collect their portion and fly away again. They scattered as he ran toward the wreckage.

He could hear screams coming from different places where wounded but living men were being attacked by ravenous beasts, and he thought them fitting for the enemies of his people, the destroyers of his race.

When he finally reached the remains of the *Saberhawk*, it was still on fire in a few small places and smoldering across most of the main body section. He found Dorian's body, but there was no sign of Tiet. Something must have happened. He would not have left her body exposed to the elements and wild beasts.

A closer look at the area revealed another surprise. There were two more androids among the wreckage that apparently had been destroyed by Tiet. He went to one that lay on the ground with Tiet's blade still imbedded into its skull up to the hilt.

He withdrew the sword, allowing the robot's head to fall to the ground and placed it into the sheath next to his own sword. Looking back to the ground around Dorian's body, Orin could see what appeared to be several sets of Horva tracks. There were no dead Horva lying in the near vicinity.

Tiet would not have been consciously engaged by these brutes without having killed at least a few. He must have been unconscious. He spotted Millo several yards away among the cockpit wreckage. They had taken Tiet for a reason, but why would they want him alive?

First things first. He buried both Dorian and Millo in a clear area among the wreckage of the *Saberhawk*. Then he kinetically pushed a large piece of fuselage over their graves to protect the site from predators.

He followed the tracks left by the Horva army's departure. He didn't know where they were headed, but he would die before he gave up on the son of his old friend. Tiet had become like his own child after all these years, and nothing was going to stop him from either retrieving the boy alive, or avenging his death.

WHEN Tiet regained consciousness, he was suspended inside a semicircular mechanism with a form-fitting black suit covering all but his head, hands and feet. What appeared to be metallic buttons covered the surface of the garment and more were attached to his feet, hands and around his head.

The room he was being kept in was fairly dark except for a light around him and the soft glow of machines beyond. He could see some movement in the darker area, but the bright light that was focused on him kept his pupils constricted, not allowing him to see much.

He tried to exert his mind upon the mechanism that held him suspended in an energy field. He heard a noise-spike from a monitor and a shock suddenly emanated from the suspension mechanism that nearly drove him to unconsciousness again. Apparently his brainwaves were being monitored.

He thought he might try again and began to feel for the people in the room. Perhaps he could seize someone controlling the unit, but the unseen monitor alarmed again and the field shocked him once more. *Man that hurts!*

He tried to contain the urge to cry out in pain. He was exhausted from the punishing energy. He knew another attempt would knock him out and he at least wanted to be conscious. Had the Horva captured him? He wasn't sure. He could only remember Dorian amid the wreckage of the *Saberhawk* taking her last breath, and then pain and nothingness.

It wasn't like the Horva to have such technology, but he remembered that the Horva he had faced on the battlefield had been much different than those back home on his own planet. And what had happened to Orin? He had not seen him since before the *Saberhawk* crashed into the valley floor. "Who are you?!" he shouted.

There was no reply from the darkness. "Where am I?! Come out and face me, you cowards!"

Behind a Plexiglas barrier a scientist tapped his communicator panel. "General? He's awake."

"Are you ready to collect your data?"

"Yes, sir."

"Excellent. Move him to the dome."

THERE had not been much to salvage from the wreckage of the *Saberhawk*. Orin had been able to obtain one blaster pistol, two working kemsticks and he had scavenged an extra scabbard for Tiet's father's blade. He had also found a locker containing several Barudii cloaks.

The cloaks were made of a synthetic material that was capable of scrambling electronic signals that came into contact with it. This had the effect of rendering the wearer invisible to scanning and sensor devices of many kinds, and was an asset when stealth was necessary.

Orin wore one cloak and carried another for Tiet stuffed inside his belt. If he was still alive, then they would need it to escape from his captors with as little fight as possible.

These intelligent Horva were much more skilled fighters than the brutish kind back home. He and Tiet would be greatly outnumbered even with their kinetic abilities. A subtle approach would be necessary in this case, if Orin was to successfully retrieve his protégé and get him home. Getting home was another problem that weighed on his mind, but only one problem could be dealt with at a time.

The trail of the Horva army had led him many miles north. It had been dark for several hours now, and Orin could see lights in the distance. The tracks of the Horva army appeared to funnel into a huge guarded compound in the distance.

The facility was massive and towered some five hundred feet above the ground. As Orin drew nearer he could see that a forcefield barrier surrounded the compound approximately three hundred feet outside the main buildings perimeter. There were intermediate, one hundred foot tall pylons placed every one hundred feet in the field that acted as connecting points. They were of an alloy Orin was not familiar with, but they looked very tough.

The forcefield looked like it could easily repel a ground force, and the large pulse cannons stationed on the ground and the building itself would be capable of repelling a large number of aerial aggressors as well.

Fortunately, he had no intention of carrying out a full on assault. He would be like a virus; a silent but deadly invader that no one ever sees coming. He approached the barrier with caution. The darkness shielded him from natural eyes while the Barudii cloak kept him invisible to the technology.

Atop of each pylon was a guard station with a Horva manning it. Orin felt for the guard with his mind. He could sense the man's body up in the tower as though his own eyes were fixed upon him; as though his hands touched the flesh. He increased pressure upon the vessels leading to the man's brain slowly and steadily until the he collapsed unconscious. Then Orin catapulted his own body over the height of the pylon and soft landed on the other side.

The Horva guard would wake up in a few minutes and would likely not realize that anything had happened save a fainting spell that the soldier would not want to report to his superiors.

Orin moved across the span of the courtyard toward an area of the structure that was shadowed. Searchlights moved across different areas, and he was careful not to be caught in them or to allow his shadow to be cast by any ambient lighting. He reached a wall and noticed that it was made of a synthetic stone material of some sort. It was completely smooth and would be difficult for an enemy to find hand or foot-holds. Luckily, he wasn't planning on scaling it.

Orin sought out with his mind, looking for any guards that might be on the roof of the complex. He found none. He leapt upwards and came to perch on the edge of the roof. He still could not see any visible guards, nor did he sense any. The roof of the complex was a maze of ventilation system outlets as well as large computer-controlled laser turrets. He began to walk across the roof cautiously; it appeared that the cloak was working well since none of the guns turned to fire upon him.

The ventilation system would be the easiest way for him to gain access to most points in the building without coming into direct contact with the enemy. There were probably scanning devices throughout, but he had to trust that the cloak would allow him to move undetected.

As he approached one of the large vent housings, he could hear the deep roar of the system working to supply fresh air to those within. He pulled out a spicor disc to get through the heavy gauge wire covering the vent, and then decided against igniting an energy weapon in the presence of the sensor-controlled guns.

With his mind he focused on the center of the criss-crossing mesh work then expanded the space so that the fibers were pushed outward just enough for him to crawl through. Once inside, he mentally controlled his descent and moved into a horizontal tunnel off of the pipe.

He slid along as quietly as possible knowing that any noise would be amplified by the nature of the tunnel. In turn, he could also hear many voices and various machine movements coming from all directions within the system, as it collected the activities of the complex and amplified them all.

Not knowing where Tiet was being held, Orin knew that he might have a long meticulous search ahead of him. He hoped that he might be able to sense him if he got close enough. His kinetic signature would hopefully be easy to distinguish among the Horva. And, if Tiet were able, he would already be trying to escape.

GENERAL Grod passed through the automatic doorway and into the control chamber. Within were various control terminals and stations for monitoring what happened in the chamber beyond. On the far side of the room was a large row of viewing windows that looked into the huge dome. Grod sat in his command chair and waited for final preparations to be finished.

"General, we have him in position."

"Is he awake yet?"

"The suspension field is active; subject is conscious. Our warriors are in place. Battle droids are in place and activated. The teragore is in place in the outer dome. All successive inner domes are secured."

Grod had a great interest in what was about to happen. He wanted to know the abilities as well as limitations of this Barudii warrior. The warrior's abilities had once been an integral part of his plan for conquest of the Vorn race and this planet. Other opportunities to utilize those abilities had been lost, but now he had another chance, and he needed to see what his prize could do.

"Release the Barudii."

TIET had not realized he was unconscious until he awoke again. His environment was different now. No longer was he inside the laboratory setting he was in before. He and the mechanism that still held him suspended inside its energy field were centered within a large dome.

The walls were mirrored like glass but the finish was peculiar; like a two way mirror. Someone was obviously watching from beyond. Near the walls were more of the Horva he had seen in the battle at Mt. Vaseer. There were twenty of them surrounding the mechanism that held him suspended within.

Each Horva soldier was wearing an armored garment and carrying various kinds of weapons, including several with pulse laser weapons. Others were armed with hand-to-hand weapons and Tiet wondered why that would be.

Suddenly the suspension field was gone and he fell about three feet to the ground. He was free from the field—but he had no weapons, and here were these Horva waiting for him. As soon as the field released him, the Horva attacked.

Tiet's feet had no sooner touched the ground before he rebounded to the air and bounced off of the top of one of the mechanism's curved sides toward the Horva. Several shots rang out from pulse rifles as Tiet sent his bare foot into the face of one of the men who tried to bring a bow staff up to defend himself. The powerful kick snapped his neck, dropping him to the ground. Tiet snatched the weapon from his hand as he fell and launched himself back into the air.

The dark-skinned warriors were trying to track his movements to attack him, but were becoming a jumble as Tiet moved nimbly through them. He came down among several bunched together and was fired upon by a Horva man with a pulse rifle. He dodged the shots with lightening speed as several unsuspecting Horva on the other side of him caught the blasts. He parried and smashed the laser weapon along with the man's hands with the spiked end of the bow. The other end quickly followed into his head, dropping him to the ground.

Tiet whirled around to block strikes from two more Horva and spun downward under their weapons to sweep their legs out from under them. They fell backward hard. Tiet struck one in the head, but was forced to evade more shots before he could finish off the other. The grounded clone tried to roll out of striking distance as Tiet pulled a large knife from a sheath on the Horva's leg and hurled it back at the other clone with the pulse rifle. As the knife found purchase, Tiet caught the Horva's rifle with his mind and leapt into the air. The pulse weapon met him there.

He landed laying down a line of steady fire on the remainder of the fighters inside the dome. There was nowhere for them to run as he mowed them down. Then he stopped firing and remained in a guarded stance to see what would happen next.

"Very good," said Grod to the technicians around him, "lower the second dome."

The dome around him suddenly split across the top and two equal halves separated and rolled back into the floor. Beyond was another identical domed room, only larger in size.

Within the dome were six battle robots that stood twice the size of a man. They were armored and were armed with large cylindrical fast repeating laser cannons. A shot rang out from somewhere on the dome that blasted the gun away from his hand.

They might have killed him, but that didn't appear to be their plan. Evidently he was meant to fight for their sport; and unfortunately with no way of escape apparent to him right now, he had little choice but to comply.

Tiet retrieved the spiked bow. He raised it into the air with his right hand and started it spinning rapidly. The battle robots locked on target as

Tiet sent the spinning bow into one of them like a buzz saw. The laser cannons that made up one of the robot's hands were smashed to pieces as the bow ricocheted into its head, sending metal shrapnel in all directions.

The others quickly opened fire on him. He only had time for an instinctive move. Without even realizing it, he formed a bubble of intensely vibrating charged air that repelled the blasts from the robots. They were raining down a firestorm upon him, yet he remained untouched. The pulse blasts were disrupted as they impacted the kinetically-formed bubble.

The robots continued to fire, trying to penetrate the mental defense. Grod looked on with intense pleasure. He had not expected the Barudii to have this much power over the elements. He knew of no such incidence recorded about the Barudii of old times. This was even better than he had expected. His eyes were fixed on the young warrior through the refraction of light and image the charged bubble was creating.

Tiet quickly regained his composure and caused the bubble to swiftly expand with great force behind it; smashing into the five working robots around him. Each one was slammed into the inner mirrored wall of the dome with enough force to crush their exoskeletons and leave them as piles of twisted metal upon the floor. Once again he was left standing alone within the arena.

"IMPRESSIVE power, is it not?!" demanded Grod to his technicians within the control room. "I really wasn't expecting him to survive the battle robots."

"Shall we open the last dome with the teragore sir?" asked one of the control techs.

Grod punched a key pad on the arm of his command chair. "Varen, do we have a viable sample of DNA?"

"Yes, General. The samples we extracted should work well for what you have requested," said the Vorn scientist from a nearby laboratory.

"Very good then. Proceed according to schedule. And Varen... remember your family would not want to see you compromise the procedure and get them killed."

"I understand, sir."

Grod tapped the communication switch off. "Golon, retract the last dome!"

The Horva technician did as he was ordered and switched the control to retract the final inner dome wall.

ORIN was trying to follow the loudest sounds he was hearing. The ventilation system was not very difficult to move through; the tunnels were fairly wide to accommodate the large volume of air that moved in and out of the facility.

He came to a branch that veered off to his right. The sounds were definitely coming from somewhere off of this branch. The shaft narrowed considerably, but he could get through on his belly.

He continued on for another fifty feet until he came to a side vent that had a lot of light coming through it and the noises intensified. Orin crawled up to it and peered through. Within his sight line was a huge creature that stood about fifty feet high. From what he could see the room was a great dome and a smaller semitransparent dome was in the center. Tiet could be seen inside it.

The inner dome was quite large also but not in comparison to the dome without that held this great beast. It was reptilian in nature and had four stubby powerful legs. A long tail, thick, with a cluster of large spikes on the end curled around the animal. Its head was fierce-looking with needle-like teeth proportional to the creature's size.

Tiet did not seem to be acknowledging the presence of the beast in the outer dome. Scattered around him were several smashed robots and a number of dead Horva men. It all looked like some deadly sport for these clones of the Vorn, and he was sure they must be watching from somewhere.

SUDDENLY the dome around Tiet began to separate in two and fold down into the floor. He looked in horror at the beast being exposed to him now. The creature also reacted to the dome dropping before it. Now the prey was exposed.

It began to step toward Tiet's position, and lunged at him with its long neck, propelling the deadly head and teeth right at him. He got out of the way fast, taking to the air. The creature lunged for him again as he landed. He threw out his hands and sent a massive kinetic blast at the predator's incoming face; knocking it away.

The beast reeled for a moment, and then regained its composure with more fury. A chemical spray issued from its mouth, which ignited in the air on its way toward Tiet. He formed another kinetic bubble to repel the flame that engulfed him. The flame was disrupted, but not the heat. It was too hot to repel this way; and he sent the bubble outward and into the creature with massive force. The animal was hurt, but only became more enraged by his counterattacks.

Grod was completely enthralled by the display. He wanted this kind of power for himself, and he intended to have it. The teragore opened its great mouth again and a long whip like tongue shot out toward Tiet. He flipped over its strike, as the beast tried to catch him.

The long tongue darted back and forth trying to capture its prey as he continued his acrobatic evasive maneuvers. Orin cried out to Tiet from behind the vent in the dome wall. He heard him and tried to pause as much as he could to locate his voice. He could see Orin's hands coming through the vent in the wall.

It was a tight place for Orin to try and maneuver. The vent was quite thick and blended right into the rest of the wall materials. He couldn't get enough room to cut through. Orin pulled a kemstick from his thigh clip and brought it through the vent space with his hand, as Tiet tried to evade the whipping tongue of the teragore.

"Tiet!! Take it!!" cried Orin.

Tiet saw the weapon in Orin's hand and leapt upward after it. The kemstick leapt away to meet him in the air. He caught the weapon just as the tongue of the teragore found purchase around his legs. It brought him full body into the ground. The impact knocked the breath out of him and the kemstick out of his hand.

The great tongue began to retract quickly, dragging him toward the beast's mouth. He realized the kemstick was not in his hand and reached out with his mind to retrieve it, as he was pulled across the ground. The kemstick obeyed and rolled after him; leaping into the air to find his hand as Tiet was lifted upside down toward the gaping mouth of the creature. He caught the weapon as the creature pulled him inside and the jaw closed after him. The teragore raised its great head and swallowed the young warrior whole.

Grod was grinning from ear to ear as the lump of flesh began to slide visibly down the creature's throat. Orin's heart was about to leap from his chest as he watched the heir of his king devoured by the animal. Suddenly the visible lump stopped its descent within the teragore's throat. A rod of bright orange light erupted from the creature's neck and quickly whirled around in a great circle from within. The teragore's massive head pitched forward as the neck separated from the rest of the animal's body. He leapt out of the orifice within, landing near the severed head covered in the creature's secretions.

"Unbelievable!" shouted Grod.

He was out of his chair on his feet in amazement. "I have never seen such a display of power and skill!"

Suddenly Tiet sprang into the air and caught a hold of the vent where Orin was located.

"Get back!"

Orin was still in amazement himself at the wonderful escape his protégé had just executed. He slid backward fast to allow Tiet to gain entrance. Tiet stabbed the ignited kemstick into the armor plated grating and cut through it with ease. The hot piece fell out and landed on the floor of the dome below as Tiet crawled inside.

Orin backed his way out of the smaller vent shaft with Tiet following him on his belly. Soon they came out into the larger main shaft.

"Good to see you again!"

"And you. Quickly, put this on. It will hide you from their scanners."

Tiet pulled on the Barudii cloak and the pair headed back down the main shaft on their knees the way Orin had come in.

"Where did he go?! And how did that weapon get into the arena?!" growled the General.

"We're searching sir. It appears he has gone into the main ventilation system but his life signature has disappeared from our scans."

"Find him now!!"

VII

ESTALL had been doing a good job getting the Vorn battle ships ready for departure. With the enemy under control here, they had been able to gain control of the ships that were still docked on the planet. Ranul had come up with technology to allow them to operate the Vorn control systems. The devices converted the Vorn computer language to Castillian and vice versa, allowing them to pilot the craft through the rift if necessary.

A number of pilots from various Castillian tribes had already signed on for the mission, and now it looked like it would be necessary to go through and intercept the fleet before they attacked as Kisch k'ta had threatened. According to Ranul's readings of the data, the rift would be stabilized within five hours and they needed to be in space waiting for it.

The Vorn fleet still had not contacted the Governor and Ranul could only conclude that the massive attack sphere was the cause of it. According to the files contained in the Vorn database, the Sphere had been constructed by the Barudii. It still blew his mind to think that on the other side of the rift there was a twin planet to his home world Castai.

He was as anxious to see it as he was to know what had become of his friends. Perhaps they might find the Vorn engaged in a battle with the Barudii sphere and be able to aid in the fight to destroy the Vorn armada. The communication link sounded. "Yes?" said Ranul.

"Ranul, all seven battle cruisers are under way. Are you ready to go?" said Estall.

"Yes. I'll meet you at the pad in ten minutes. How does everything look?"

"Everything seems to be operating smoothly so far. Those translation devices are allowing everything to go smoothly."

"What about the Vorn?"

"They're tucked away nicely in one of their own prison compounds, guarded heavily by my men. The other Aolene warriors are settled in on the warships and ready to join Orin and the others in the fight across the rift."

"Very good. I'll join you shortly."

He did not mention to Estall that the *Saberhawk* may very well have been destroyed by now. He assumed that Estall could have figured out how dangerous the mission was in the first place, or maybe he just had that much confidence in Orin and Tiet.

The Barudii warriors were powerful, but in a space battle that would make little difference. He hoped Estall's optimism was well-founded. He also wanted to see his friends again—alive.

Ranul glanced over the data screens once more as he grabbed a pack of his own technical gear and headed for the exit to the lab he was working in. He boarded a nearby transport tube and was whisked away toward the main launch platform where he was to meet Estall.

Within three minutes he was across the large compound and exiting the tube to find Estall waiting for him with a shuttle. They greeted each other unceremoniously and climbed into the small ship. Estall, a capable pilot himself, operated the shuttle controls as they ascended to the Vorn battle cruiser hovering one thousand feet above the compound.

The other warships were already en route for the transdimensional rift and would be leaving the atmosphere by now. The small six man transport was dwarfed by the ominous size of the Vorn ship which received it into itself like a mother pulling in its young.

The battleship was easily ten times the size of the *Saberhawk* and much more heavily armed. These same types of ships had destroyed the Castillian space fleet in the early years of the war with the Vorn. Now, they would allow the Castillians to exact retribution for those losses and more.

They made their way to the bridge where a Castillian crew piloted the ship with the aid of Ranul's translation devices. They had all spent so many years under the heel of the Vorn, that it was a tremendous feeling to have taken so much control back from their oppressors. The ships were quite powerful and Ranul was pretty confident that if they had to face the Vorn fleet they would fair well in the battle.

The cruiser soared upwards toward space breeching the atmosphere. The rest of the ships appeared on the main monitors with the Castillian language equivalents. The new Castillian space fleet pushed onward toward the transdimensional rift. Neither Estall nor Ranul had ever been in space. The sight of the rift, as they approached, was ominous. It was so huge in comparison with their ships. Absolutely nothing could be seen beyond the void.

Ranul checked the science station readouts on the stability of the rift. It would still be several hours before it became permeable enough to cross. He continued his work on communication with the Barudii sphere. If the Sphere was in the area of the other Castai, then they would need to quickly establish contact with it to show themselves as Castillian and not more Vorn ships to be attacked. The void lay before them, and everyone wondered what they would find beyond.

WITHIN the ventilation system, Tiet and Orin were making good time, as they passed under a vent coming from above. Tiet, who was bringing up the rear, heard a clattering sound like something coming toward them. He looked upward into the tube and saw a mechanical beast of some sort coming fast at him. There was no room to have a full out confrontation in this vent, and the insect-like robot was going to have the advantage.

He scrambled out from under it as it fell into the same vent tube he was in. Suddenly he saw more appearing behind it, coming from the way he and Orin had already been. The robotic beasts had multiple legs on each side of their slender cylindrical bodies. Several red eyes were spaced across the slender heads that contained small compressed air jets.

As the creatures took up pursuit, scurrying along the vents, they began to fire small spikes from the air jets. The spikes were clattering along the metal sides of the vents as they tried to move as fast as they could through the curves of the system.

The spikes imbedded into the metal where they hit, injecting acid cores, causing the walls to sizzle as the acid burned into them. At this point, they didn't know if they were on track for the outside or not, but the robot insects were gaining on them. If they tried to blast the mechanical creatures kinetically they might shatter the entire vent tube and drop themselves right into the middle of an army of Horva.

The tube that had previously provided many twists and turns to help them avoid the spikes now opened up into a long straightaway. Orin almost paused, but there was no time to find another route. He picked up the pace as fast as he could, but the creatures were quick and the spikes they were firing were even faster. With a straight shot at them the creatures would no doubt hit them multiple times.

Orin could hear Tiet behind him, dogging his heels. The smaller man definitely had the advantage running in these tubes. Suddenly the shaft closed ahead of them. A security door had come down in front of them and the only outlet was a connecting tube from above. Orin came to a halt below it and turned to see if he could hold the creatures off while allowing Tiet to go up first.

The moment he turned to fight, the entire ventilation tube between themselves and the approaching robots, collapsed inward as though a giant hand had grasped it from without and crunched it. They couldn't believe what had just happened in their favor and had no explanation for it. The integrity of the tube seemed to be intact. They could here the robots on the other side of the collapsed tube clattering against the crumpled metal trying to get at them, but to no avail.

Without wasting anymore precious time, they shot up the outlet tube using their kinesis to propel them. The tube appeared to keep going and it looked like they might even reach the roof again by way of it. But how had the Horva known their location in the vent system to close that door in front of them?

Orin wondered if the robots had been transmitting images and navigational information back to the Horva once they had happened upon them. He couldn't come up with anything else. The Barudii cloaks had been working when he got into the facility; he had no reason to believe they had failed to hide them now.

But if the Horva were looking at their own schematics of the system, they might well know where this tube was taking them and be waiting. Still, they had no choice but to try and exit the facility or be potentially caught in a battle they couldn't win; if more Horva were waiting they would have to deal with the problem then.

The pair continued upward at a high rate of speed upward as the end of the tunnel came quickly into view. Orin blasted the vent cap with a kinetic burst. The power rippled the air causing odd refractions of the available light, like a wave of heat rising off a hot road.

The vent cap shot off the tube as they flipped out of the vent and landed with weapons ready on the roof. Orin's suspicions had come to fruition.

Several hundred Horva warriors were closing from all directions, but the automatic gun turrets still had not picked up on their life signatures. The cloaks were working but nothing was going to hide them now; The Horva were closing fast and beginning to fire their pulse weapons.

The pair blocked several shots with their ignited blades and each one began to send out kinetic blasts in various directions trying not to hit each other in the process.

Suddenly from somewhere within the Horva masses, a huge kinetic bubble erupted, sending many of the Horva over the sides of the crowded rooftop to their deaths. Tiet and Orin looked at each other in surprise, as neither had caused the incident.

From within the area a new fighter could be seen utilizing twin ignited Barudii blades; whirling with complex precision, slicing into the Horva around him. The mystery guest in this battle was taking down Horva in all directions and with a complexity and speed that captivated the tiring pair.

This fighter was moving nimbly among Horva and reaching out in all directions with ignited twin blades—blocking incoming shots as an after-thought to his own offensive attacks. It was terribly precise fighting that smacked of a highly trained Barudii; beyond even Orin or Tiet's skills.

Suddenly the auto-guns swiveled around and began to fire not at them, but at the Horva warriors. In particular, the guns were picking off Horva around the new unknown fighter almost as if they were coordinat-ing with his sword attacks. For a brief moment Orin thought the warrior must be controlling the guns somehow.

But surely this warrior was not so powerful as to be able to execute such precise and amazing hand-to-hand fighting along with the mental stamina required to precisely operate five or six computer controlled laser cannons all at the same time—was he?

The action had gone away from Orin and Tiet by now, but they didn't know whether to make a getaway or wait to see what or who this person was doing all the amazing damage to the Horva. They hesitated toward the latter. Then the figure, having cleared away most of the Horva around him with swords and the auto-guns, launched high off the rooftop and came to a landing in front of Orin and Tiet, still crouched in their defensive positions.

The person was wearing a sand-colored garment that seemed oddly pedestrian for a warrior of this caliber, and he was hooded, with only glaring, penetrating eyes visible. "Do you want to live, Barudii?" he asked with a distinctly masculine voice as the Horva regrouped behind him with more reinforcements adding to their numbers.

The warrior ran to the edge of the roof and launched out away from it with such power as to completely clear the compound's energy wall three hundred feet away from the buildings perimeter. Orin and Tiet barely took enough time to glance at each other as they stood and followed after the mysterious man. They each made the jump and soft landed next to the warrior.

"What about the perimeter cannons?" asked Orin as they all broke into a paced run away from the compound.

"We're all cloaked from their sensors by our garments," said the warrior.

Well that answered one question, thought Tiet. Now who in the world was this person?

"Who are you?" asked Orin.

"There isn't time now. The Horva are already mobilizing attack fighters to come after us. We must keep moving."

"Where are we going?" asked Tiet.

All he could see in the direction they were running was desert. Against the pale sand, the attack fighters he spoke of would easily spot them without sensors.

"Just keep moving!" urged the warrior.

As they continued on toward the open desert, the terrain began to shift from the rocky terrain where the facility was located to shifting sand and large dunes. The trio had been running for nearly fifteen minutes when they heard the sound of fighter engines coming toward them from the rear. Despite having covered approximately two miles at a high running speed, the fighters were still closing in.

The men began to enter the dunes as Tiet looked back to see at least ten aerial fighters coming into view about a mile behind them and moving fast. As they entered the dunes, the sand began to swirl around them. He wasn't sure what was going on, but kept running. The whine of fighter engines got louder and louder. Orin knew they must be within visible range by now. Only the warrior's tan attire seemed appropriate now as they ran through the whirling sand.

Then suddenly a wave of sand seemed to billow up around them all and swallow them whole. The fighters zoomed past where the men had been and kept on going on the assumption that their targets must be hiding around the dunes, or had made it further away from the compound than they had anticipated.

TIET, Orin and the mysterious warrior now found themselves in an odd shaped underground alcove. The sand was above them without being on them. It was as though the desert had opened its mouth and swallowed them, depositing them within its bowels. The sand parted before them to reveal an underground cavern of immense size.

"Don't be alarmed gentlemen. We are quite well hidden down here," said the stranger.

"Who are you?" insisted Orin.

"Ah, yes," said the man as he untied his hood and slipped it away to reveal a man of more years than Orin with a partial beard and short completely white hair.

"It can't be! I thought you were killed in the sector seven battle—Wynn Gareth."

Orin was shocked and Tiet was clueless. Who was Wynn Gareth, that Orin would know him? He had never mentioned the name to Tiet before.

"Well, I see you've heard of me, though I don't remember either of you. I wasn't killed in that battle obviously. One of the big Barudii carriers exploded in the vicinity of my fighter, which disabled my controls; the shock wave pushed me through the Transdimensional Rift.

After I emerged on this side I was able to affect repairs to the damaged system and make my way to the planet. It took me awhile to figure out what had happened to me. At first I didn't realize my ship had even gone through the Rift."

"My name is Orin Vale and this is Tiet Soone, the son of our late king, Kale Soone."

"Really? The birth of the king's son was announced only days before we went into battle against the Vorn at sector seven. And here you are all grown up—and a very promising warrior from what I could see."

"How long have you known we were on the planet?" asked Tiet.

"I have been watching you both since you emerged from Mt. Vaseer and entered the battle against General Grod's forces. After you escaped the dome, I aided you in your escape a little."

"Then it was you who crushed the vent tube?" asked Orin.

"Yes. Kinetically. I tracked you and thought you could use some assistance."

"That was some amazing fighting on the rooftop. How—?"

"Young master Soone, you may have noticed that on this side of the rift our kinesis is greatly enhanced beyond what we knew back home on Castai. There is something about being on this side of the Rift that increases our power."

"We began to notice it after we passed through the Rift two days ago," said Orin.

"I have been on this twin planet of Castai for twenty years and there is much that you and our people back home don't realize about what has been happening in this war with the Vorn. Also, the forces that overlapped into our dimension through the Rift have a much more potent effect on our abilities than you are probably aware.

Back home, we Barudii were receiving the misting rain from a far off storm; here on this side we are in the thick of it. What you may have thought amazing back at the compound is within either of your abilities. With proper training you two will also be able to control the energies that are in play on this side of the Rift."

"But what about the Vorn and these Horva…" asked Orin?

"Orin, things are not as they may appear to be. But no more questions now. I will explain the situation after you have refreshed yourselves. Come, there is food and drink," insisted Wynn as he began to walk a path through the cavern. Fueled torches lit the way as they made their way deeper.

It had been while Orin was still in training as a warrior that he had studied some of the battle techniques of Wynn Gareth. He had been a formidable pilot, but was studied for his mastery of the warrior art of Barudii kinesis. But what Wynn had been known for all those years ago back home paled when compared to the display they had witnessed today.

Orin was curious to learn what Wynn was referring to with the war and the greater abilities that were within their reach, but Wynn was right, they did need to eat and rest and prepare for whatever lay ahead.

DAOOTH Pasad stepped in front of the retina scanner located near the exit of the lab facility. He was an assistant to one of the head scientists located within General Grod's compound and there were very important goings on of late. He had proven himself to be trustworthy to the Horva while they were fighting the oppression and rule of the Vorn military; and he had the privilege to leave the compound at will.

The scanner cleared him for exit. The computer-controlled door opened, allowing him to pass through to the outside. While some of the Vorn scientists had been captured and put to work under the general, others had come voluntarily—hoping to find safety and protection, as they allied themselves with the Horva commander. Among them was Daooth, and he was well-favored in his occupation at the compound and his liberty was a result of that favor.

The tall, slender-framed Vorn man made his way to his transport with his personal supplies from the compound and loaded them into the storage compartment. He climbed into the cockpit and then closed the canopy as the engines came to life.

The compound had not been built to house civilians, so many of the Vorn loyal to Grod and his campaign were allowed to live in a nearby area that was close enough to the base to enjoy the protection of the Horva.

Recently, the Vorn military had not been striking offensively very much. They had been preoccupied with defending their interests on many fronts. They needed to reinforce their conquest of the twin Castai across the Rift and there were terrible losses because of the Barudii sphere; as well as the great losses sustained at the hands of General Grod and his clone army. The Vorn military was very near collapse, and it seemed nothing would be able to prevent it.

The transport headed away from the building perimeter and passed through a security portal in the shield, heading for the wasteland. The settlement given to the civilians was far from luxurious, but its location underground provided a better weather environment and added protection.

After several miles the transport came to a large protrusion of rock in the desert that lay to the west of the compound. The transport came to a metal door that was the entrance to Daooth's residence.

The door responded to a transmitted code from the transport and opened to allow it entrance inside. The transport settled down on a platform area, and then Daooth retracted the cockpit canopy, gathered his supplies and headed into his domicile. He made his way to a closet along the corridor and triggered a switch inside. The back wall released and moved aside.

He went through the portal, which led into a large cavern beyond. The closet wall waited a moment then smoothly slid itself back into place. He hurried down the cavern to a place where another smaller tunnel intersected with it. He took the passage and came to a room. Inside were three men. They were eating as he came into the entrance of the hollowed out chamber.

TIET spotted the dark-skinned man first as he appeared in the entrance to the chamber where Wynn had served them all a meal. Tiet launched out of his seat at the sight of the dark-skinned man standing there. His blade was in his hand as he lunged for one of his sworn enemy.

Daooth deftly dodged the first strike and parried with a strong fist blow to Tiet's side. Tiet came back quickly; ready to deal a death blow to the man. Suddenly Wynn was next to him and had grabbed his sword arm. Instantly he was disarmed of his father's blade, and it fell to the floor. The look on his face was astonishment. Had he and Orin been led into a trap by a traitor?

"Stop it! Daooth is a friend. He is a civilian I have known for many years. He saved my life shortly after I came to the planet, when I was captured by Grod and his Horva," said Wynn.

Neither of them could believe what they were hearing. But they stood down and listened to what Wynn had to say.

"Forgive my startling of you," said Daooth in a vaguely familiar dialect.

"I told you that things are not what they appear here," said Wynn. "There are those among the Vorn who would gladly live at peace with us, but the military has control over them—just as they do our home world.

Daooth is one of many who want that control to end. There is also General Grod who is the leader of the Horva armies you saw at Vaseer and at their main compound at Nagon-toth. Grod and his clones are of a breed that was discontinued due to the threat they began to pose to the Vorn's control.

They were engineered to be stronger, but it became obvious to the military—as well as to Grod—that these Horva were capable of rising up against their Vorn masters. Grod quickly took the opportunity to lead them in revolt and that rebellion has been building in strength steadily since before I arrived on the planet.

Grod had been capturing important cloning scientists from among the Vorn cities on raids; then he conquered cities as his power increased. Not long after I arrived, I was captured by the General and he took samplings of my DNA to use in a new experimental process by which he could regenerate his cloned body and splice my Barudii DNA with his own in the hopes of gaining our kinetic abilities.

Daooth helped me to escape, and caused an accident which destroyed the genetic material Grod was going to use. He has hidden me here all these years since.

It is my hope to somehow free his people from the control of the military and Grod."

"Why haven't the civilians risen up for their freedom against these two," asked Orin?

"My people have not fighting skill to face these armies, and they are not the only threat," said Daooth. "Baruk clan is also enemy, and more fearsome than Vorn military or Grod. Now they control Vorn military from distance. Vorn do what they want, further Baruk interests, they leave them alone. But now Vorn nearing defeat by Grod's forces and Baruk are sure to try and come."

"Yes, and Grod knows that as well," said Wynn. "That's why he's so desperate to complete his DNA experiment so he can power up his clones with Barudii kinesis."

"But you said that Daooth destroyed the sample of your DNA that Grod needed to do the experiment."

"Yes, but now he has yours," said Daooth.

Tiet was taken aback; he had no idea what had occurred before he had awoke within the confinement field in the Vorn lab.

"Then we have to infiltrate Grod's compound and destroy the samples," said Orin.

"It not that simple anymore," said Daooth. "Grod already moved out with scientist for project and samples, and headed to a rendezvous with his army at Baeth Periege."

"Baeth Periege is the main city for the Vorn military and it houses their most advanced cloning facility," said Wynn. "Grod needs to have control of this facility to perform the regeneration of his army. He will have to defeat the Vorn and if he does he will have taken away the main power base and last refuge of the Vorn military."

"What can we do?" asked Tiet, "if he takes that city and the cloning facility—how can we hope to stop him and a whole army of clones with our power?"

"There's the problem my friends," said Wynn. "We are up against formidable odds, two armies and time itself. If we fail to stop Grod, which must be our first concern, then I fear only the Baruk themselves will be able to stop him."

"If only our clans could have made peace," said Daooth, "men should act as brothers—not this killing of other races. Skin color is only difference between you and me," Daooth pointed at Tiet. "My blood is red like yours; my heart beats same as yours. Even Grod, he a clone of my dark-skinned people; fierce, strong, but he wants freedom just like us."

"My friends, I realize that I have involved you in a seemingly suicidal goal. It may seem overwhelming and I cannot ask you to endanger yourselves for this cause…"

"We're already involved," said Tiet. "That's my DNA he's using." Tiet looked at Daooth. "I guess, I never though about your clan's side of things. We need peace between the clans, but how?"

Orin nodded his agreement. "It's easier said than done. We had better stay focused on what we can handle now."

"We have a transport and some explosive charges that we could use to destroy the equipment Grod needs to conduct the regeneration," said Wynn. "It's just about the only way we can prevent Grod from coming into power."

"I've been sorting things out Wynn," said Daooth, "I think I have way to destroy facility. We try to infiltrate city in transport we having to fight our way through Grod's army then Vorn military guarding city. In these caverns is link to old magnetic rail system. System used to connect Baeth Periege with military compound at Nagon-toth, before Grod captured it.

Vorn military have detonated charges to bring tunnel roof down and cut off route into city. System still has power, but Grod did not want to take time to clear all of debris, it remained unused. System runs right into cloning facility. It used primarily to send troops from main cloning facility to compound."

"How fast is the rail system?" asked Wynn. "Baeth Periege is nearly one thousand miles away."

"It is a frictionless magnetically suspended rail car system. It will travel approximately six hundred miles per hour," said Daooth.

"That's pretty fast. It wouldn't take us long to get there at all," said Tiet.

"Yes, but Grod already has the jump on us," said Orin. "And where is the break in the system?"

"Break occurs approximately one hundred and fifty miles from city perimeter," said Daooth. "Only problem how to clear debris and pass through in time to stop Grod. Defenses of Baeth Periege will not hold him long. He has massive clone army and Vorn military already very weak in their resources."

"I think that with our kinesis we might be able to clear the debris but we will need time to work," said Wynn.

"My people long for freedom," said Daooth.

They all shared the sentiment. They gathered the explosive charges necessary and followed Daooth through the various side passages to access the magnetic rail system. But the thought lingered for Daooth and Wynn that with Grod defeated the next enemy would be the mighty Baruk.

VIII

IT did not occur with the fanfare Ranul had expected, but the fleet had successfully passed through the Transdimensional Rift. The passage was surprisingly quick and uneventful.

Estall's cruiser the *Esyia* took the lead of the group. Ranul scanned the area for other ships, but found none. They had no contact with the *Saberhawk*, which he had always guessed would be the case—but there were not any ships within scanning range at all, not even in orbit of the planet.

Kish k'ta had boasted of a space fleet on their way to wipe out the remaining people on Castai, but there was no evidence of it at all. Even from the Vorn computer records, Ranul had expected to possibly find a battle between the Barudii sphere and the Vorn; but there was nothing. Nothing.

"There isn't much to see out here is there," said Estall.

"I know. That's what bothers me. I suppose we better head for the planet and see if that's where the action is. If Orin and Tiet are still alive there will be something going on."

Ranul signaled to the helmsman, "Let's proceed to the planet."

The ships glided forward on course for the strangely familiar planet.

"Lets get those shields up," said Estall to one of the control technicians. "If that Barudii sphere weapon is out here somewhere, I don't want it mistaking these Vorn ships for targets."

"I agree, but we don't know if it's here or not. The Vorn fleet was not responding to Kish K'ta's messages, but we don't know why. If the

Sphere is in the vicinity, it could be cloaked from our sensors. The Barudii on this planet built it right from the schematics I have here.

That thing could very well have already destroyed the Vorn fleet Kish K'ta spoke of. I don't know if it would have attacked the *Saberhawk* or not. It's a computer, so I would expect targeting intended targets only, but who knows."

"If the *Saberhawk* didn't face anything out here, I bet they would have gone straight for the planet," said Estall. "I don't know any warrior who wouldn't rather face a fight on the ground, rather than be cooped up inside a space ship."

"According to the records the planet is now inhabited completely by the Vorn. They have colonized it since wiping out all the other Castillian clans there. We'll have to get closer to the planet before we can scan the surface."

VOLLEY after volley of pulse fire blazed across the sky toward the perimeter defense shield surrounding the Vorn city of Baeth Periege. General Grod watched with great satisfaction as his forces mounted the assault upon the city. "How long will it hold?" asked Grod.

"Probably another twenty hours at the rate of replenishing."

"Good, that gives us plenty of time. Is the team ready?"

"Yes sir. They're waiting for you to join them for the assault."

Grod headed away from the firing line toward an area to the south. The pulse cannons continued to pound away at the defense shield as the city's gun systems attempted to repel the attack.

He made his way to a work site away from the main group. Malec was waiting for him with three hundred warriors outfitted for battle. The work site was relatively hidden from view of the city; just as Grod had planned.

"I've sent an advance team ahead of us sir, to begin the breach on the tunnel barricade."

"Excellent Malec. The intercepts on the local transmissions show that the Baruk may have already answered their distress calls. They could be here within the twenty hours it will take to breach the perimeter shield."

"Once we have come into the city from this position we will be very close to the cloning facility. We should be able to disable the shield and allow our forces to continue the main assault while we begin the regeneration process," said Malec.

"Let's go."

He moved to the head of the group and into the tunnel they had been working on. It went down into an old magnetic rail system tunnel that had previously connected the city to the compound now controlled by Grod's forces hundreds of miles away. Once inside, the Horva warriors began their rapid move to enter the city beneath the perimeter shield.

The tunnel had been barricaded at the city entrance but the small team ahead of the main group would have it breached by the time they arrived. It was imperative to Grod to get to the cloning facility in time to complete the regeneration process before the Baruk could arrive on the planet. If he was to have any hope of success against that fierce race, he would need the advantage of the Barudii kinesis.

The tunnel was dimly lit by the emergency lighting that was still powered by the city. Main power to the entire system was split between Grod's compound and Baeth Periege, but with the tunnel collapsed many miles from the city perimeter; it had been left abandoned.

Grod's forces moved swiftly toward the perimeter barrier that had been put in place by the Vorn military. The demolition team Malec had sent would have everything ready by the time they arrived. They were going to use some old salvaged Barudii technology to get through the barrier. It involved dispersion fields and would, with the power they were supplying to the device, completely vaporize the barricade in a moment of time.

It took them about twenty minutes to make it to the position where the demolition team was waiting.

"Is everything ready?" asked Grod.

"Yes, sir," said one of the team, "we can remove the barricade at any time."

"Excellent. My brother Horva," said Grod to the entire group of warriors, "it is time for us to go beyond the designs of those who created us as improvements of themselves. We shall remake our own image with a far greater power than we have known before. We shall conquer our oppressors and be free. And if the Baruk should come, we will defeat them as well."

It was on everyone's minds that the Baruk were going to come in response to the uprising now that Grod and the Horva were beyond being defeated by the Vorn military. But they would not arrive in time to save their principle base of power here at Baeth Periege.

"As soon as we are beyond the barricade and come into the open square of the city I want my team with the scientist Varen, to accompany me to the cloning facility. We will take it and begin the regeneration process, while the rest of you attack the main power couplings for the perimeter shield generators. With the shields down our brothers will swarm in and the city will quickly fall. We need not worry if any ships try to escape. It is the city and the cloning facility that we want, not Vorn prisoners. Their time of rule is at an end no matter what."

He turned to the demolition team and gave the final order. "Detonate the device!"

They complied and up ahead a brilliant blue burst flashed down the tunnel at them. The entire barricade to the rail system tunnel was engulfed in the dispersion field flash causing the metal and stone to disassociate every molecular bond within the field. The light of the sun shone into the tunnel, and the troops immediately rushed ahead toward the opening.

As they came out of the end of the tunnel and crossed the semicircular smooth crater left in the tunnel floor by the dispersion blast, they could see the rail systems above ground system of magnetic rings that were spaced out along the remainder of the distance to the cloning lab compound. The rings allowed the rail cars to continue above ground while still being propelled magnetically.

Grod's group maintained its push down the track toward the cloning lab with Malec personally bringing Varen. Acting as both protector and jailer to Varen, Malec carried the cryo-pod that held Tiet's genetic samples for use in the regeneration procedure that Varen would be performing on Grod and his Horva.

The hinder group, composed of the remaining two hundred Horva warriors, was splitting off to attack the shield generators. They were already coming under fire from the Vorn military and many of the Vorn's brutish Horva clones were coming in for the fight as well.

The shield attack group laid down heavy firepower as they advanced steadily; blasting many along the way. Clearly the Vorn military had not expected to be attacked from behind their own positions at the city perimeter, allowing the attack team to make steady progress towards its goal. The pulse fire from without the city continued to batter upon the perimeter shield as thousands upon thousands of Grod's Horva warriors waited to enter Baeth Periege.

Grod and his team had very little resistance in getting to the cloning lab complex entrance. Only a few of the brutish Horva slaves had stood between them and the entrance to the facility. He did not enjoy the fact that they had to be killed. He really did pity the poor creatures. But as they could not be brought from the loathsome state they had been created in—as brutish dumb beasts to be exploited by the Vorn—he thought that truly death was better for them.

Grod and his one hundred warriors rushed into the complex and quickly secured the lab facility they needed for the regeneration. Varen's identification card, which remained active, had allowed the group quick access to the interior of the facility. Malec gave the cryo-pod to Varen and led him to the control boards.

"Varen," said Grod, "remember your family! I want this done perfectly or they will suffer."

"I understand General," said Varen with a nervous voice.

Varen tapped the controls and a multitude of the cloning pods opened up allowing Grod and fifty of his warriors to climb into the horizontally situated units. They first removed their weapons and battle gear with the respective items of clothing and then positioned themselves individually within the pods.

The remaining warriors would ensure that no one interfered with the approximately three hour procedure. No doubt, the shield attack team was getting all of the attention within the city.

Varen secured the pods once they were all situated inside and removed the Barudii genetic material from the cryo-pod. He inserted it into the matrix chamber that housed the parent cloning material during normal procedures and inserted a command disk containing the necessary changes in the standard processes to bring about the automated sequences for a regeneration of the already cloned tissues and the very genetic structures that were embodied within them.

The material within the matrix chamber would be used as an enhancement of the cloned warriors within their own bodies. Once the data was received by the automation system, Varen activated the program and the process began even as the thunderous battle continued to rage within and without the city.

Grod drifted off into a medicated sleep as the system prepared him and his warriors for genetic enhancement and regeneration. His drifting thoughts were of the glorious spectacle he had witnessed in his battle dome of the young Barudii warrior skillfully vanquishing all the combatants, Horva and robot alike, that had been arrayed against him in the dome; even the teragore beast itself.

WHEN they arrived in the rail system chamber they found minimal power available. Daooth located the grid controls and brought the system online. The rail cars were kept in a docking bay apart from the magnetic propulsion tunnel. Daooth brought one of the cars from the bay on a loading arm as Wynn and the others brought the explosives into the loading area. It was quite a bomb they had rigged; almost too much for the hover carrier to support. It consisted of two containers of inert chemicals that became volatile when mixed; Trilithium matrix and B7 accelerant.

"Two of us will need to go ahead of the car with the explosives and begin clearing the rubble from the tunnel," said Wynn. "After that, one person needs to accompany the bomb in case there are any other obstructions in the tunnel."

"Tiet, why don't you go with Wynn and I will take the explosives on through after you," said Orin.

"Are you sure Orin?" asked Wynn.

"I'll make sure nothing interferes with the car reaching the facility," said Orin.

"Daooth can load the cars into the propulsion tunnel and send us through from the control chamber here, so you will not need to operate the rail car yourself, but you will have to escape after it comes above ground inside the city. The rail system becomes a series of magnetic rings that are spaced along the track until it enters the cloning facility. However you will be inside the city at that point so you will have to be careful. Grod's forces have undoubtedly already begun their assault."

"What about our rail car that will be setting in the tunnel?" asked Tiet.

"Daooth can move our car into a passing cell located at different positions along the tunnel. They allow for cars to be displaced while others pass," said Wynn. "We will go on ahead in this car and then I'll communicate with you when its time to come through with the explosives."

Wynn and Tiet climbed inside the rail car which was quite long. It must have measured nearly thirty yards in length. Tiet and Orin exchanged glances as the door closed on the car. Orin tried to look reassuring.

He knew if anything happened to him, that Wynn would be able to continue Tiet's training even beyond what he had been able to accomplish with the boy. But he had no intention of riding that rail car to his doom. He did wonder what would be waiting for him in a city full of Vorn military and potentially a Horva army led by Grod. Hopefully they would be so busy with each other that they wouldn't even notice him.

The door of the car secured itself in a locking position as they sat down and fastened their seat harnesses for the trip. Daooth worked the controls causing the hoist arm to move the rail car into the propulsion tunnel. Once inside the mouth of the tunnel, a safety door constricted into place behind the car so that the magnetic field would not harm anyone in the loading area. The field was powerful enough to pull a person with any metallic garment into the tunnel and potentially to their death.

The safety door sealed and the rail car was bathed in a magnetic field. The hoist arm released the car, which was then suspended within the magnetic field.

He hit the send command and the car began to propel forward down the tunnel; rapidly increasing speed to six hundred miles per hour. Within the car, Wynn and Tiet noticed little effect from inertia because of the damper systems in place.

"The trip will take a little over an hour to complete. I would suggest we both try to get some rest before we arrive. You'll need it."

"If you say so."

The journey from his home on Castai seemed like an eternity ago and nearly the whole time now without much sleep. He was glad they had at least had the opportunity to eat some food and clean up back at Wynn's base in the caves.

He didn't like being separated from Orin, but he had to stand on his own at some point and he sensed it may have even been done on purpose when he sent him with Wynn. He rested his head back, noticing that Wynn already looked like he was asleep. Within moments he had also drifted into much needed sleep and not even his old nightmares could break through his exhaustion.

ORIN made his way to the car holding the device. He boarded and found a seat, unconsciously glaring at the weapon as though it might blow at any moment. Daooth watched him from the control booth and manually closed the car door so he could secure it with the boom arm for loading into the tunnel.

He noticed an odd power fluctuation on his panel. It was something he had seen before but he couldn't...*wait they're monitoring the system!*

"Orin! I have to send you on through quickly," his voice came through on the rail car intercom.

"What's wrong?"

"They're monitoring the power emanations back at Nagon-Toth. If they've already noticed it they'll be sending a squad to investigate. Strap yourself in, we've got to hurry."

Orin didn't waste any time with further inquiry. He located his safety harness and secured himself to the chair.

The boom arm swiveled over to attach to the car and he could hear the magnetic seal apply through the roof with a snap of metal. Daooth watched carefully as he guided the arm and placed the car inside the tunnel for departure. Once inside he released it and closed the safety door behind it. It took only a moment for the magnetic field to charge and build inside the tunnel and then the rail car was speeding down the tunnel.

Daooth secured the control station and locked out the system. Hopefully Grod's men would not be able to disable it when they arrived to investigate. He ran out of the chamber and back through the secret tunnel entrance they had come by. It was time to get back to his quarters before he was missed.

TIET was shaken by the slowing and stopping of the rail car. He saw that Wynn was already out of his harness and looking through the front window at the tunnel blockage ahead. He removed his harness and joined him at the window. The lighting in the tunnel was adequate to see the large pile of heavy stones that were piled three quarters of the way up to the roof of the tunnel. A large hole that looked like the source of the rock could be seen going upward into the tunnel roof.

The rail car came to a halt approximately fifty yards from the blockage. The side door unlocked and opened automatically, no doubt under the watchful eye of Daooth hundreds of miles away in the control chamber. Tiet followed Wynn out the door and they bounded up the tunnel toward the rubble.

"Well, let's get started," said Tiet as he began to concentrate on the individual stones.

"I want you to move all the stones at once."

"What do you mean? Are we able?"

"If you remember when we were on the roof of the General's compound…."

"Yes," interrupted Tiet, "you were controlling the automated weapons while simultaneously fighting the Horva! That was amazing."

"It was easier than you realize. It is not in the amount of power but in the technique for wielding it."

"What do you mean exactly?"

"I mean that when you use the kinesis you are reaching out with your mind. You are probably used to reaching out in one direction at once. But you must learn to reach in all directions at once; as though you were surrounded in a sensory field and everything within the boundary of it were susceptible to your senses and your control. When these things are comprehended at once in your mind you're able to manipulate them, and the kinesis carries out the thought with action."

He was enthralled by this new understanding of the Barudii power insomuch that he nearly forgot why they were even here.

"When I was on the roof, you were in the dome with that teragore. I could reach out throughout the compound and in my mind I could see you fighting that beast. I admit it takes discipline and a lot of practice to begin thinking in this fashion, but you do have the ability. Of course it's all made possible by the energies in play here. We don't understand how, but the fact remains. It was the overlap through the Rift that gave us Barudii what power we had, but on this side we are much more powerful."

"Could you teach me?"

"Within you I believe is the last hope for the Barudii to carry on as a race. We must do what we can to preserve what is left. You're young and if you survive this war our people have hope to live again. I want to make as much of a contribution of what I have learned to that future as possible."

"Now, raise the rocks Tiet. Reach out in all directions around you, feel the tunnel, the ground, the hole in the roof, even me standing here beside you, and then move the picture in your mind with determined intent."

He tried to let go of the way he would have normally gone about the task by trying to lift the boulders individually. He began to feel more and more around him. The picture of his surroundings was in his mind as though he had eyes on all sides, and even more he could feel his surroundings in a way he had not previously realized.

He could sense the temperature of the air in the tunnel, the rhythms of Wynn's bodily functions—heart rate, blood pumping, neurons firing—and he could feel it in a way that gave him confidence that he could manipulate any of it if he desired. His kinetic power felt like another appendage of his body. In his mind he searched over the surface of each piece of rock in the pile of rubble and could sense with exacting precision where it fit in the crumbled tunnel roof above.

He exerted his will upon the rock and it disassembled in his mind and in reality. It moved apart and seemed frozen in a moment of time with even the dust suspended in the air. Wynn was in awe, not at the possibility of performing the task, but in Tiet's quickness to apprehend the concept and be able to apply it so skillfully. He was his father's son indeed. The rock began to ascend upward and reassemble into the places it had previously occupied in the cavernous hole.

Once it was all in place, Tiet held it there but was unsure what to do to keep it all in place. Wynn fused the joints of the rock with his mind and Tiet could feel them supported by it. He released the structure and it held.

"I could sense your power working within the same space as my own and I could sense my susceptibility to your mind. Was that real?"

"It was real but not indefensible. If I were to attack you kinetically, you could shield yourself from the intrusion and prevent such an attack and possibly even counter it if you sensed that I was unprotected in some way."

His communications link beeped to life on his wrist.

"Daooth here. How are you progressing with the repair?"

"It is already complete my friend."

"Good. Orin is already en route with the other rail car and the explosives. He should be arriving at your location; within half an hour. I had to leave the station because I realized they are monitoring this place from Nagon-Toth.

I have been monitoring transmissions from the compound about Baeth Periege. Grod's forces have already penetrated the city and were able to disable part of the city's perimeter shield. The Vorn are attempting to keep them at bay, but from the communications among the Horva they are probably well on their way to entering with their main group of forces."

"The sooner we send that rail car into the cloning facility the better," said Wynn.

"I agree. You will need to reenter the rail car. Now that the blockage is cleared, the automated system will take control and position your car safely inside a passing cell in the tunnel wall."

Tiet followed him back into their rail car. The door closed automatically and an alarm sounded to notify the passengers of an approaching car in transit. The computer began its procedure for clearing the path of the other rail car in the system as a hoist arm moved away from the tunnel wall to magnetically grasp Wynn and Tiet's car; pulling it into the recessed portion of the wall known as a passing cell. The car locked in place as it prepared for the passing of Orin's car; counting down now from twenty two minutes.

IX

ORIN sat uneasy within the second rail car as it made its way down the dim tunnel traveling at hundreds of miles per hour toward Baeth Periege. The explosives setup, located in the car, was rigged for an explosion upon the car's stopping and Daooth had wired its trigger directly into the auto sensor panel for that purpose.

The computer controls for the magnetic rail system would automatically bring the car into the cloning facility for unloading and stop it at a preordained station within the compound. When the auto sensors signaled a full stop it would detonate the care package. All he had to do was make sure nothing prevented the car on its journey and then escape himself where the system comes above ground.

Daooth had sent the car into the blocked tunnel under repair conditions, but with the removal of the tunnel blockage, the automated system had assumed control again. Orin was glad to know that they had been successful in clearing whatever debris had been up ahead.

Now he just had to keep his mind centered on the tunnel up ahead so that he could make sure nothing else happened to prevent the car from reaching its destination. If this was their only shot at stopping General Grod from completing his DNA regeneration of his troops then he had to make sure nothing would trigger the automated system to stop the car.

He could sense the other car up ahead as he projected down the length of the tunnel. It was out of the path of his car and he was approaching their position rapidly. In a few moments he had passed their car tucked away in a recess of the tunnel wall. Orin continued to project his mind up ahead. Nothing appeared to be in the way and within ten more minutes he felt the car and tunnel begin an upward ascent. Daylight came into the car abruptly as it emerged on the surface within the city of Baeth Periege.

He quickly made his way to the front window of the car and could see what must have been the cloning complex in the distance ahead. The speed of the car was rapidly declining as it entered the city. Overhead, he could see the massive magnetic rings that Wynn and Daooth had spoken of.

A barrier came halfway up the height of the rings and stretched between them on either side. He supposed it must have been a preventive measure to keep someone from inadvertently falling or climbing into the path of the rail cars. Otherwise, there was open space between the rings from that height upward and this would be his means of escape.

Orin looked over the bomb mechanism once more then raised his blade from this scabbard and cut a circle into the roof of the car large enough for him to pass through. He shot up through the hole and came to stand on the roof of the car. He could feel the tingling of the magnetic field around the car and beneath the rings. Several items including his blaster pistol flew off of his person toward the rings as he passed underneath them. Fortunately the adomen that formed his blade was not magnetic.

Around the rail system on either side was a massive open area that separated the main city from the outer perimeter. It was lavish, with decorative pools and gardens of every sort and Orin thought how surprising it was to find such things in the Vorn city.

He had never considered the peaceful or artistic side that the Vorn might possess. They had been the enemy for so long that he had never looked beyond any characteristic that wasn't oppressive or linked with this war.

On the right of the magnetic rail he could see where Grod's army had knocked out a large portion of the defense shield and had secured the area just inside. It appeared they were making a definite effort to push the Vorn away from the cloning facility.

Perhaps Grod had already gotten inside and begun the process to re-generate himself with Tiet's DNA. If any of them were inside, they were about to get a big surprise.

To the left were several ships docked upon a huge landing platform. None of them would have made Orin look twice except one. It was a Barudii ship. A strider. It sat within a number of Vorn military ships, some of which were powering up to escape the onslaught of Grod's army.

He picked his moment and leapt away from the rail car. It continued on without him toward the cloning facility, but he wasn't watching it anymore. He was transfixed upon the Barudii ship. It had been his ship and had been stolen previous to the massacre of his people.

It was nearly five hundred yards away from him and he began to run toward it. He could see it exhausting from the engine's cooling vents. Whoever was inside was planning on leaving very shortly.

Behind him, the rail car came into the station at the cloning facility. Several of Grod's men who were guarding the entrance raised their weapons as they saw the rail car coming into the docking site. The car slowed and the men moved toward it, but they couldn't see anyone through the windows. The car stopped and the doors opened for unload-ing.

Orin was closing within two hundred yards of the strider. Behind him came a flash of light that cast his shadow upon the ground running in front of him. The sound came less than a second later along with a blast wave that knocked Orin off of his feet. He tumbled and looked back to see the cloning facility blossoming like a flower with petals of debris and flame. The job he came here to do was done, but now there was some-thing more.

Orin quickly got back to his feet and turned back to the landing plat-form he had been heading for. To his amazement, the gateway was down and someone was walking out to see the devastating explosion. Orin had started to run but stopped in his tracks when he saw the man standing there. Then the man caught his gaze and they locked together in time.

Each of them recognized the other in a way few could ever under-stand. Rage flooded every fiber of Orin's being. He surrendered to it and sprinted toward the man standing under the strider. At nearly the same instant the man ran towards Orin. He removed a blade from a scabbard under the long coat that he wore. Orin pulled his own blade.

They took to the air as they approached one another. Their ignited blades struck one another as they passed and Orin struck the other man's face with a quick jab. They both soft landed and turned to face one another with blades on guard.

The other man staggered a moment, from the hit, as he landed. He touched his face with his hand and looked at the blood when he pulled his hand away. The cloning facility burned behind him.

"So, what I was told was true!" shouted Orin. "You murderer! You're a traitor to your family and your people!"

The man did not answer the charge. He raised his blade and leapt again at Orin, who stood his ground. The man came down with a powerful blow and Orin matched his blade. They exchanged several quick blows then Orin was knocked backward by a kinetic blow from the other man. He flipped over and recovered himself quickly; bringing his blade to bear.

"So Kale, I see you have been training. You rejected your people, but not their ways?"

"I was rejected by my father and my people!" said Kale angrily, and he blasted at Orin again with his mind, but the mental attack was countered and nullified.

"You betrayed your father the King! And for what? So that you could join up with the enslavers of our planet?!"

"No! For revenge. What loyalty did I owe to him when he dishonored me, his only son, before our people?!"

"Not your people anymore. And not his only son," said Orin sarcastically.

Kale struck again and again but Orin did not let his blade through. Suddenly he sensed someone else and quickly evaded another blade in flight. He launched himself up and away and came down to find two more Barudii surrounding him with Kale.

"So you led away other traitors as well?"

Kale and the other two Barudii rebels closed in on him simultaneously with blades drawn and ignited. Orin pulled a kemstick from under his cloak and ignited it. He did not wait for them to strike, but took the fight to them.

He struck at one of the two Barudii, while simultaneously attacking the other man with his kinesis.

The first defended himself with his blade while the man under Orin's mental attack failed to perceive his own weakness. Orin caused a massive firing of pain neurons throughout the man's body, especially in his hands and arms.

He buckled under the mental attack and threw his sword away as though it were on fire. Orin immediately sent his kemstick spinning behind his body at the newly vulnerable target. It caught the man directly in the chest. He seized and fell to the ground dead, as the kemstick fell away.

Orin diverted between his two remaining opponents, striking and countering as each came at him. He tried a mental attack on the other unnamed Barudii, but found him protecting himself kinetically. Kale moved in again as Orin defended a strike from the other. He tried to mentally pull the kemstick from the ground, but Kale intercepted it in flight and cut through the handle of the weapon, destroying it.

Orin wondered in passing thought if he would lose this confrontation. The other Barudii man was not nearly as skilled, but having to deal with both at the same time was tipping the scales out of his favor. Suddenly explosions began to erupt on the air field around them.

They each looked to the direction of the attack to see the army of General Grod beginning to move toward their position. Large war machines were firing volleys from some distance away at the ships on the huge landing platform apparently in an attempt to destroy those preparing for lift off.

Orin used the distraction to strike again at Kale who skillfully intercepted his strike but did not anticipate the leg sweep that Orin caught him off guard with; sending him backwards to the ground. The other Barudii renegade took advantage of Orin's move against Kale to strike at Orin from behind. As Orin turned to counter the strike, something flashed behind the man and a blade shot through his chest.

Orin looked toward the point of origin to find Tiet and Wynn emerging from the magnetic rail safety wall and running hard toward them. He was glad to see them, but for a quick moment the tragedy of Tiet seeing Kale and vice versa flashed in his mind. He turned to strike at Kale again who was still on the ground trying to get up.

He locked eyes with the younger man in that instant, and then Kale glanced behind Orin to the blade that had been hurled into his comrade. Orin did not have time to discern what had caught Kale's attention. The Barudii blade catapulted away from the fallen man's body under Kale's mental control and pierced Orin from behind. He lurched in shock and pain; his eyes still locked on Kale's face. He could hear Tiet shouting from some distance away.

Kale looked at the young man approaching with an older man following close behind. He was dressed in the same Barudii cloak as Orin. Kale stood over Orin's fallen body and extracted the blade from his back.

He knew the weapon very well. It was the blade of his father the king. He crouched down near Orin's body, which lay on his side bleeding profusely from the uncauterized wound. "This is Father's blade, Orin," he whispered in his ear. "Where did that person get it?" And then insight seemed to light upon his mind and it was seen in his expression.

He knelt close to Orin's ear, who was now gasping for his breath as his life poured out. "Is that my brother, Orin?" But he did not wait for an answer from the dying man.

The Horva were still reigning down a heavy volley of fire upon the platform; threatening to destroy his stolen ship and Orin's companions were closing in as well. He decided he could not afford another confrontation right now and ignited his father's blade long enough to drive it into the pavement next to Orin.

There it remained; imbedded halfway up the blade length as he extinguished it. He took another stolen stare at Tiet as he approached; then turned to run for his ship before it was destroyed by the approaching war machines.

Kale managed to reach his ship as another not far away on the platform was struck by a powerful blast from the Horva. He got to the cockpit and retracted the ramp as the engines powered up for lift off. He could see his brother reaching Orin's body and he wondered if the boy even knew that he had an older brother. The thought that his own younger brother might have no knowledge of him, bolstered the resentment and fury he had carried so long against Orin and his father.

The child had been so very young when the old incident had occurred, but Kale remembered him. He had supposed that all of the family, including little Tiet, had perished in the great battle that had been said to have completely wiped out the Barudii as a people. It was obvious that the report had been premature.

Kale had seen his father's body upon the battlefield after the battle was over and remembered his crown, but the king's blade had been missing. Now he knew why. He pushed the memories back in his mind and brought the engines to power. The old Barudii strider lifted off the platform and tore upward through the sky toward open space.

ORIN was very close to death when Tiet came upon him. He knelt in his mentor's blood to try to help him, but it was nearly over. He tried to speak as he coughed up more blood. "Who was that person? Who did this? Tell me so that I can avenge you!" said Tiet frantically.

Orin's voice was weak. He could only manage one word before his life ceased. "K...a...l...e..."

He was gone. And the pain of losing him on top of the loss of Dorian was only delayed momentarily by the bewildering last word he had given in answer to his question.

Wynn was beside him as Orin died. His own reaction to the name was one of realization rather than bewilderment. But there wasn't time now for any hesitation. The Horva were on the move toward their position.

"Tiet, we must go!" urged Wynn.

He seemed not to even hear him. Wynn pulled him to his feet against his will and urged him away from their fallen comrade. He went along knowing he must, and paused only a moment to ignite his father's blade and free it from the ground.

Wynn urged him on as they ran toward the cloning facility. He wanted to be sure that the equipment Grod wanted was destroyed. As they approached the building it became clear that the facility was in total ruin. Many fires were still blazing within and there was no way to get inside to investigate further. It certainly appeared that the bomb had done the job adequately.

The Horva continued to lay down heavy firepower as they approached the cloning facility. Tiet and Wynn ran back toward the magnetic rail and took cover behind the safety wall as the Horva strafed the area with pulse laser fire. They were now within four hundred yards of the rail and many of the ground forces split away toward the cloning facility to attempt to rescue any of their forces who might have survived the devastating explosion.

The safety wall was crumbling around them. There seemed to be nowhere to go. Tiet ran to the nearest of the giant magnetic rings and used his blade to make multiple cuts to the support as it rose above the safety wall.

Wynn discerned his intent and sliced away at the support for the same ring on the opposite side of the rail. As the supports gave way, they both combined their mental power to support the ring and then quickly sent it up into the air in a great arc toward the forces approaching their position.

Seeing the approaching section of the ring, most of the ground forces stopped firing as they attempted to scatter. The huge section of metal came crashing down into their frontline and smashed many of the warriors as it tumbled through their ranks. Some of the war machines caught in the path of the ring were crushed and burst into flame.

RANUL continued the scans of the planet surface trying to close in on the disturbance the computer had picked up. The sensors concentrated on one city in particular. The database identified the city as Baeth Periege There was a very intense battle being waged from within and without the city perimeter.

"Helmsman, get us to that city immediately," he ordered.

Estall signaled for two of the other cruisers to follow them to the surface while the rest remained in orbit. The large Vorn warships began their descent through the atmosphere with shields at maximum for reentry. The sheering forces of the atmosphere beat upon the vessels but did not harm them.

As the three large battle cruisers came closer to Baeth Periege, Ranul was able to pull up a more detailed visual: several Vorn ships were leaving the city and heading away for open space as the battle raged on.

Ranul tried to locate the beacon from the *Saberhawk*, but was unable to locate it anywhere in the vicinity. He did however notice an old Barudii ship climbing through the atmosphere, but it was of the smaller strider class of vessel. They needed to get to the city soon; hopefully his friends could be found safe.

WYNN and Tiet stayed pinned down in the trench of the magnetic rail. The Horva had regrouped and were laying down more pulse fire against their position. Large blasts from the war machines were closing in on them. They looked at one another trying to figure out what to do next. "The tunnel!" shouted Wynn over the explosions going off around them.

Tiet got up and followed the elder man toward the magnetic rail tunnel they had emerged from earlier. The explosions continued all around them as the Horva persistently moved in on their position.

The tunnel was nearly eight hundred yards away from them and the enemy was tearing into the rail trench with everything they had. Pulse laser fire was shredding the safety wall all around them as they ran. They shielded themselves mentally at different intervals as large chunks of concrete and metal flew at them.

Suddenly, large beams of energy shot overhead from another direction, but the shots weren't aimed at them. They stopped a moment as the firepower coming down on them halted. As they surveyed the scene, they could see several large Vorn battle cruisers coming in over the city from the southeast. The cruisers were firing upon the Horva army.

The Horva tried to return fire but it was useless against the shields on the cruisers. After several heavy volleys of laser fire, the Horva began to retreat away from the approaching warships. Many of the Horva began to scatter into the wasteland beyond the city perimeter while the greater majority either retreated into the tunnel of the magnetic rail or stood their ground and died.

Wynn and Tiet watched as their own escape route was being used by those trying to kill them only minutes before. They were still hunkered down in the rail trench below a section of the crumbling safety wall approximately four hundred yards from the escaping Horva going into the tunnel. They didn't dare run from their position for fear the Vorn cruisers might pick them off with large pulse cannons.

From the shuttle bay of the lead ship, they noticed a large troop carrier coming down very near their position. They remained where they were as it landed, not having anywhere else to go. To their surprise, when the back of the transport lowered and the people inside came out it wasn't Vorn military but Castillians.

The warriors filed out of the transport and took up a defensive stance around the ship. Behind them came Ranul. He jumped out of the trench when he recognized them. Wynn followed behind him. The warriors took aim on him until Ranul called his name and came out of the formation to meet them.

"Tiet! Where are the others?" asked Ranul over the sound of the cruiser's cannons; still firing on the retreating Horva.

Tiet's face gave away the news before his voice did. "Dead!"

Ranul was shocked by the news, but he hesitated only a moment; a battle was still raging around them. They entered the transport and took seats near the cockpit. The Aolene warriors filed back into the transport and took their positions inside. The ramp lifted as the pilot brought the ship off the landing platform and headed back to the Vorn cruiser.

Tiet could hear Wynn and Ranul speaking with each other, but he wasn't really paying attention to them. He felt safe again as they climbed skyward toward the waiting cruiser still blasting away at the Horva.

The tension of the fight began to be relieved somewhat, but with it came a flood of suppressed emotions. He began to weep bitterly as he pressed his head against the bulkhead. Ranul and Wynn left off their conversation with one another, but did not engage Tiet.

The Vorn cruiser received the transport and continued to clear the city of Horva combatants. They fled into the rail tunnel in droves while others continued into the wasteland on foot or in damaged war machines. They were pursued no further than the limits of the city.

A lone and injured figure watched as the Horva army retreated under heavy fire from the battle cruisers. He wondered where they had come from. All of those large ships were thought to have been destroyed by the Barudii sphere. The battle at Baeth Periege had taken a turn unexpected.

He wasn't sure how the cloning facility had been destroyed. The last thing Grod remembered was going to sleep in the cloning pod. He awoke to utter devastation, and all of his men in the cloning pods, with him, were dead. Malec and the scientist Varen were also dead.

Grod could see his army was on the run without him. This battle was lost. But at least he was alive.

He spotted a personal transport vehicle near a section of debris and confiscated it. Firing up the engine, Grod climbed onto it and bolted away from the smoldering wreckage of the cloning facility toward the open wasteland beyond.

ONCE he was clear of the atmosphere, Kale scanned the space of sector 773. He quickly found the signal he was looking for. He plotted the course into the navigation computer and activated the auto pilot. The strider took off for the preset coordinates at three quarters of its maximum speed. His thoughts were returning to the surface and his fight with Orin.

He had thought the man dead for so many years now; the man who had come between him and his own father. Now he was sure that Orin was dead. But it was not at all satisfying to him. He even felt some regret.

He had not had such feelings since he saw the body of his father lying dead on the battle field near Mt. Vaseer. The betrayal of his own people, though they had rejected him, had not been as satisfying as predicted either.

He had wept over his father and mother and brother on more than one occasion, secretly. His years among the Vorn military had not been able to erase the memories he had of better times before the incident that changed everything for him.

Regret once again tried to settle upon his mind and once again he fought to push it away. After all, what was done was done. He had chosen his path and things could never be what they were again. As for Orin, he had initiated the attack on the landing platform. Kale had only been defending himself. There was nothing he could do about that. At any rate, it had been clear that nothing had changed in Orin's mind either.

But, his younger brother was alive on this Castai. It did not matter. To change course now would be a death sentence for him. He had betrayed his people to the Vorn and now the Vorn to the Baruk.

In the distance, scanners picked up the large vessel he had fixed the navigation system upon. The strider automatically slowed its pace as the docking bay of the Baruk vessel locked onto it and guided the ship inside. Kale prepared himself to give report of the battle. He pushed lingering thoughts of home and family as far away from him as he could and proceeded down the ramp to the waiting Baruk.

INSIDE the Tiet's cabin, Ranul and Wynn discussed the events leading up to this battle at Baeth Periege. The Vorn cruiser under Estall's command was still in position guarding the city, but the Horva had fled hours ago.

Still, the western portion of the city was in ruins from the battle. The space port and surrounding buildings including the main cloning compound were devastated almost completely.

Tiet stood in the shower stall of the washroom, letting the hot water pour over him. He wished the steamy water could cleanse away the recent memories in his mind; even that he himself could be dissolved in it and washed away never to be thought of again.

When the heating cell in his quarters ran low on stored hot water the temperature began to change and so did his desire to stay there in it. He turned off the faucet and stepped out to dry himself. He noticed in the wall mounted mirror that his body was covered in cuts, scrapes and bruises.

These last few days had been the most exhausting and punishing experience of his young life. He stared into his own face reflected before him. Why had he lived while others had died? And did he really want to go on living without them?

He clothed himself in a simple garment and came into the other portion of the cabin where Ranul and Wynn were still talking. Tiet caught Orin's name mentioned before he entered the room.

"Who killed Orin?" asked Tiet abruptly.

Both men gave him uneasy stares, as though the answer was known but they weren't sure of whether to give it.

"Wynn, I saw your face when Orin said the name. He said Kale killed him. Kale was my father. But he could not have meant my father. You seemed to know who he meant by your expression."

Ranul looked at Wynn also.

"Ranul, do you know who this person is? I think the time for secrets is over."

"You're right. You need to know the truth. The person Orin named is not your father, but your brother."

"What!?" Tiet could hardly stand at the statement. "Wynn, I don't have a brother!"

"Actually Tiet, you do," confirmed Ranul. "He's your older brother."

"Why have I never been told these things? Why didn't Orin tell me this?!"

"Three years after you were born there was an incident," said Ranul. "While under Orin's command, your brother was to guard a certain village of three thousand people with a squadron under his command. He had always been a brash young man and given to conflict with his superiors.

Kale decided that there was no real threat to the village and took the majority of his fighter squadron onto the battle front, while leaving only a few to guard the people. The Horva attacked during that time and almost two thousand men, women and children were killed as a result of his irresponsibility.

Orin was furious with him and petitioned your father to remove his rank as a warrior. Your father was ashamed of him and did so and Kale was dishonored before the people. Shortly after those events, he disappeared; he was nearly eighteen years of age at the time."

"I still don't understand why he killed him," said Tiet.

"About five years later Kale was found to have conspired with the Vorn military. He gave them the information on the effects of the Transdimensional Rift upon your people and how they were greatly weakened by its random collapsing. It was all they needed to know to mount an appropriate and devastating campaign at the Barudii's weakest time."

Tiet dropped his head into his hands as he sat down upon his bed. "Does any of this get any better?! My father and mother and my people massacred by the Vorn conspiring with my own brother! And now Dorian and Orin are dead because of all these things!! I do not think I can bear to know anymore of it!" shouted Tiet.

They got up to leave. "I cannot say I know how you feel young master," said Wynn as he put his hand firmly upon Tiet's shoulder, "but I'm here for you. You must go on despite what has happened. Your father the king is dead…but you, the heir to the king…you live on and our people live on with you. I hope you will not let their legacy die now after all that has happened."

He followed Ranul out the door, leaving Tiet on his bed to ponder all that had happened. It was so horrible. Everything was worse in reality than he could have ever imagined in his worst nightmares. Yet he was still alive. *Now what am I supposed to do?*

He thought of Orin. Back when they lived in the cave far in the wasteland, when he had taught him to be a man and a warrior, he had told him that to resolve a difficult problem or situation, resting the weary mind was the best way to clear one's thoughts and be able to approach the situation with new vigor.

He thought upon those lessons for some time. Orin had always been very wise. He wondered if his own father had perhaps imparted his wisdom in some way to Orin. Now both men were gone, but their wisdom was still living in his memory.

He got up from his bed and walked to the portal window of the chamber. He could see over the city of Baeth Periege below. Much of it lay in ruins from the battle with Grod and his army.

Wynn had said that these people, the civilians, had longed for peace, and had hoped for it even through years and years of oppression under their own military government. That government was gone; defeated by Grod's Horva. Grod appeared to be dead, the Horva were defeated and fleeing from Baeth Periege. Maybe, just maybe, he thought, there was something left that was good after all.

X

DATE: The Year 9028 (planet: Castai III-Rex)

THE bright red glow of the binary star Casiss glided across the surface of defense probe #2041. Its mission, to hold a position in this quadrant and maintain continuous long range scans toward the home system of the Baruk, had been uneventful for the last six months since its launch. The probe sailed through a vast sea of silence. Casiss was calculated at nearly one quarter of a light year away, with none of its uninhabitable planetary bodies visible to the eye, save the electronic eye of probe #2041.

Something entered into its sensor band one tenth of a light year away from the probe. #2041 closed in on the object with its sensors to distinguish whether it might be a naturally occurring object such as a meteor. It had been the case fourteen times already since the probe took position there.

The object was quite large, but it was not following the normally erratic flight pattern of a natural space body. Quickly the sensor field was penetrated by even more similar objects; fifty in all. Each of the objects followed virtually the same flight path putting the group on a direct course for the planet Castai.

WYNN walked through the courtyard of pools outside of the newly ap-
pointed combat training facilities. The artwork was pure Vorn from different eras he was unfamiliar with. He took note of the rich detail present
in the forms; some of natural things such as native animals, and some of
the Vorn race. As he came through the serene area into the main courtyard, he could hear the sounds of battle. He saw hundreds of warriors
from among the Vorn race intermingled with many Castillians from
nearly every tribe that had migrated across the Rift after the battle of
Baeth Periege eighteen months ago.

The migration had been rather unexpected, but there had been a rally
cry to join the Barudii king. The Vorn had been defeated on Tiet's home-
world by Estall. The people had begun to refer to it as Castai-Ori, for
origin. The twin Castai here across the rift had similarly begun to be re-
ferred to as Castai-Rexus, illustrating the presence of the Barudii king.
There was at present, no king at all, but Tiet being the heir to that throne
had chosen to remain on this side of the Transdimensional Rift following
the battle at Baeth Periege. His desire was to remain on the sister planet
of his own home world because of the likelihood of further conflict with
the Horva and the impending attack of the Baruk.

Tiet as yet had assumed no formal power, but both the Castillian
tribes remaining on Castai-Ori and the recently freed Vorn civilian population of Castai-Rexus were looking for leadership.

The Vorn had originally looked to Daooth or Wynn as potential leaders to unite them to face future conflicts, while the Castillians had looked
to Estall as the victorious leader of the Aolene who had brought about
the capture and subordination of the Vorn military on Castai-Ori.

Wynn had emphatically refused, while pointing out that he could
never assume power under any circumstance so long as an heir to the
throne of his people lived. With Daooth backing Wynn, and a history of
relations between the Vorn and the Barudii kings of the past before the
Baruk created conflict, it brought about a consensus among the Vorn to
follow Wynn in backing the throne of the Barudii. Estall had also de-
ferred to the throne of the Barudii, and hoped Tiet would step up to the
task.

It all seemed a wonderful change of events to Wynn, but Tiet had not
consented to ascend formally to his father's throne. It had become a matter of great frustration both to Wynn and those among the Council of the

Twelve Cities that he remained reluctant. Wynn himself had spent hours trying to persuade the young man, who at times he thought might cave in to the pressure, but he realized that Tiet doubted himself. The deaths of his friends were still weighing heavily upon his mind.

Tiet had taken great interest in organizing civilians from among the Vorn and the migrating Castillians to form a large ground force in training. He had become obsessed with the task in fact, leading Wynn to the conclusion it was in part to relieve himself from his own troubling thoughts concerning recent events and the deaths of those dearest to him.

Wynn ascended a stairway leading to a very long balcony that overlooked the training courtyard. He couldn't help but be delighted to see his own Castillian people training with the Vorn to fight a common foe. A dream in part had been realized with the uniting of these people and he hoped nothing would tear them apart again; but he thought it vitally important that they have the necessary leadership and that leadership could not be served better than in the Barudii King.

Swords clashed on the courtyard as instructors from among the Aolene guided the trainees in various sparring exercises. The handsome new uniforms Tiet had designed were of the same material used in the old Barudii cloaks and rendered the wearer electronically invisible.

Various improvements from Vorn technology allowed for the E.M. shields to be reduced in size and incorporated directly into the garments along with components that provided a real-time holographic data display and nano-sensory components. These helped to mimic the Barudii kinetic ability to sense information such as number and position of combatants within a certain range.

The data created pressure sensations in the garment to alert the warrior and in effect give them perception in all directions simultaneously. Other nano-components provided scanning of one's surroundings and feeding the information to the holographic display.

Today, the trainees were practicing Barudii blade techniques. Much progress had been made in the eighteen months since Baeth Periege had been engulfed in battle. Daily more trainees appeared as the migration from Castai-Ori continued despite the threat of the Baruk. The city had been under constant repair by numerous robot construction crews, although the cloning facility that had once been such a jewel of science for the city was never rebuilt. The Vorn Council of the Twelve Cities, named for the twelve large cities now housing the population for unification and safety concerns, had outlawed the cloning of Horva as servants.

General Grod's Horva troops provided little interference to reconstruction after their defeat. There had been a few raids on smaller cities that were nearly abandoned, but it appeared they sought supplies rather than conquest. Grod himself had been proven to still be alive; a fact that had brought considerable alarm to the Council. While there seemed to be no immediate threat, it was a definite possibility that Tiet's new recruits might face a war on two fronts if the Horva resurfaced with attacks on the twelve cities.

Wynn continued to walk the length of the balcony until he could see a group of recruits surrounding one unarmed man. The young man was blindfolded but not bound. Several of the recruits moved in to strike.

The first strike went for the face. The victim's head bobbed to one side as the strike passed before him. He quickly struck the mid-section of the attacker then swept the feet while countering another strike from a different recruit.

As the recruits moved in quickly, trying to overwhelm the man, the whole situation seemed to revert to chaos. In a matter of a few seconds, all of the recruits were tossed to the ground, leaving the man standing alone. Wynn chuckled a bit to himself as Tiet removed his blindfold and beckoned his students to their feet.

He could not hear the instructions given at that point, but soon the recruits disbanded to other exercises in the courtyard.

Tiet raised his blindfold again and replaced it over his eyes. Wynn noticed a flash of light as something caught the sun between Tiet and himself. Something whispered and kissed the railing of the balcony next to his right hand. He could see a spicor disc lodged there.

He looked back at Tiet, still blindfolded but curling his index finger in the air toward Wynn. He smiled then stood waiting. Wynn dropped to the courtyard below as Tiet leapt at him. Wynn caught Tiet's foot and sent a fist to the groin, but Tiet's other leg had already come up and over to catch Wynn in the side of the head. Wynn stumbled as he let go of Tiet's foot, but quickly regained his composure. Tiet was standing ready and on guard; he liked training with his mentor.

Wynn smiled back at the younger man and began to think he had taught him too well in recent months. They exchanged a quick moment of fists and kicks with neither man landing a blow with advantage. Tiet was still smiling behind his blindfold.

"I've come to urge you to speak with the Council," said Wynn.

Tiet's smile disappeared. He was never pleased when this subject came up; which it often had since the Council had pressed for leadership in the months following the battle at Baeth Periege.

"We've been over this before," he said. "I am not the man to lead these people, Wynn."

Wynn could sense that this hardness was not as deep as he was trying to make it appear. They exchanged several more blows, with Wynn the more playful now. He noticed that all the commotion on the courtyard had ceased. Nearly all the recruits in the area were focused on the sparring between the Barudii.

"You've become very powerful in recent months. Far more than when we first met," said Wynn.

"All thanks to your training, I'm sure."

"Would you be up to a wager with an old man like me?" he baited.

Tiet smiled again and raised his blindfold. "Wynn, if you're trying to get me to—"

"Of course if you doubt your ability to knock me to the ground in hand-to-hand combat, I suppose I understand," Wynn interrupted.

"And if I do?"

"Then I won't bother you with the matter again."

Now he was intrigued. "Do you really mean it, Wynn?"

"I do."

That was the last word needed. Tiet launched an intensely fast barrage of attacks at Wynn. He managed to match them all, but with difficulty. The younger man had the age advantage and he was powerful. If this kind of attack continued, he might wear him down. Wynn considered it and Tiet hoped for it.

Tiet was younger, but Wynn had decades of specialized training. He deliberately faltered and Tiet took the bait. He landed a strong blow to Wynn's face. The elder man stumbled and went to one knee. Tiet approached. "Looks like you're about to lose this one, Wynn," he boasted.

"That's too bad. Do you think Orin and Dorian would be proud of your lack of resolve to assume your rightful place?" he asked with a mocking tone.

Tiet's countenance flashed through surprise and then anger. He lunged. The elder man took the opportunity and rose to meet him with a knee to the stomach; three consecutive quick blows that knocked the wind out of him. He followed the ambush with a backhand to the side of the head that sent him to the ground gasping for precious breath.

He looked up at his mentor, who was smiling at him again. He remembered the old lesson to refrain from anger in battle, as it can foil one's concentration.

"You tricked me," he coughed out.

"My dear young king, it was only for your own good and ours."

Wynn offered him a hand, helping him to stand again. The pride and anger were gone, replaced with the knowledge that Wynn would never let the issue die.

"The Council meets tonight at dusk. Don't be late."

Wynn smiled and turned away to leave the courtyard and its stunned audience who began to whisper about the outcome. Tiet looked after the elder man, thinking himself foolish to have been baited so easily. It was so important to Wynn, this matter of the throne. He did not understand why, but a promise was still a promise.

He heard a slow clapping coming from behind him and looked to see its source. Ranul was sitting under the shade of the balcony overhead clapping sarcastically with a sly grin on his face.

"Yes, yes—very funny," said Tiet as he turned to gather up his sparring weapons from the ground.

Ranul got up and walked over to him. The soldiers were renewing their training on the grounds; pairing up as they prepared for the days to come should the Baruk actually attack.

"Now don't be mad young master; after all, Wynn means well. The people do need a leader and you are the natural choice. I'm sure Orin would have agreed."

Tiet turned to look at him. "Well, I don't know about that. Orin tended to be very protective of me."

"Maybe, but he cared a great deal for you. And whether you realize it or not, he was quite proud of you."

"How do you know that?"

"I knew Orin very well back before the Vorn came. It was written all over him. He treated you like the son he never had. He would have wanted you to take your rightful place as King."

Tiet looked at him, not sure how to answer. He was rubbing his stomach; Wynn had really laid into him.

"You should get over to the medical complex and have my daughter take a look."

Tiet smiled. "I'm not really hurt Ranul; he just knocked the wind out of me."

"It's still worth a visit, just to see Mirah. Haven't you two been talking recently?"

"A little, but…"

"But what? She's a nice girl Tiet…"

"I know."

"And she's moving up now that she's completed her residency. You're going to have to think about taking a wife someday."

Tiet looked at the *donjarr* on his wrist. He had still not removed it after losing Dorian. "You're a bit direct aren't you Ranul?"

"I don't mean to push Tiet, but you have to go on with your life. Dorian is gone and Orin is gone—you have to assume your responsibilities for your own good and the good of those around you."

"I just don't want to fail everyone, like I failed them."

"You didn't fail them. You fought back against those who had enslaved our people and you won. I owe a debt to you I can't repay in giving me back my daughter. If you hadn't been set on freeing us from the Vorn she would have died in that prison cell along with the children they had captive with her. She was able to go on with her residency work and now she's turning into a fine physician; you haven't failed."

Tiet thought about it for a moment. His words were kind, but they cut him to the heart. He felt unsure of himself yet convicted of the need to serve the people.

"I had better get going Ranul. I've got to get ready for this meeting if I'm going to keep my promise."

He shook Ranul's hand and started to walk away from the courtyard.

Tiet, don't forget. If you get a chance, go by and see Mirah. She really would like to see you. You know, she was very complimentary of the man that freed her from prison.

He laughed under his breath as he continued to walk away. "Subtle, Ranul, very subtle."

GOVERNOR Tal tapped the communication panel to end the transmission to his ship. He was onboard the flagship of the Baruk space fleet. He had assured his wife of his safe arrival and the time for his meeting with the Council of Three. He was quite anxious about the meeting. Since their rendezvous with the Baruk battle convoy months ago, he had not been given much information at all.

The Baruk were far too secretive for his own tastes. After all, the Vorn military and the Baruk were supposed to be allies. This meeting should have taken place just after their arrival, he thought. But he wasn't about to push the issue with the Council.

The Baruk were the most blood-thirsty clan Tal had ever known. It was dangerous enough to be their ally and the Baruk's supposed deal with the fallen angel Lucin was the stuff of legend. He was terrified of this mysterious clan.

One of the Baruk warriors came into the chamber. He was fierce looking to say the least. His black body armor was a part of him; a symbiotic coexistence. Whatever the living armor was, all of the warriors of the Baruk were joined to them. Somehow they covered and intertwined internally and externally with the Baruk forming a living exoskeleton that protected them. Tal had seen the warriors in action before. Their exoskeletons were capable of repelling light pulse weapons fire, and the various weapons they utilized were part technology and part bio-weaponry.

The warrior motioned for Tal to follow him. They both entered the chamber of the Council of Three. Tal had only seen them once before. They were of a different caste than the warriors and they ruled the Baruk as one.

Tal came before them where they were seated upon a raised platform. They were sitting on a wide throne that seemed more organic than craft. Tal waited for them to speak, not daring to show any disrespect to them.

"You have desired and audience with us, Governor Tal?" asked one of the Three.

"Indeed, my lords. I would inquire as to your plans for retaking the planet of Castai on our behalf. We looked to you for assistance in quelling the rebellion of the Horva under General Grod, but we were overrun at Baeth Periege before you could arrive."

"Should we retake the planet it would be unwise to reinstate control to your regime, Tal. You lost the planet and most of your people were killed. You lack the capacity to reign over the inhabitants."

"But we are allies. Surely you will want to help us to regain control. It is for your benefit as well—"

"Our benefit does not concern you, Tal," interrupted another of the Three. "You are weak. It is time we assumed possession of Castai ourselves."

"But you can't—" He almost bit his own tongue trying to stop the words.

"Can't?" they all questioned simultaneously.

"What I mean to say, my lords, is that we have always tried to govern the territory in accord with your interests as well as our own. It would be unfortunate to dissolve that relationship now. I still have a thousand people aboard my ship who can lead the way in retaking the planet from these rebels. At your command, of course."

"Our command has already been issued concerning your people," said one of the Three.

A holographic image of Tal's vessel gliding along with the Baruk convoy appeared in the room above him. One of the Baruk ships heaved a large projectile out of one of its cannons. Tal's heart sank as the object impacted with his ship, smashing it like a glass upon the floor. A thousand-plus people, including his own wife and children were dashed to pieces in a moment. He gasped and could not breathe. He almost didn't notice the white hot needle-stick of the neurotoxin injection. He lost sensation almost instantly as he numbly fell to the ground at the feet of the soldier who had administered the poisoned weapon. His breathing slowed, and then stopped as his muscles ceased to function. He was suffocating but couldn't move to help himself, though his mind was still clear.

"We have no further need of treaty with you or your people Tal," said one of the Three. "Now that your strength has been diminished, we see Castai as ripe for the taking."

Tal could not respond. His body began to spasm from lack of oxygen. The Three hissed with delight as the Vorn Governor entered the throes of death before them.

"Housra, see to the traitor," the Three said to the soldier.

"I obey."

THE food aboard the Baruk vessel was barely palatable. Kale detested almost everything about their clan. If the Vorn military had been able to suppress the various uprisings, then he wouldn't be in this mess, he thought. Kale had been turned against his Barudii people, by Lucin himself, all those years ago and now he was paying for it.

He understood the desire of the Baruk to control the planet of Castai. It was rich in resources and perhaps, even more importantly; it was the perfect location for control of the Transdimensional Rift.

None of that really mattered to Kale at all. He had no allegiances to anyone. He took another bite of the carusk meat. It was bitter to his tongue. The Baruk loved this meal as a delicacy but that didn't surprise him. The bitterness of the meat seemed ironic to him as he thought about it. What had seemed right and good for him at one time so long ago had become ashes in his mouth.

He could not push out the thought of his brother running across the tarmac to try to save Orin. He realized that Tiet almost certainly didn't know who he was at the time; but did he now? And what if they had come face to face then, he wondered. Would Tiet have embraced his long lost brother, the betrayer of their people and their parents?

No, of course not. He would have gladly struck with all the fury he could muster. Suddenly Kale felt disgusted with everything; or perhaps only with himself. He spit the hunk of meat back onto his plate and pushed it away across the small table.

The Baruk could not be trusted. They were completely sold out to the wicked one, Lucin. The Vorn had very little understanding of the true nature of the Three that ruled the Baruk clan and their planet. They were merely a vehicle for the fallen one; a way for him to move among men and control their minds in his symbyte form.

It was Lucin that had promised him vengeance upon his father and Orin for the dishonor they had shown him; a prince of the Barudii. He only had to provide the weaknesses of their mountain cities and great power would be his. But it was a lie from the prince of lies. The death of his people and his family had brought him nothing but regret and sorrow. But he had bound himself to a fallen angel; how could he escape from such a power?

The Baruk certainly had no way of escape and they didn't want any as far as he could tell. The symbyte form of Lucin, inhabiting their bodies, gave them great power and the ability to drive out their enemies before them. Now they were on the move to Castai. Lucin would conquer it and move on through the rift to conquer the twin Castai. Only God could stop an angel and though he thought of dropping to his knees to pray; Kale knew that he was probably the last person God would want to hear from.

Normally, he might have suspected his food to be poisoned, but his personal scanner had detected nothing dangerous in the meal. It did little to console him about the possibility of the Baruk killing him. He looked at his blade upon the hard slab the Baruk called a bed. Picking up the blade he examined it a moment; this blade was his life. He knew he could never trust the Baruk and even if he could, he did not want to remain among them. But how could he escape? They had control of his ship. He heard heavy footsteps approaching his quarters.

THE door opened up before the Baruk warrior. Housra quickly moved inside with his compression gun ready to terminate the Barudii on sight, but he wasn't there.

Kale looked down on the Baruk warrior from the ceiling of the compartment. He clung there via kinesis. The compression weapon used by their clan swung from side to side as the warrior surveyed the compartment, stopping to examine the half eaten meal.

Kale dropped down, igniting his blade as he landed. Housra whirled around bringing his gun to bear upon the Barudii. The ignited blade divided the weapon before he could fire. The living exoskeleton sprang outward from the Baruk, striking Kale.

He was smashed backwards into the door of the compartment but managed to strike back furiously with his kinesis. The Baruk crashed hard into the other wall, but was stabilized quickly by the morphing exoskeleton. It had appeared solid, but now morphed into obscene appendages to protect its host.

Kale brought his blade between himself and the Baruk. The symbiotic creature was reared up in a posture of aggression as it sought to strike.

One of the appendages lashed out and Kale struck it with his ignited blade. It recoiled. He moved in again, striking at the hovering tentacles and landing a blow to the warrior's leg. He severed it completely.

Another appendage knocked Kale to the ground into the table as the Baruk fell from his wound. The morphing tentacle smashed the table flat as Kale rolled away. If Lucin had sent this warrior to kill him, more would quickly follow. He needed to get off of this ship as fast as possible.

He bolted out the door, leaving the maimed warrior and his symbiotic protector as far behind as he could. Now he just had to figure out how to get to his ship and off of this vessel alive.

ESTALL stared at the information coming onto the display as Ranul keyed in the various retrieval commands. Probe #2041 was transmitting its information on a coded band. He studied the incoming data carefully. Looking over Ranul's shoulder, Estall attempted to understand what the transmission contained, but Ranul was scanning the data too fast for him to put it together.

"Well?"

"Well, what?"

"Are you going to share with the rest of us?" he asked.

"Oh!" he said as though he had forgotten others were in the communications room with him. "The probe beyond the star Casiss has picked up a group of objects. After long range scans, it has concluded that the objects are in fact very large space cruisers on a path for Castai."

"The Baruk, I suppose."

"Well, I don't think there's any other possibility. According to the Vorn records, it's along the flight path to their territory."

"Well, we've been training for a fight; looks like we've got one."

THE council buildings were as luxurious as any Tiet had seen among the Vorn cities. This one in Baeth Periege was perhaps the most beautiful of them all. He passed through the main hall on his way to the meeting chamber. It was lined on either side by troops he had helped to train in recent months. They looked very sharp in there uniforms, he thought. It was nice to see the peace between the Castillians and the Vorn illustrated in the new standing army.

Why did Wynn insist on trying to push him onto the throne? He certainly did not see himself as a king. He was just a young man, still in training himself—not a great man like his father. Tiet wished his father was still alive to lead this great people. He would've known what to do.

Tiet wished he had been able to really know his father, but his brother—the thought cut him to the heart. If he ever saw his brother again, he would avenge his father's death and Orin's.

Too bad the coward had taken off before he realized who he was. Tiet would have killed him. That thought gave him little joy, but seemed to satisfy his anger to some degree. Two of the acting guards opened the large main doors that allowed him into the main council chamber.

The ceiling was three stories high in the main hall and he could see that it was even higher within the meeting chamber as the doors parted before him. They revealed a very large circular room with a dome at the top. The Council of Twelve, along with their various advisers, was seated along the outer portion of the room slightly above the place where Tiet was to stand in the middle of the room and be addressed by the council.

As he made his way into the large room he could see that the session was already beginning and apparently everyone was waiting for him to arrive. As he entered, many began to cheer and clap. This was not the sort of entrance he had expected or wanted.

He didn't feel he deserved any applause. What had he done to deserve it besides being born to a certain family and people?

He could see Wynn now. He was seated near the delegate for the city of Baeth Periege and Daooth Pasad was next to him. Daooth was a good man. He could still remember his first meeting with the Vorn in Wynn's underground dwelling and almost taking his head off, supposing him to be an enemy.

That day had been a wake up call for Tiet; learning how the Vorn were a friendly people enslaved by their own military. He had hated them for so long, blaming them for the murder of his family and his people—not realizing things were rarely as straightforward as they seemed.

He approached the podium in the middle of the chamber and waited. A glass of water was sitting on the side and he wondered if it would be inappropriate to take a big drink of it right now. His throat was getting dryer by the moment.

Everyone became quiet as the delegate from Baeth Periege stood to address the gathering. He was an elder Vorn man named Licoure. His translator pin came to life as he spoke in his native Vorn language.

"Master Soone, we are honored by your presence at this gathering and are happy you have accepted our invitation. I realize you have been approached numerous times with our offer to support your ascension to the throne Castai. I would ask that you to hear us out collectively on the matter with patience, understanding our sincerity."

"I am honored by the support of all of the delegates assembled here," said Tiet, "but I fear you have placed your confidence in the wrong man to lead. I do not feel I am experienced enough in necessary matters to be worthy of such a calling."

"Then I hope we may further persuade you," said Licoure.

Another Vorn elder stood as Licoure seated himself again. Tiet recognized him as Ush, the delegate from the city of Thalidi. He appeared to be very old, although Tiet wouldn't guess his age.

"Master Soone, I was in the Vorn military when the war between our peoples first began more than four generations ago. It had been a peaceful relationship during the times before. Our peoples were like brothers. The Barudii king of that time was Isic. He was a very wise man and was instrumental in the exchange of information and technologies between our peoples.

He and our leader were the best of friends and there was open trade and socializing between our planets and peoples. Many Vorn lived in the cities of this Castai and many Castillians lived in our cities on our home planet of Demigoth.

Trade negotiations had only recently begun with the Baruk when a tragedy occurred. Our leader, who was greatly beloved by our people, was assassinated. When an extensive investigation was conducted, the evidence all seemed to point to a plot among the Barudii to gain trade agreements with the Baruk and push us out. The Baruk had come forth with the information, and though King Isic denied it vehemently, our people felt genuinely betrayed.

Not long after, a group of Castillians living on Demigoth was massacred by vigilantes seeking revenge for our fallen leader. King Isic himself journeyed to Demigoth in an attempt to quell the misunderstanding and persuade the new military leadership to reenter the relationship of peace that had so long been enjoyed between our peoples. The Vorn military leadership seized Isic and his entourage and put them to death for crimes against our people.

This was an outrage to the Castillians and war was declared. The Baruk pretended to be neutral to the conflict and made their technologies and information available to both sides. It would not be understood until much later what role the Baruk had played in instigating the war.

The struggle lasted nearly ten years with the Vorn appearing to be the victor. We had decimated nearly all the major cities of the Castillians on this planet before a new weapon was revealed. We would learn much later that the Baruk had provided technology to the Barudii, who created the giant Sphere weapon. By the time it was launched against us, the Castillians were all but wiped out. It would be their last attempt against us before they were extinguished as a people on this planet. The weapon's mission was to hunt down and destroy all Vorn targets; we lost millions of troops to it. It was at this time that the Vorn military turned to the scientific community in a desperate attempt to rebuild our dwindling forces. They created the Horva clones.

The first generation clones were similar in capacity to normal humans with the exception of much greater physical characteristics. They were very superior warriors and; it soon became apparent that the Horva themselves were becoming too powerful and might well get beyond our ability to control them.

The first generation Horva, including Grod, were replaced with a brutish new type of clone that could be easily controlled by our leaders."

"Do you mean, Ambassador Ush, that the Horva were created as slaves to the Vorn?" asked Tiet.

"Yes, exactly" replied Ush. "The Horva under Grod would, as you have seen, eventually rebel against the military. However, the brutish Horva were very useful to them in keeping the civilian population under military control.

At a later time when, the role the Baruk had played became apparent to our people, there arose and outcry among our people to break ties with them. However, the military had treaties with the Baruk, and were determined to maintain their own power. Our people rebelled and called for new leadership, but the rebellion was quickly crushed with help from the Baruk.

It has been their plan to gain control of this system all along. It is very rich in natural resources and they played our people against one another in hopes of destroying both. They've managed to nearly obliterate the Castillians except for those escaping across the rift to the twin planet and the have so severely crippled the Vorn that we have gone under their dominion almost completely. They were just waiting for the Sphere weapon, which continued its attacks, to wipe out the Vorn completely before moving in for the takeover.

The Vorn military's strength diminished as the Sphere attacks continued and the Horva under Grod mounted campaign after campaign of deadly attacks upon our cities that were established here on Castai. The military attempted to push through the Transdimensional Rift to other worlds when scouts came back with data to support the proposal.

After conquering the twin Castai on the other side, it was hoped that the remainder of our people might escape the Sphere by migrating through and somehow collapsing the Rift permanently.

During that conflict with your people, Wynn was displaced here and has worked with our resistance leaders in hopes of finding some way to overthrow the military's control over the remaining population even while Grod's forces gained more and more territory and threatened our lives.

Now that you are here, Master Soone, we have seen some of your ability. Both Wynn and Daooth Pasad have put overwhelming confidence in you. Not only do we trust their judgment, but we have also considered the opportunity presented to us by returning an heir to the Barudii throne.

Our people once revered your leader as much as our own, and we feel compelled to ask you to ascend to your rightful place as king and lead both of our peaceful peoples against the threat we are faced with from the Baruk and Grod."

Tiet was stunned by the whole account of Castillian and Vorn history. It was much more than he had expected. The pieces to a vast puzzle seemed to fall into place now. The Baruk had begun it all and had very nearly destroyed all the clans in their greed for conquest.

Tiet now began to understand the importance that was being placed on the Barudii throne. Perhaps it was a matter of redemption for the Vorn after falsely accusing and executing their ally of long ago; or more importantly, maybe they genuinely believed that the Barudii king was so great an icon to rally around that the peace might even last and these two races could engage the threat wholeheartedly, maybe even victoriously.

Orin had taught him years ago that the confidence you take into a battle may well determine the outcome. Tiet still did not feel confident in himself, but he did have confidence in this great people. If he was what was needed to unite them and hold them together in the face of the coming conflict then perhaps he should reconsider.

Just then, Ranul and Estall appeared in the council chamber.

"Forgive our interruption, Ambassadors," said Estall.

"We have new information from one of our long range probes near the star Casiss."

"Tell us," said Licoure.

"The Baruk appear to have amassed a battle fleet of some fifty large vessels and many smaller ones. They're on their way," said Ranul.

"When?"

"Maybe two days, if we're lucky," said Ranul.

A wave of murmuring enveloped the large chamber of delegates and guests as the realization of the coming storm hit them. Tiet thought further on the situation as the focus left him. The delegates began talking amongst themselves and the whole assembly generally became disorganized.

Little was known about the Baruk's true capabilities; only that they were very fierce in combat employing various kinds of technologies and bio-weaponry. It would be very difficult to fight a war on two fronts, even though Grod and his forces were weaker than before. If Grod seized the opportunity to attack en masse again with the coalition simultaneously fighting the Baruk, it could quickly turn out for the worse.

Then Tiet was struck with a new thought. The threat to this planet was also a threat to the Horva. They had no allegiance to the Baruk and had helped drive off the Vorn military presence, which held treaty with the Baruk. This fight was Grod's fight, whether the General realized it or not.

Tiet needed the assembly's attention, and he needed it *now*. Then he decided to get their attention. He kicked the podium off of the raised platform. It crashed down the few steps to crash loudly on the stone floor. All eyes were suddenly upon him.

"Forgive me for the interruption, Ambassadors," he said, "but I have reconsidered and decided to accept your endorsement."

Shouts began to erupt from the audience. He interrupted them again.

"Please...my acceptance is conditional!" he said over the crowd. Everyone became quite again at this point. Tiet could see Wynn considering him.

"I will accept—on the condition that the Council endorses my going to General Grod in an attempt to broker a peace agreement and convince him to fight with us against the Baruk."

He waited after that statement expecting a reaction. The ambassadors were all looking at one another to confer. The room was now awash in low murmurs concerning Tiet's dangerous request. Tiet stood fast and waited. After a few moments Ambassador Licoure turned back to address him.

"Master Soone, your request is troubling to say the least, but I am curious why you would think the Horva would join us?"

"I believe the main thrust of Grod's campaign and the Horva's desires all centers around wanting their freedom and a fight to attain it. I think he might be willing to listen to what I have to say. He wants what we want; I just have to make him see it."

"With all due respect, we have never known the Horva, especially Grod, to be open to negotiations," said Licoure.

"I only ask for your endorsement and the willingness to work with the Horva peacefully if I am successful, nothing more. If you agree, I will accept your motion that I ascend to the throne of my father."

Licoure looked back at the other delegates in the council and at Wynn who was still fixed on Tiet. The other ambassadors gestured approving nods to Licoure.

"Well, Master Soone, we will agree, against my better judgment."

"I appreciate it, Ambassadors." With that, Tiet turned to leave the assembly.

Wynn made his way quickly to catch up to Tiet as he walked back down the great hall.

"Wait, Tiet!"

Tiet slowed, but did not stop.

"Tiet, what are you up to? Grod won't negotiate with you. He's a brute who loves conquest."

Tiet stopped then, surprised by the statement.

"Wynn, you told me things aren't always what they appear to be. I hated the Vorn who were actually peaceful—"

"Yes, but that's not Grod at all, he—"

"He and the Horva were slaves wanting their freedom. And as for being a brute…well, he managed to destroy the Sphere weapon no one else had been able to defeat, so he must be pretty smart and he must be a great leader to have generated the successful uprising against the Vorn military."

Wynn stood silent; surprised at the wisdom pouring out of his apprentice and king.

"Besides, we cannot afford to fight a war on two fronts; without him, I think we'll lose."

Wynn had considered that aspect before and remained silent as Tiet turned to continue out. "I've got to get going on this while we still have time," he said as he punched the button to open the lift door.

"Do you really think Grod will listen or even answer your transmission?"

"I have no intention of transmitting anything. I'm going to Nagon-Toth personally."

"And do you really think he will let you just walk in?" asked Wynn sarcastically.

"We'll see."

"You realize if you go and confront him he might just decide he should join the Baruk against us. Did you consider that?"

"I'm not giving him the opportunity," Tiet said matter-of-factly. "If he doesn't join us then I'm going to kill him."

And with that Tiet let the lift door close in front of him. Wynn stood there speechless. He was certainly his father's son. The same brash determination was something he remembered from serving under the king years ago. He was glad to see these qualities emerging finally, even though he was worried about the likelihood of Tiet being successful.

XI

THE hangar bay of the Baruk flagship was teeming with warriors. Unfortunately, they were congregated very near Kale's ship. Kale watched from a shadowed position high above the massive tarmac. There were many ships inside the bay, mostly Baruk fighter craft. Then he spotted one that was different.

It was Tal's ship; he was surely either imprisoned or dead by now. Kale knew the Baruk were going to remove the remaining Vorn military from the equation very soon. Tal's presence on the flagship likely meant that was already in process.

Nevertheless, the Governor's ship was some distance across the bay from his own, and still better, it was unguarded. Kale deftly made his way to an area above the vessel. It was quite a bit larger than his.

He pulled a spicor disc from his garment and flung it downward at the hull of the ship. When it impacted, a hole was created all the way through the hull. Kale dropped in fast. He landed inside and quickly made his way to the bridge.

He had learned a few things about Vorn spacecraft during his years with them. He pulled a palm-sized device from his coat and then fitted the mechanism to an interface panel at the helm.

The area around his ship was still quite crowded with warriors. Kale keyed in a sequence on the touch screen, and the ship hummed to life.

The group of warriors surrounding the strider noticed engine sounds coming from across the bay. From above the long lines of Baruk fighter craft they could see a ship rising off the platform. It was the ship that the Governor Tal had arrived in with his aides—all of whom had since been executed.

The Baruk warriors brought their personal weapons to bear as the commander received his order from the Three telepathically; attack the fleeing ship.

The warriors began to fire on the Vorn ship floating above the docking platform as it prepared to leave the bay. The ship began to drift as the warriors closed in on it. The vessel crashed into Baruk fighters docked nearby, and then attempted to rise again as the warriors concentrated more firepower on it.

It was starting to spin out of control. The tail end was knocking Baruk fighters all around the bay, causing the warriors to scatter for cover while still trying to maintain their assault.

The shields on the vessel were not active. As it spun wildly out of control many Baruk were pummeled to death by flying debris from the ship and the destroyed Baruk fighters.

Kale sat calmly at the helm and adjusted the controls. The engine responded accordingly. He pulled up his handheld control and tapped in a new sequence. The Vorn craft drifted further down the bay toward the hangar control center. It tumbled and smashed into the area.

As the control center was engulfed in the fireball of the ship, the hangar force field window deactivated, allowing the influx of open space into the hangar bay. The entire hangar bay's contents rushed into the vacuum; carrying the Baruk warriors with it.

Kale laid aside his remote device. By remote piloting the Vorn ship he had been able to get to his strider. He launched the strider from the platform as debris impacted against the ship's shields. Baruk warriors sucked into the void bounced off of the hull as he proceeded through the mass of bodies and wreckage swirling out of the hangar bay. He activated the ship's hyper coil and pushed away from the Baruk formation at high speed.

THE lush scenery that was common near the twelve cities had given way to the desolation of the territory around Nagon-Toth. Tiet was getting close now. The land was war torn and they had made no effort to revitalize it. No wonder the Horva were conducting raids for supplies. They might be starving to death otherwise.

He felt sure now of his motives for conducting this mission. The Horva were just trying to survive. They had their freedom from the Vorn military now, but this was a bad start.

The display showed another fifty miles before he would reach Grod's fortress. He made adjustments to the helm, as his small craft glided over the barren landscape. It was well-designed and fast. The mileage deficit clicked away rapidly on the display.

He slowed the fighter as he approached to within one mile of the facility. He realized that they must already know he was there, but he wasn't planning on a surprise visit; only a memorable one.

He brought the ship to a complete stop on a rise that overlooked Nagon-Toth in the distance. He got out of the cockpit and then strapped on his blade. He quickly checked his weaponry: two thigh mounted kemsticks and a few spicors in addition to his father's blade. He intentionally left his blasters in the ship. He didn't plan on killing anyone but Grod—if it came to that.

Tiet closed the cockpit of the ship and took a deep breath. This wasn't going to be easy. He had to get to Grod and then hope the general would listen to what he had to say. He had never even met the man, but he supposed it wouldn't be that difficult to distinguish him as the leader.

He began to walk toward the facility. Tiet made no effort to conceal himself, but the same could not be said for his attackers. From an outcropping of rock nearby his path to the compound, no less than ten Horva jumped out to ambush him. Tiet was ready for them.

His E.M. shield hummed to life as the first pulse shot came at him. He blocked several more then dodged into the middle of the warriors. He swung his blade with absolute accuracy, cutting the pulse weapons through with the charged tip. Immediately he set off a kinetic burst that knocked the warriors to the ground around him as he replaced the blade in his scabbard. They were stunned but otherwise unharmed.

"I don't intend to harm you," he said. "I have business with General Grod."

"You'll never see the General," said one of the warriors as he leapt to his feet and charged. As he came toward Tiet he drew a large dagger. Tiet grabbed the warrior's arm with one hand and with the other he brought two fingers to the warrior's throat and tapped a particular nerve with the right pressure to bring him down. He laid him down gently as the dagger slipped out of his hand. The warrior was unconscious; the others were staring at him with apprehension.

"As I said, my business is with your General Grod. This really doesn't have to be anymore difficult than you make it."

They all looked at each other not knowing what to do next. Then one of them rushed him and the others followed. As they attacked he moved among them and created quick chaos throwing some off balance and into the others while hitting them with blow after rapid fire blow with his hands and feet. Within twenty seconds they were on the ground again but less aware of their assailant than before. Tiet gathered himself and continued his trek toward the complex, leaving his victims to their induced slumber.

WYNN'S com-link blinked to life on his wrist. He set the fighter on automatic pilot as he answered. "Wynn here."

"Sir, we've picked up a ship entering our system. It's a Barudii ship, strider class."

He was very surprised to hear this. "What's the heading?"

"It's on a direct course for Castai-Rex sir."

This was puzzling. It was almost certainly the ship that Kale had used to escape the planet months ago. So why would he return, and why now?

"Sir?"

"Yes?"

"We're receiving a transmission from the ship...it's an intent to surrender, sir."

Now he was very puzzled. Why in the world would he come back and then surrender? It didn't make sense, but he didn't have any time to deal with it personally.

"Captain, forward our acceptance of their surrender and meet the ship with a full squad of our best. Take the ship into custody. If you meet with any resistance from those onboard, terminate them."

"Yes, sir."

This was a twist Wynn hadn't counted on, but other matters were more pressing at the moment. He adjusted the controls again and the ship careened south toward Nagon-Toth. He quickly located Tiet's ship by scans. He hadn't put up a sensor cloak or anything. What was he up to?

Wynn brought his ship down in an area facing another side of the complex. He was out of the cockpit quickly and left the ship sensor cloaked and shielded. He wore his own Barudii cloak to keep him invisible to the Horva's sensor sweeps. He did not intend to be seen. If Tiet meant to boldly walk into a deathtrap, he was going to at least give him a fighting chance of getting out again.

KALE keyed off the display. The Command Center at Baeth Periege had formally accepted his surrender. He set the autopilot to the coordinates given to him to dock his ship. He almost felt relief at the thought of giving himself up. His long run from all he had known was almost over.

He wondered if Tiet would be there to meet him as he landed. Perhaps he will run father's blade right through my heart, he thought. Even so, the running was over.

Perhaps Tiet would imprison him for life to watch his traitorous brother rot on a daily basis. It didn't matter. If that was God's will, then so be it. He knew he deserved it anyway.

Father, Mother...forgive me. Emotions, long pushed aside, threatened to flood in.

The computer soon sounded the alarm as the strider began to penetrate Castai's atmosphere. Turbulence was quick as the vessel passed through and came around on course for the city of Baeth Periege. He noticed on the approach how much damage had been repaired within the city. Even the surrounding area had begun some renewal as far as the destruction of the ecosphere during the battle for the city. He had not seen the ending of the battle. The city's defense shield was back in place and fully operational.

As he flew over the southeastern portion of the city he could see many large pulse laser batteries. They looked as though they were expecting a fight. And whether they knew it or not the Baruk would soon be here to give it to them.

A beacon flashed on his display showing him exactly where to bring the ship down on the huge landing platform near the Command Center. The building looked more imposing than before with its added weaponry adorning the outside.

The area he was being led to below was being guarded by what looked to be an entire squad of troops. He did not recognize the uniforms they were wearing, but as he drew closer to the platform he could clearly see that the troops were a mix of Castillian and Vorn.

So they've formed an alliance, he thought. Maybe they stand some chance of survival with the Baruk this way; but it's going to be a terrible fight.

The strider touched down on the platform and the squad of alliance troops surrounded the vessel. Kale looked out at the soldiers with their pulse rifles focused on him. It's not too late to fight, he thought. No, this was the right thing to do; no more running.

Kale lowered the platform and descended. Daooth met him with two armed escorts flanking him on either side.

"Kale Soone, I presume?"

"Yes."

Kale recognized the insignia on the Vorn man's uniform distinguishing his rank.

"Commander, I offer my formal surrender to you," said Kale.

"Your weapons, Kale."

"Of course." He removed his coat slowly. Then Kale unbuckled the strap for his blade and scabbard, handing them to Daooth. "My other weapons are on board, Commander."

Daooth stepped aside to allow the soldiers with him to secure the prisoner. He had never seen Kale Soone before, but he could see the family resemblance very clearly. Tiet looked very much like him.

"Sergeant, secure the prisoner."

"Yes, sir."

The two soldiers with Daooth secured Kale with a binding around his hands and a hood over his head. They didn't want him to recognize the layout of the holding facility if he tried to escape. The two soldiers now flanked Kale and then with each holding an arm, they led him to the holding facility. Daooth fell in behind them with the Barudii blade in his hand and the other soldiers in the squad followed close behind them.

Kale couldn't resist thinking of how he might escape from these men; if he had really wanted to. As a Barudii warrior it was just natural for him to try and resolve such problems. He could sense all of them around him with his kinesis and he could tell the layout of the building even though they deprived him of his sight with the hood. It seemed kind of funny in a way; how easy it would be. Of course he wouldn't attempt it. That would only make everything worse than it already was.

They led him to a holding cell deep within the complex. The square chamber was approximately ten feet by ten feet. It was heavily armored on every side except the open front entrance. The soldiers placed him inside and walked back beyond the entrance.

A charged field was activated to seal him in. Someone he could not see tapped a keypad that caused the binding around his hands to release.

With his hands free he removed his own hood and surveyed his surroundings. There were ten guards still in the room outside his cell. They were heavily armed and watching him like a hawk. He had the feeling they understood the damage a Barudii warrior could do.

Kale was tired. He stretched out on the padded bed that was the only furniture in the chamber. Surely Tiet would be down to confront him soon. He thought it was very strange he had not met him on the tarmac. But he would be here. Now all he had to do was wait.

THE blasts came fast and furious from the towers along the length of the compounds perimeter shield. Tiet ran hard toward it dodging along the way. By his kinesis he could sense the laser fire coming in at him as he ran the open space before the shield wall.

He speedily approached within range of one of the towers then ran right up to it and began to kinetically scale it as though he continued to run upon the ground. The guard in the tower tried to fire upon him from close range.

He pulled his blade, igniting it as he passed the large gun turret. The barrel and main chassis of the gun fell away as his weapon kissed it. He went on never pausing, never killing any of his attackers. As he reached the top of the tower he leapt away from it, flipping end over end down to the ground below.

He hit the ground still running. More shots were coming at him from ground soldiers firing with their weapons. Warriors from all directions seemed to be closing in on him. He ducked and rolled fast across the ground to dodge more laser fire, then rolled out, back to his feet running. He hit the main gate and drove his blade deep into it cutting a portal as laser fire raged upon the wall and ground around him.

He dove through finding a great hall beyond. Many Horva were already in the great room. Tiet could hear hundreds of weapons cocking their firing bolts in readiness. He stopped dead in his tracks. He stood at the ready with his blade ignited and his E.M. shield charged. Mere seconds seemed like an eternity. Then a voice shouted over the silence.

"You will go no further, Barudii!"

"My business is with your General Grod," said Tiet. "Why is it that with so many brave warriors that he will not face me?"

"He will face you," replied the voice again as warriors parted before him. From among them Grod came forth. He was easy to distinguish as Tiet had guessed. The Horva leader was an imposing person; a good foot taller than himself and of a regal stature. He looked quite strong physically and there was an air of confidence he exuded.

"Why did you come here Barudii? Do you mean to assassinate me?"

"No. I've come to propose peace between our people. Surely you must know the Baruk are coming to destroy us all."

"I have no use for your peace. You are a fool to come here and your folly has caught up with you."

Grod drew a large broad sword.

"We've discovered something of your people's technology on our explorations through your cities," said Grod.

He slid a catch on the hilt and a dispersion field enveloped the blade. Grod smiled then charged him. There was a quick exchange of sword strikes between the two. Tiet concentrated on Grod's broadsword; on the hilt.

The field on Grod's sword failed. Tiet's next strike divided it in half as planned. Then Grod did something unexpected, he moved in fast grabbing Tiet's sword arm. He had expected the Horva to back away with his weapon destroyed, but the fearless old warrior had surprised him.

Grod held his right arm with one hand preventing any further strike while delivering his own hard blow to Tiet's face. He was stunned and almost staggered but Grod still had his sword arm. It was all very fast. Grod's next strike was to his forearm.

Tiet felt his right arm break at the Horva's powerful blow. His hand went limp and the blade fell to the ground. Grod did not even go for the weapon. The look in his eye was as though he meant to kill him with his bare hands.

He could hear the crowd of Horva warriors cheering Grod on as the sword fell to the ground. Grod left Tiet's arm and grabbed the young man's throat while pulling a dagger from his side. But his weapon stopped as though frozen by an unseen hand. Grod tried desperately to bring the death strike home, but could not move his arm at all. Tiet stared into his eyes, "Killing me will not be that easy, General."

Grod tried to bring the blade down, and then tried to crush the young man's throat; but he could not. He also realized that he could not move his body in any way; his will was not his own.

"Look down, General," said Tiet. "Your life is in my hands more than you realize."

Grod looked to find the Barudii holding a short rod between them with the business end across his own belly. He had seen the weapon before. The Barudii had used the same thing to kill the Teragore in the dome.

"Kill me then, if that's why you came here."

"I told you already, that is not why I came here Grod. I want peace between our people. I know and respect your struggle against the oppression of the Vorn military, but the civilian populace had nothing to do with that. I proposed this alliance to them and those people have sent me with the same hope.

Our people need peace. We already have enough of a fight on our hands, the both of us, when the Baruk come; and they are already on their way. Join us, and let's fight them together and hopefully live to have peace on our planets."

Grod just looked at him listening and studying the young man. His dagger was still frozen in mid strike above Tiet's chest; held by the Barudii's mental power. Finally after a long silence between them Grod spoke. "And if I refuse your peace?"

"Then I came prepared to kill you; I do not intend to fight a war on two fronts between you and the Baruk."

"Then kill me, I don't care about peace with you or the Vorn."

Tiet only had to activate the kemstick to kill him and Grod knew it as well, but he stood stone faced looking into his eyes, waiting for him to do it. Instead, Tiet pushed him away and released him from his mental grip. Grod looked surprised by the turn of events.

"I don't want to kill you," he said. "Believe it or not, I respect your skills and your mission to be independent of those who enslaved the Horva. I still think it's a shame I may have to face you on a battlefield some day instead of around a peaceful table breaking bread as friends, but that's your choice; I tried."

Tiet brought his broken arm to his torso, it throbbed terribly. He could hear the room full of warriors raising their weapons again, bringing them to bear on him. Grod raised his hand quickly to halt them.

"As you said Barudii, we may see one another on the battlefield someday; but this is not your day to die. Now take your peace and go in it."

Tiet gave him one last look then backed away from the room full of warriors. The main gate opened up behind him allowing him to exit as Grod walked slowly after him, watching him leave. The Horva were falling in behind him with their weapons still at the ready just in case, but none were aggressive toward him.

Wynn watched from the support beams above the chamber where Tiet had fought with the General. He couldn't believe what was happening. Tiet had said he would kill him. Grod was within his grasp and he spared him.

Even with the broken arm he probably still could've made it out if he had wanted to. The young king was surprising him more with each passing event.

His gun was still trained on the General from his perch. Wynn waited for Tiet to make it back over the defense field and head back for his ship over the ridge before he left his hidden position and made his way back to his own fighter. The Horva never knew he was there; his Barudii cloak had seen to that. He hoped Tiet had not been aware of his presence either.

IT took Wynn several hours to make his way back to Baeth Periege in his ship. He had arrived nearly at the same time that Tiet's fighter was reported to have docked in a different part of the city, near the main medical facility.

He was going to have to see to his broken arm. The medics would put him through the standard osteoblast enhancement. What used to be done in weeks back home was now done in two hours with Vorn medical treatments. It would be enough time for Wynn to get to Kale before Tiet was able to. Hopefully he would be undergoing the treatment before anyone even told him about his brother being captured.

Wynn sprinted out of the lift of the holding facility. He wasn't sure why Kale would just surrender himself, but he needed to find out as much as he could before Tiet heard of his brother's arrival. From what he knew about Tiet's feelings concerning Kale, he would be fortunate to even get a quick death.

Wynn placed his hand on the DNA scanner and entered the room of Kale's holding cell. He was still there sitting quietly with two armed guards watching him carefully. The cell was such that any tampering with the mechanism, even mentally, would cause another separate system to fire a charge within the cell that would stun the prisoner and potentially even kill them. The energy field comprising the front wall was still functioning properly.

Kale stood to his feet as Wynn entered the room. He did not know the man, but he remembered him from the platform, running behind his brother after the battle with Orin. He perceived him as Barudii. He could sense his power before he had even entered the room.

Wynn stood before the energy field to face Kale. He could sense the power of the Barudii. He almost felt like he was in Tiet's presence, the intensity was so powerful.

"Kale Soone, my name is Wynn Gareth; I served under your father."

"I have heard your name, but I do not know you."

"I would like to know why you came back to this planet and why you surrendered to our forces."

Kale waited a moment before answering, studying Wynn's face and considering the question. "It doesn't really matter. The Baruk are on their way. I'm not one of them. I didn't have anywhere else to go."

"But you didn't have to come here. You realize that you are facing a death sentence by coming here. I just want to know why," said Wynn.

Kale's guard seemed to soften at that point. "I'm guilty of killing my own family Mr. Gareth. I betrayed them to the Vorn. My brother is the only one of them who escaped. If he wants to kill me then I'm sure I deserve it."

Wynn could see the emotion in Kale's eyes as he spoke. He meant what he was saying. "Perhaps if you told Tiet then he might—"

"He'll never forgive me. And I really don't blame him. Whatever I receive for my crimes against my people will never be enough," said Kale.

Wynn wasn't sure what to say. He could sense truth in the man and genuine remorse for his past crimes. He stood there, watching the son of his former king and he felt sorry for the man. Not because he might die as a traitor, but because he was genuinely repentant and had no way to repair the damage he had done.

Suddenly the door to the room was opening and in walked Tiet.

"So it's true!!" he shouted.

He pulled his blade from his scabbard as he crossed the small room toward the cell. This was exactly what Wynn was hoping would not happen. He noticed Tiet's arm still tucked to his side. He hadn't made it to get the repair yet. Tiet was already bringing his broken arm up painfully to place his hand on the DNA scanner.

It was a moment frozen in time. The energy field went down to the cell as Tiet raised his blade to strike his brother. Wynn knew it now; he was really going to kill him. He looked at Kale. He was just standing there with his eyes closed like it was going to be a relief to his own inner pain.

Tiet thrust his father's blade toward Kale, and then it was landing on the ground beside him. "What are you doing?!" shouted Tiet.

Wynn had caught his arm in mid-flight and disarmed him. It was a split second decision to save Kale's life; to save Tiet from the regret and torture of having killed his own brother. "Tiet, if you kill him you'll never forgive yourself," said Wynn as they struggled.

"He killed my father, my mother and Orin; our people were slaugh-tered because of him!" shouted Tiet.

"It's alright, Wynn," said Kale, "I deserve this, let him go."

"You shut your mouth, traitor!!" shouted Tiet as he attacked Kale with his mind.

Kale was pushed backward into the wall. He slumped to the floor in pain under the kinetic attack; he wasn't trying to shield himself at all from his younger brother's righteous fury.

"Tiet, he is still your brother, all that you have left of your family!" shouted Wynn.

Tiet shook free of Wynn's loosening grip on his arm. "Stay out of it, Wynn."

He looked back to Kale still groaning on the ground trying to breathe. Something snapped in his expression as he looked at his brother bent to his will on the ground in pain. He released him from the attack and backed away with a bewildered look on his face.

He turned away to walk out, looking very disturbed. Tiet extended his good hand behind him and caught his blade as it leapt from the ground, flying across the room after him. The door closed behind him.

Kale began to recover himself. Wynn did not help him up. Instead he stepped back outside the cell and scanned the lock to reactivate the cell's energy field.

"Watch him," he said to the guards, who were stunned by the event.

He looked back at the cell to see Kale climbing back to the small bed against the cell wall. There wasn't time to worry about the pain either of the brothers might be feeling; the Baruk were still on their way.

XII

RANUL rushed into the power lift heading for the bridge of the Vorn cruiser *Esyia*. The Baruk were headed into the sector where they were patrolling. The probes along the way were being destroyed systematically as they journeyed toward Castai-Rex. With at least fifty large warships, they were flaunting their power and moving quickly.

The level indicator clicked away as the lift carried him toward the bridge where he could analyze the latest data. There were only two Vorn battle cruisers assigned to each sector from among the twenty-three that had been confiscated on Castai-Ori and left on Rex after the departure of the remaining Vorn military during the battle of Baeth Periege. The *Onicule* was traveling with them nearby.

All the Vorn battle cruisers were heavily armed and highly maneuverable, but with the greater number of Baruk vessels approaching, many serving aboard the cruisers were expecting to fight a losing battle. Still, morale among the crews remained strong. If they were going to lose, then they would take as many of the Baruk with them as possible.

Suddenly the whole ship reeled. Ranul was tossed into the ceiling of the lift then down to the floor hard. The lights flickered then faded as low intensity emergency lighting came on. It felt like an impact to the ships hull, but he couldn't tell. The lift continued its climb soon arriving at the bridge.

When the doors opened up, he could see the bridge crew locked into their chairs prepared for battle. On the display they were tracking several objects heading in their direction. Estall was barking out orders to the crew from the command chair.

"Estall, what's happening?!"

"The Baruk have launched some sort of projectiles from outside the sector; the shields are having difficulty with them. They're not strong enough to repel these things—they're some sort of grossly dense alloy."

"The shields would have to deconstruct and disperse the matter; very difficult with objects of the density you're talking about." Ranul jumped to a science station and began to look over the data. An alarm sounded on the bridge.

"Incoming!"

"It's another one of those projectiles," said Estall. "Ranul, what do you have!?"

"It's some kind of Tritarium variant, super density. Its normal molecular arrangement would put it at one thousand times the current size."

"Evasive!!" shouted Estall to the helmsman.

"It's tracking with us!" said one of the science officers.

"I'm having trouble with the helm, sir. It's like we're being pulled into it."

"It's exerting a localized gravitational pull on the ship; gets stronger as it approaches!" shouted Ranul from his station. "Wait, wait! It's tracking on the *Onicule* now!"

"She's going to take a hit!"

The projectile shifted the flight path of the *Onicule* as it approached, pulling the Vorn cruiser into its path at the last moment. The shields on the ship activated as the object passed into field; trying to vaporize it. It seemed to sheer off half of its mass in vaporized layers but the remainder passed through the shield and crashed into the hull of the *Onicule* near the rear of the ship.

"She's hit!!" shouted Estall.

"Analyzing," said one of the science officers. "The *Onicule* took a hit just behind mid-ship; several decks destroyed; they're sealing them off. It's not a fatal blow."

Ranul continued to monitor the ship. "Wait! Something is happening! That thing is like a gravity bomb," he mumbled as he turned to Estall.

On the main view screen the *Onicule* was beginning to crumble inward, imploding upon itself.

"Ranul, what's happening to them?" he asked as he watched.

"The localized gravitational field around the object is pulling the ships structure inward upon it."

They all watched helplessly as the *Onicule* caved in upon itself. Gases escaped in flame as the superstructure crumpled around the gravity projectile within.

"Sir, we are being hailed by the other fleet ships," said the communications officer. "They're all on a rendezvous course to this sector."

"Estall, the Baruk formation of ships is entering the sector now," said Ranul "They're splitting up; spreading out against us. Another gravity bomb is approaching our position!"

"Evasive maneuvers!" shouted Estall.

"I'm trying to recalibrate the ship's shields to repel the object rather than vaporize it."

"Twenty seconds to impact!" shouted another science officer.

"Hurry, Ranul," gritted Estall as he watched the incoming object on the view screen.

"I think I've got it."

The gravity bomb slammed into the shields of the *Esyia* and sent the ship reeling off of its flight path. The bridge crew would have been tossed about the chamber had they not been strapped into their flight chairs.

"How bad are we?" asked Estall over the groaning of the engines.

"The object did not penetrate!" shouted Ranul. "It was deflected away. But the impact still damaged our hull by causing a reverberation in the shield."

"How bad are we?" asked Estall.

"The hull is intact."

"Are the Baruk within range yet?"

"Just now," said the weapons officer.

"Lock and fire the dispersion cannon on the nearest ship."

The large weapon swiveled upon its mount located on the topside of the *Esyia*, aiming off into the black of space toward the Baruk, still out of visual range. The weapons officer locked on target to the nearest Baruk warship and fired. The beam from the Castillian and Vorn engineered weapon flashed out into the darkness.

The Baruk warship *Kosinok* veered away from the formation of cruisers toward its designated heading. A beam flashed from ahead of its course and hit the ship, strafing across the surface. It vaporized everything it touched across the surface of the massive hull.

"Direct hit!" shouted the weapons officer.

"They're raising their shields!" said Ranul from his station.

"Fire again," said Estall.

Once again the weapon adjusted slightly to reacquire the same target on its trajectory. Once locked, it fired again into the blackness of space. The beam hit the *Kosinok* square on, but its shields responded in kind.

"Their shields are drained significantly but it didn't go through," said Ranul.

"The rest of the fleet is heading for the Baruk formation," said the other science officer.

"Take us in with them, shields at full power, all weapons systems at the ready. Garret, fire all weapons systems at will as we come into range," ordered Estall.

TIET sat uneasy on the exam table. His arm was throbbing terribly now, but his conscience was hurting him more. He had wanted so badly to drive the blade through Kale and avenge his family; his people, but it wasn't what he had expected. Seeing his brother standing there in the cell just waiting to receive his fury was very unsettling.

Tiet had expected a fight; he had wanted a fight. After attacking him mentally and seeing him writhing in pain from the kinetic grasp, Tiet had, for an instant, felt pity for him.

Wynn had stopped him from killing his own brother. At the time he would have struck his mentor for interfering, had he been able, but now he knew he would have regretted that as well. Wynn was no fool and he had no reason to protect Kale. There had to be a good reason for him to step in between them, and save his life.

The med-lab door opened allowing Mirah K'ore to enter. "So…the king has returned."

"Hello, Mirah."

"That's Dr. K'ore to you. Father said you were going to accept the Council's nomination to the throne...I haven't seen you lately."

"I'm sorry. I've had a lot on my mind."

"I understand. But don't think that gives you an excuse in the future. Now let's see that arm."

Tiet raised the arm for her inspection. The sleeve was already cut away up to his shoulder. The med tech had managed to get that far before the message had come through to Tiet's com-link that Kale was a prisoner. His arm was severely bruised and swollen but there was no bone penetration.

Mirah picked up a hand held scanner and passed it over his arm. "Well it looks like a clean break, ulna and radius. I won't ask you just how you managed this."

"How long to put me back in action, Doc?"

"About two hours of osteoblast therapy and another half hour to bring down the edema."

"Let's do it then."

"OUR ships are really taking a pounding up there commander," said Lieutenant Davers. "They're outnumbered two to one. They've been using the new dispersion cannons, but the Baruk shields are too strong."

"What's the current shield status for our ships?" asked Wynn.

"Ten ships below 70 percent shield power, eight below 50 percent power and two are under 20 percent power and three have already been destroyed."

"What about the *Esyia*?"

"She's approaching 30 percent power and still taking a pounding sir."

Wynn continued to sort through the incoming images on the war room displays. The armada was really getting beaten to death up there. They were tough ships, but the odds were against them. If they failed to stop the Baruk in space then the fight would hit the ground.

"Sir, another of our ships has been destroyed, the *Kyrysk*," said Davers.

The other four soldiers manning the war room control systems paused briefly to look up at Wynn then continued with their work.

"What about the Baruk fleet?" asked Wynn, "what kind of damage are they taking?"

"They're going blow for blow, but our ships are grossly outnumbered," said Davers.

"By the time they do any significant damage, their shields will be down and it will be over very quickly. Have we notified Tiet yet?"

"He's in the med lab; the alarms don't sound in there."

"Put me through."

"Online, sir."

"Dr. K'ore, may I help you?"

"Mirah. Wynn Gareth here. I need to speak with Tiet immediately."

"My patient is still undergoing treatment under sedation," said Mirah.

"I need you to wake him up. We've got a situation; he's needed."

"What he needs is to get this treatment completed without duress, Commander."

"Doctor, our fleet is getting burned out of the sky. The Baruk will begin a ground assault as soon as they get the chance. Please, we need him on his feet now."

"I'll do the best I can, Mirah out."

The communication link was terminated at that point. "I'd better make sure of it," said Wynn. "Davers, what's the status of our troops?"

"All division commanders report ready and awaiting deployment instructions."

"Tell them to hold positions and the king will instruct them personally," said Wynn as he headed out the door.

MIRAH returned to the control panel monitoring Tiet's treatment. He was coming out of his sedation as the procedure finished up. Everything was precisely computer controlled. She walked into the treatment room as he began to come around.

"How are you feeling?"

"A little groggy, but I feel alright. My arm feels a lot better; just a little sore now."

"Well, that will pass soon enough. You've got plenty of pain meds on board."

"I appreciate the fix up Doc."

"You don't have to be so formal."

"I know. There's just been so much happening recently Mirah."

"Well the arm looks fine," she evaded.

"Thank you Mirah," he said not pursuing. Tiet flexed the arm, trying out the repair. "You do wonderful work."

"Tiet I uh…." She started to speak as the door to the med lab opened to let Wynn inside.

"Well I see you're on your feet again," he said quickly.

The two dropped their gazes to the ground and then to Wynn and he suddenly realized he might have interrupted something. The thought might have delighted him more had it not been for the present danger; deadly business was at hand.

"Tiet, we've got to get you to the main deployment area. The Baruk are hammering our ships and it looks like we'll be looking at a ground assault somewhere very soon."

"I'm ready, let's go," he said as he gathered the upper body portion of his uniform from the counter nearby. They both headed out the main door as he called behind to Mirah.

"Thanks again Mirah, we'll talk soon," he said as the door closed behind them.

"I hope so," she whispered to the empty exam room.

THEY walked quickly together to the nearest lift. "Tiet, I want to apologize for the situation with Kale."

"Wynn, don't worry about it. You did what was right. It's just that…he betrayed everything we knew, and yet he's my brother."

"I know."

The lift opened allowing them in. "Main deployment area," said Wynn.

The computer complied with the settings and away went the lift through the city.

"You could have killed him and he wouldn't have made any effort to stop you. I think he even longed for you to do it, to end his pain and guilt."

"Why should I care about his pain? He betrayed us—all of us. Including you, Wynn."

"That's right. And I am still asking you to consider the situation with your brother despite that fact."

Tiet looked at him sternly then looked back at the city without saying anything.

"I don't mean this in any insulting way, but Kale did not need my help to save himself from your sword."

"Do you think he's that powerful?" asked Tiet more thoughtfully.

"Well, he did defeat Orin and if I have any sensibility about these things I believe he is very powerful."

"I don't want to hate him Wynn, I just don't know how to handle this right now…"

The lift slowed as they entered the deployment area and its control tower.

"…but we have a war to deal with; everything else will have to wait."

AS Wynn and Tiet entered the control center of the city's main deployment area, the data techs were busy monitoring the current situation with the fleet as well as troop status and the readiness of the twelve cities and their defense systems.

Each city had a large portion of the new army assigned to defend it in the event they came under a Baruk attack. At the least, they hoped to hold on until the other legions could arrive at whichever city became the main front.

"What's the status of the fleet?" asked Tiet.

"Ten of our ships have been destroyed sir. The rest are trying to out-maneuver the Baruk ships, but they're dangerously low on shield power," said one of the techs.

"Can you patch me in to Estall on the *Esyia*?" he asked.

"Yes sir, one moment. Baeth Periege ground control hailing the Captain of the *Esyia*."

"CAPTAIN, the ground control at Baeth Periege is hailing us," said one of the communications officers.

"Put them through," said Estall. "Ranul, have you got the system re-configured yet?"

"I'm still working on it, just a few more circuits to re-route."

The intercom on Estall's command chair sounded with Tiet's voice. "Estall, what is your status?"

"We've lost ten ships so far and it's not looking good. Some of the Baruk are veering away from the main group. They look to be troop transports. I don't know if we can stop them, we're barely hanging on up here."

"Estall, I want you to get your people out of there. Do you hear me? I want you to withdraw your remaining ships immediately," said Tiet.

"I want to send out the weaker ships first. Ranul is working on a re-configuration of the dispersion cannon that may just allow us to penetrate their shields."

"Do what you think is best, but don't take any chances," said Tiet.

"Affirmative. If this doesn't work we'll withdraw the remaining ships to the surface; *Esyia* out."

Estall clicked the switch on the intercom panel of his chair as he watched the stats for the fleet on a smaller window of the main screen. "Mellar, give withdraw commands to the ships below twenty-five percent shield power."

"Yes sir," she replied.

"Ranul what's the status on that reconfigure?"

"I've got it!" said Ranul from his science station. "The cannon will now cycle through one hundred thousand shield frequencies per second and lock on the one that matches theirs'."

"Excellent. Garret, lock the cannon on their shield generator and fire."

"Yes, sir!"

The dispersion cannon swiveled on its base and locked on the approximate position of the shield generator on the closest Baruk vessel. The cannon fired its rapid multi-frequency blasts at the ship. The Baruk shield repelled the blast for a fraction of a second then it got through and struck the generator's position; vaporizing it.

"Shield's dropping on the Baruk vessel, Captain!" cried the main science officer.

"Garret, fire at will, targeting the bridge area first! Ranul, transmit that reconfiguration sequence to the remaining ships!"

"Already on it!"

"Then let's do some damage," Estall said with satisfaction.

"Those carriers are already passing into the atmosphere," said Ranul from his station.

"Well, they're out of our reach now. Contact Tiet on the surface with the information. We'll do what we can here while they deal with those on the surface."

"SIR, we're tracking a group of approximately ten carriers entering the atmosphere," said one of the data-communication techs in the control center.

"What is there course heading?" asked Tiet.

"Descent projection is that they are heading for the Usai Valley beyond the borders of Thalidi. It's just about the only area large enough to land that group of ships," said the tech.

Wynn and Tiet watched the computer model with the respective tracking data coming in on the group of Baruk ships.

"I think you're projection is right," said Wynn.

"Get me the Troop Commander for Thalidi," said Tiet.

"Online sir."

"This is Commander Erib, sir, what can I do for you?"

"Commander, I want you to order an immediate civilian evacuation of the suburban area beyond the defense wall and then mobilize your troops there. The Baruk are heading your way. We project an attack launched from the Usai Valley within twelve hours," said Tiet.

"I trust we'll be launching a cooperative attack with the city's defensive batteries?" asked Erib.

"In part. What I hope to accomplish is more of an ambush. The Baruk will be expecting our civilian population to withdraw behind the city's defense wall. Hopefully we can lay in wait for them to take up positions in the suburb area and then come out on them in force."

"Yes, sir. Erib out."

"What about me?" Wynn asked.

"I want you to deploy more troops on this side of Thalidi and set up a front approximately ten miles away. Let the other troop commanders know to send you 50 percent of their forces to make up that frontline. I expect the Baruk to try and go for Baeth Periege beyond Thalidi. They'll want the capital."

"I wish you would allow me to lead the first strike at Thalidi and you remain here to set up the front," said Wynn with concern. "The battle there is going to be nearly a suicide mission and we need you to survive and lead these people."

"Trust me, Wynn, this is how to lead them; by going into the fire with them. And I don't intend to die at Thalidi if I can help it. But if I should fall, you must assume command."

Wynn remained silent. There was wisdom in the young man's words and he knew it. "I'm only sorry we couldn't enlist Grod's Horva to help us in the fight. If we can't defeat the Baruk, they'll be the next target," said Tiet.

"Well, I think your broken arm speaks all to well for Grod's intentions," said Wynn sarcastically.

"Maybe." Tiet looked at his mentor. "I better get going; I hope to see you again."

Wynn didn't say anything. His concern showed on his face. Tiet turned with a small wave and walked out of the control room, heading for the main deployment area to arrange troops to join with him in the journey to Thalidi.

Wynn thought about the extreme danger Tiet would be facing there outside the walls of Thalidi. An ambush was very ambitious against the Baruk. He just couldn't understand why Tiet wanted to face them that way. Even with crack commandos from among the best trained troops it was going to be hairy. He wished he could be there to at least keep an eye on him and try to protect him. Then it occurred to him that if he couldn't do it, someone else just might.

WHEN Commander Mendle had assembled his troops, he opened the door to the private assembly hall allowing Tiet to enter. Though no formal ceremony had taken place to crown him as such, everyone knew full well the authority that had been granted to him by the Council as the new Barudii king. And they were glad for it.

Tiet walked to a place before them where he could address the recruits.

He said to all, "I don't know if you realize the mission we are about to undertake. We are going to reinforce the troops already stationed at the city of Thalidi, where it has now been confirmed that the Baruk have landed and are deploying their own forces. The Baruk are coming at the city from the Valley of Usai. It will be our mission to take up positions within the suburban district that lies between the Baruk and the defensive wall of the city."

"Excuse me, sir," said Commander Mendle. "Did you say outside the defense wall?"

"We're going to provide an ambush in the hopes of at least giving the city officials enough time to evacuate the civilian population. This isn't much time to evacuate a city full of people, but we have no choice. With the number of Baruk forces that will be thrown at us in this first assault, we likely will not be able to hold them from entering the city."

"So this is a suicide mission, sir?" asked one of the soldiers.

"Not at all," said Tiet. "I have no intention of wasting lives, but we need to buy some time. We have security tunnels within that sector that were intended to allow the civilian population living there to evacuate to within the defensive wall perimeter if an attack came.

We will take up positions well ahead and fight and fall back as we have to. When we can't hold our positions anymore we'll evacuate through the tunnels and help the rest of the civilian population in the city to get behind a defensive front. Wynn Gareth will be putting that together with the majority of our security forces from all of the twelve cities. That is where I intend to face off with the Baruk."

"Make no mistake soldiers, this will be an extremely dangerous mission and some us may fall in the battle, but I for one would rather lose my life fighting the Baruk than to live under their rule," said Tiet as the recruits began to shout a cheer of support.

"Trust in your training; it will save your life and the lives of your fellow soldiers. Now let's go."

The troop commander barked a few quick orders at his men and then they all made their way to the transports ready to take them to Thalidi. Tiet watched the elite trained group of five hundred file into the carriers as he made last minute checks to his own uniform and weaponry. The last item he checked was the secure latch on the hilt of his father's blade. He was ready.

He boarded the lead carrier as the ramp began to ascend. Within moments they were all in the air en route to Thalidi and the Baruk.

KALE watched the monitor that his guards were watching, as different images and information on the coming attack was displayed. The two soldiers were talking amongst themselves about what was happening and even how they wished they could get into the action rather than remaining on guard duty.

"Look at that, the king is going to be leading the first strike at Thalidi," said one of the soldiers.

"Yeah, but this says Thalidi's population is going to be evacuated to Baeth Periege," said the other. "That doesn't sound like they expect to hold the city."

Kale was concerned now. His brother was heading into an attack against overwhelming forces and probably would not survive it. He had to do something, even if Tiet hated him.

The two soldiers still weren't paying any attention to him, but his eyes were fixed upon them intently. After a few moments they both collapsed into the floor unconscious. The hand of one of the men raised in the air away from the limp body which began to be pulled across the floor toward the security scanner to Kale's cell. The hand glided through the air dragging the soldier underneath, and planted itself on the scanner. The computer responded by lowering the security field to the cell.

Kale quickly moved across the room to the storage locker where his weapons were and broke open the lock kinetically. He removed his own weapons and his blade, then using the hand of the other soldier nearby, he opened the chambers main security door.

When Kale stepped into the hall, he found Wynn Gareth standing propped against the wall about ten feet away. He froze, not sure of his next move.

"That was faster than I expected," said Wynn sarcastically.

Before he could respond, Wynn held out a security code key. "You'll need this if you're going to get to the hangar and take my personal fighter to Thalidi."

"How? How did you know?" asked Kale

"I'm the one that fed the information to the monitor in there. Tiet hasn't allowed me to be there to watch out for him—but he can't stop his brother, can he?"

"You'd better get going," said Wynn. "And Kale? It's not too late."

Kale gave him a thoughtful look as though he was surprised at Wynn's insight into the situation as well as grateful for it. Then he turned and made his way quickly toward the hangar bay. Wynn watched him go before he looked in on the two unconscious soldiers.

He sensed they were unharmed and left them there asleep. To wake them now would set off the alarms to Kale's escape and the battle at Thalidi would be underway all too soon. Wynn wanted the young king to have a watchful older brother on hand to help him stay alive.\

XIII

THE *Esyia* careened around several Baruk ships firing its dispersion cannon at the targets. With the weapon able to adjust to varying shield frequencies the damage was now mounting. Still, the flagship of the Baruk remained distant to the battle, but Ranul was watching it from his science station.

He had noticed the vessel remaining away from the main group while the others made great effort to intercept any of the Vorn cruisers trying to get near it for an attack. He was conducting multiple scans on the vessel, but one piece of information continued to puzzle to him.

A very unusual waveform was emanating steadily from within the ship somewhere. It was more biological than mechanical and it seemed to envelope not only the Baruk ships, but also the surface of the planet near the Twelve Cities.

The *Esyia* shuddered as blaster fire blazed across its shields again. The few remaining Vorn ships were holding their own now against the Baruk. A number of enemy vessels had already been destroyed with multiple direct hits from the dispersion cannons, but they were still outnumbered three to one.

Ranul shifted as the ship quaked, then continued on with his observations.

"What are you doing? I haven't heard anything out of you recently," said Estall.

"Why, did you need something?" he asked without looking away from his data screen.

"Helmsman, head for that group on another attack run," he said as he climbed from his own chair to join Ranul at his science station.

Few things could have caught his full attention during a full on space battle with their lives at risk, and he wanted to know what it was that could be so important.

"What is it?" he asked as he braced himself against the bulkhead next to him.

"I'm not exactly sure, but I think I might be picking up some sort of coordinating signal being used by the Baruk."

"What?"

"It's a signal, I think biological, and it's coming from that Baruk flagship. I can't decode it at all and it seems focused on the movements of the Baruk only. It could be telepathic in origin."

"Telepathic? Do you mean something on board is controlling the Baruk forces?"

"Well, I can't be sure," said Ranul, "but it would make since; at least with the data I have. And if we destroy that control source we might be able to disorient the Baruk long enough to win this battle, especially on the surface."

"Transmit what you've got to Control on the surface. Let them know we're going after the flag ship with everything we've got," said Estall. "Helmsman, plot a new course for the flag ship of the Baruk. Notify our remaining ships to concentrate all firepower on that vessel."

"Command being transmitted to the remaining ships, sir!"

The *Esyia* came around setting her course for the Baruk flagship. The dispersion cannon rotated on its base as the gunner set up the targeting information.

"Fire dispersion cannon at selected targets," said Estall.

The first volley of cannon fire struck the shields of the flagship. The cannon compensated for the appropriate shield frequency within milliseconds and the blast penetrated to strike the ship. A large portion of the hull on the port side was vaporized with the hit. Within moments a heavy firefight issued forth upon the *Esyia* from other Baruk ships coming to the aid of their flagship.

"Where are those other ships?" shouted Estall.

"Sir, they're being engaged to heavily to aid us at the moment. The Baruk ships are attempting to ram them now!"

"Estall!" shouted Ranul from his station. "The signal I've been monitoring, it just increased its intensity tenfold in the direction of the Baruk ships."

"Then it is some sort of control signal."

"Almost certainly," said Ranul. "Whatever is aboard that ship wants to be protected even if it means using the other Baruk ships to ram into us."

"Sir, more Baruk ships are coming at us on collision course!"

"Evasive maneuvers!" shouted Estall. "Fire the cannon at them."

"We've got to destroy that signal source!" shouted Ranul.

"I know, but we can't do it if we're dead," said Estall. "Helmsman, keep us elusive. Look for any way to get near the flagship again."

"They're forming a perimeter to protect it," said Ranul as he watched the data screen.

"Tell the other ships to keep trying to break through. I just hope they can hold out on the surface until we can succeed out here."

TIET watched as his forces moving throughout the suburban area of the city of Thalidi, outside of the shield wall. The shield was operational with the old thick alloy wall standing behind it. He wasn't optimistic that even that defense could hold the city.

The soldiers moved quickly and quietly in and around buildings as they set up positions from which to ambush the Baruk. They were well-armed and well-trained despite the limited time the new army had been in operation. As he watched them deploying, Tiet wondered how many would be going home after this was all over; even wondering if he would.

He pulled his long range lens to his eye and peered out toward the valley of Usai. He could see the Baruk forces approaching already. The range was five miles. Their projected speed would put them in contact within twenty minutes. The image was obscured by an increasingly large cloud of dust being churned up from the valley floor by their army; making it difficult to get much detail on exactly what they were going to be up against.

Tiet spoke into his communication mouthpiece. "Fire the cannons at will."

Above him, from positions on the defense wall, large pulse cannons began to rain down a firestorm out upon the approaching Baruk. He looked at them through his oculars again. Multiple blasts were erupting from their location, but it was difficult to tell if they were doing much damage or to what number.

Tiet moved with those near him to their positions as they drew their pulse rifles and prepared to wait for the Baruk.

KALE watched his brother from behind a nearby wall. He had made it this far with Wynn's help, now he just had to keep Tiet alive. It was hard to believe that Wynn had helped him to escape.

Wynn must have really cared for Tiet and believed that Kale would actually follow him here and try to protect him. The man was quite insightful, and Kale was determined to give his life for his brother if necessary. He would never betray him again.

Wynn had apparently thought this out and had provided a uniform to allow him to blend in with the other soldiers. He activated his own datascope lens and watched the image as he scanned out to where the Baruk were approaching from.

Flipping through several different image perspectives, he noted something odd. The main group was apparently approaching under some sort of large shield that went before them like a barricade. It appeared to be automated, and put off an easily recognizable power signature. But something else was showing up ahead of their formation.

Kale tapped his wrist pad for an analysis of the odd signature that was showing up as multiple trails heading in their direction.

Insufficient data, said the computer display.

Looking with normal vision he could see nothing. No dust trail, no visible anything. The trails continued on a steady pace along the ground as the Baruk began to close in on the outskirts of the suburban housing area. The area at that point began to slope upward toward the perimeter defense wall behind him.

Kale noticed the others getting ready to fire and Tiet's voice came over his headset. "Lock on your targets and use multi-burst setting. Fire on my command."

That was smart, because the symbiotic creature that provided the exoskeleton for the Baruk could take several direct hits before allowing a burst penetration. The multi-burst would likely get shots through the living armor.

The large shield dissipated as the Baruk came into closer quarters in the housing area, as did the cannon fire from within the perimeter wall. They were too close to be hit by it now.

There was a town square with a fountain and an open area that lay between themselves and the Baruk. Tiet had given an order to wait for the enemy to reach it before firing; and only on his command. Kale could see the forces that opposed them more clearly now, and they were fearsome indeed.

It was mostly infantry, but they had large carrier vehicles that carried supplies for the troops as well as large projectile cannons that were mounted to the top with various other arms. A number of large alien beasts were mingled among them as well; they all looked like the kind of mutated ravenous brutes that the Baruk were known for.

The Baruk were fanning out through the streets below, and all of them were rapidly making their way toward the defense wall. It looked like there had to be at least five thousand warriors storming toward the city and the hidden Castillian army. Kale readied his own pulse rifle and looked over his weaponry.

He was well-armed with spicor discs in rows along his chest attached to magnetic bands. His two kemsticks were magnetically clipped to each thigh and his blade was safe within his scabbard across his back. They would need every bit of this firepower and it probably still would not be enough.

The enemy forces began to pour into the town square and come around the fountain as they advanced. Kale heard the command from his brother, "Fire!" and the battle was on. All of the Castillian soldiers blazed to life from their hidden positions, as a massive wave of pulse laser fire erupted down the slope against the advancing Baruk. Immediately they scattered and sought cover from the onslaught. Many were cut down as the multiburst laser fire punched through the symbiotic exoskeletons.

Kale noticed once again the strange signature of moving lines as he peered through his data-scope lens. They were moving very close to their position now, almost as if they were underground! But the thought occurred to him too late. Just as he raised from his position amid the return projectile fire from the Baruk warriors, the Hurutai erupted from beneath the ground.

Kale had seen them one time before, but had only vaguely remembered the capabilities of the huge worm-like creatures. They moved very fast and as their heads pushed upwards through the surface they caught the Castillians completely off guard.

Around the neck area of the creatures were hundreds of six inch spines that shot forth in every direction from the vesicles that produced them. Kale could see about ten of the worms emerging among the troops as he leapt behind a barrier to escape the spines. Soldiers all around the creatures were hit by the spines which contained a fast acting neurotoxin.

That was what Kale had remembered the most; the Hurutai paralyzed the voluntary skeletal muscle functions of their prey so that they could feed on fresh meat without a struggle. He had seen one eat up to ten men at once, holding them within its long wormy body for a slow digestion over several days.

As he peered back at his previous perch he saw it pierced with poison needles all around. He remembered his brother then and searched visually for him amid the chaos.

TIET fired his pulse rifle at every target he could find. The multiburst setting was allowing them to penetrate the Baruk armor; which looked like some sort of exoskeleton. Suddenly something blew up out of the ground nearby.

He turned from his crouched position to see a huge worm-like head pushing through the ground. He had never seen anything like it.

His men fell in every direction as needlelike spines erupted away from a colored ring around the creature's head. Tiet raised his weapon to fire at it but his own arms began to go limp.

He looked down as the pulse rifle fell out of his hands and he saw a spine fixed in his lower left abdomen. He pulled it out as his vision went blurry and the buildings and terrain began to spin. He felt the ground smash hard into his face as he tumbled over helpless. He tried to cry out for help but could not.

The beast reared its head around and slammed into the ground as it brought more of its body out on the surface. It opened up a huge orifice allowing long tentacle like tongues to issue forth across the ground. It latched onto various Castillian soldiers lying on the ground and quickly pulled their paralyzed bodies into its own hulking mass, consuming their paralyzed bodies.

Tiet could see it all, but could not move. He tried to use his kinesis, but he was too dizzy and disoriented to concentrate. It looked like this would be his end; eaten alive by this monster of the Baruk.

Around him, soldiers he had trained personally from among the Castillians and the Vorn were being pulled into the gullet of the creature. He would have wept for them if he could or risen to save them, but it was no use.

He could see pulse fire still being exchanged with the firepower of the Baruk and other creatures like this worm that were spraying their venomous darts at his forces as they tried to fend off what was quickly becoming a slaughter.

In the near distance he could see the approach of the Baruk as they made their way up the slope. If the worms didn't take him, the Baruk certainly would.

A coiled tentacle swept over his body as the creature moved its head in his direction. The horrid appendage latched onto his leg and began to pull him toward the gaping maw of the creature. It leveled its head to his position as the tentacle pulled his limp body through the dirt.

This was it. It was over. A brand new coalition of Vorn and Castillian people working together for peace and safety, him made the King on the family throne once occupied by great men including his own father, and now it was going to end.

The Baruk were winning. They had lost most of the Vorn cruisers trying to prevent the ground war that now was probably going to destroy the Twelve Cities and he was ultimately responsible as their leader.

A flash of light blazed across his visual field and suddenly the tentacle was hanging from his leg, severed. From above the head of the great worm beast he could see a lone figure coming down on it with an ignited

Barudii blade that was quickly driven straight into whatever brain it might possess.

The creature reared up as the soldier drove it deep again. The beast gave up the fight quickly and the head crashed with tremendous force into the ground near Tiet's paralyzed body.

Without warning, this person picked him up somehow, almost as if he had levitated up to him. And then they were off and running. He heard a voice as the scenery kept changing before his fixed eyes. "Don't worry; I'll get you out of here, brother."

It couldn't be. Kale? But he was in detention at Baeth Periege. And suddenly with the realization he felt no anger, only relief that somehow and for some reason his brother was here to save his life.

He could hear Kale as he called for a retreat to behind the defense wall. "Abandon your posts and return to the city immediately, by order of the King!"

Tiet was glad Kale was taking charge. The men were getting slaughtered and he would have called the retreat himself had he been able. Hopefully, the remainder of the civilian population had been able to get behind Wynn's ten mile front by now. They had been nearly out by the time the defense cannons were set to auto track and left running as long as the Baruk were within target range.

Kale joined other soldiers who were now in full retreat from the advancing Baruk. They had to reach the access portals quickly to get inside the wall before the enemy caught up with them. Fortunately it appeared that the creatures were busy still feeding, leaving only the Baruk warriors on their trail.

The clatter of their projectile weapons could be heard all around, as the metal shells pounded the surrounding buildings and took down more of the Castillian soldiers as they retreated toward the defense wall. Of five hundred elite warriors that had come to the battlefield with their king, fewer than a hundred remained standing.

Kale tried to put as many structures between himself and the advancing Baruk as he could to block the storm of shells swarming around them. He found them easier to detect mentally than pulse blasts that traveled much faster, but it was still difficult to evade all the gunfire with his brother limp across his back.

He was supporting the majority of Tiet's weight kinetically but his movements were still cumbersome. With the masses of Castillian soldiers dying all around him all he could think of was getting his brother safely behind the defense wall up ahead.

Some of the other soldiers had already reached the wall and accessed one of the portals through. One of the Vorn was standing at the doorway waving other Castillian warriors inside. Kale followed the others through the passageway that took them beyond the defense wall into the city. Several of the soldiers guarded the portal until they could see no other Castillian soldiers; then they followed the others through, sealing the doorway behind them.

The Baruk were locked outside of the city now. As Kale came into the open city he spotted a place where a med station had been set up and left for anyone that might be wounded in the battle. The other soldiers were congregating around several of the stations that had been set up while the city's population was being evacuated to Baeth Periege.

Kale laid down his brother and examined him. He passed a med scanner across his limp body and determined that he was alive and well despite the neurotoxin that kept him paralyzed. He took one of the needle leads from the scanner and pushed it into Tiet's deltoid muscle. It may have still hurt him but he needed to do a cellular muscle scan to determine how best to treat the poison. The scanner began to run through a series of tissue and function tests over several minutes. When it had finished, a series of instructions came across the screen to instruct Kale on what medication combination would be effective in reversing the paralytic effect of the Hurutai neurotoxin.

The gunfire beyond the wall was quickly quieting down which disturbed him; they were up to something. He rummaged through the med box in the station tent looking for the prescribed drugs called for. Only two were needed, but the dosage had to be precise. He located more supplies to mix the concoction and went to work. Tiet remained seemingly lifeless on the ground.

Beyond the med station tents something was happening. The men were yelling and then he heard the screeching of the Hurutai. He went to the tent door to look out just as a spray of Hurutai spines pierced the flaps. Kale jumped back and could see several of the spines in his body.

He had the injection in his hand called for by the med scanner and immediately jammed it into a vein in his arm and pushed it systemically. He quickly began to get dizzy but within moments the effects of the neurotoxin appeared to be prevented.

He went to work mixing another dose for Tiet. He could hear more than the just the Hurutai outside now. Kale fixed his mental senses on the area around him and found the Baruk warriors coming through the Hurutai tunnels into the city. Gunfire was erupting again as the remaining Castillian warriors tried to defend themselves against the steady stream of Baruk warriors pouring through the tunnels.

Kale worked fast to get the mixture prepared and when he had it he injected the medication into a vein in Tiet's arm. He could sense the Baruk closing in on where they were now and he didn't have the time to wait for the paralysis to be reversed on his brother. He quickly lifted him up kinetically and moved to the rear of the tent where he sliced down the cloth wall with a kemstick and plowed on through to the outside.

The battle was raging again but there were hardly any of his comrades left alive as the Baruk began to capture the area the Castillians had been recuperating in. Kale ran for cover toward the large buildings ahead, but the Baruk were closing on him fast.

He could feel Tiet beginning to shift on his back as the paralysis wore off.

Ahead in their path a Hurutai worm erupted through the surface, leaving the brothers with no where to go. Kale dropped to the ground fast with Tiet as the reflexive spray of toxic spines sprayed away from the beast and sailed over their heads. Tiet was moving on the ground now trying to regain his own muscle control as Kale drew his blade to defend as best he could.

Suddenly a flash of light appeared between the Hurutai and the buildings behind. Kale could see what appeared to be a huge window, to another place, materialize with the figures of men coming through it into the city. He could begin to make out the people as Horva warriors and General Grod was leading them through.

They each wore a metal glove with wires trailing along the length of their arms to a small pack across their backs. The gloves were being held before them as they ran into the area, alerting the Hurutai to their presence. Streams of plasma energy shot forth from the gloves; some of them hitting the Hurutai. The creature screeched in pain and within seconds it fell over dead.

The Horva were running straight at him and Tiet, who was still trying to stand for battle. Kale raised his blade as he ignited it and prepared to fight the Horva coming at them. More streams of plasma energy issued forth like lightning from their fingertips but the attack passed them and hit the advancing Baruk head on.

He was dumbfounded as the Horva warriors ignored them completely to fight off enemies behind him.

General Grod came right up to the pair of warriors as they stood there exhausted from the fight they had already faced.

"Come with me, we need to get you to safety," he said speaking directly to the young king.

Tiet responded now, appearing to realize more of what had just happened than Kale did.

"I knew it, Grod," he said weakly as he tried to catch his breath. "I knew you were a man of honor."

Tiet could still barely stand and Grod helped Kale support the young man as they made their way back toward the energy portal standing in mid air.

"My warriors!" said Grod into his own communication headset. "Return to the transgate!"

Grod, Kale and Tiet all proceeded through the portal and found themselves immediately inside the fortress at Nagon-Toth.

"SIR, we've been unable to confirm how many troops have off-loaded inside the city since the other transports began landing," said Sergeant Corbin.

"What about the power?" asked Wynn. "Have you had any success getting to the main supply conduits?"

"No, sir. The Baruk are still fortifying that area very heavily. We can't get through."

"It's been two hours now and nothing from Tiet or anyone from the preliminary team."

"With all due respect, sir, it seems clear that no one survived and the Baruk have the city now; how could they possibly have made it?"

"I understand the circumstances, Corbin, but I don't want to give up hope. And don't start that rumor among the men. It won't do anything for morale, and our fight is far from over. Now get the units mobilized, those Baruk aren't going to remain in Thalidi for long."

It was a fact, the Baruk were mobilizing their ground forces for the inevitable push toward Baeth Periege. For an hour they had seen troop carriers coming down from space into Thalidi. The defense wall was still in place and the Baruk were sitting safely behind it for now.

Somehow they had gotten into the city without disabling it and had apparently decimated the entire team that Tiet had taken to ambush their army. It looked like Kale had failed to protect his brother and considering the circumstances it really wasn't a surprise. The Baruk were mounting a formidable ground force behind that wall and he wasn't sure whether they could stop it or not.

Frustrated, Wynn tapped the communication panel that was locked in with the *Esyia*. "Estall, what is your status up there?"

"We're trying to hold our own up here, Wynn, but we still haven't been able to blast that flagship," said Estall.

"We've been seeing a lot of troop carriers landing inside Thalidi…"

"I know, but we're completely outnumbered up here," said Estall. "We just don't have the ability to guard the surface and try to get to that flagship!"

"I understand Estall. I don't mean to accuse, I know you're doing everything you can," said Wynn apologetically. "Bad news. We may have already lost Tiet."

There was a pause for a moment before he answered. "Are you sure?"

"No. I can't be certain, but it appears the whole unit was wiped out as the Baruk made their way into the city. We've not heard any word from them. I don't want to believe it, but…"

"I understand. Let's just keep up the fight and hope we can manage to drive them back. It's all we can do," said Estall.

Wynn tapped the communication panel again. The scans of the city were still inconclusive. The Baruk were jamming them somehow to hide their next move.

"Sir, the units from the other cities have arrived at the staging area," said Corbin.

"Good. We'll need all the help we can get. It looks like this is where our future is going to be decided."

IT had been several hours since they had come through the portal into Grod's compound and they were still being confined to the medical lab under guard. Tiet had been relieved to see Grod's aggression aimed at the Baruk, but what was his intent now? He wasn't sure. Kale was pacing and examining the room discreetly looking for a way of escape.

They had not spoken since their arrival and neither seemed to know what to say to the other. Kale had been the last one he had expected to see coming to his rescue out there against the Baruk, but he was glad to have him.

After all that he had said and trying to kill him inside his confinement cell, Tiet was unsure what he could say at this point to even begin a dialogue with him.

"How's your equilibrium? Your head hurting?" asked Kale suddenly.

"It's fine. Thank you for saving my life out there."

Kale stopped his pacing and just seemed to be listening, like the words were something he had wanted to hear but never expected to.

"Look, Kale, I'm sorry for what I said and did when you were in confinement. I just don't know what to make of all of this. I mean, you betrayed us...our parents, our people...how am I supposed to react?"

"I know. Believe me, I wish I could undo all that I've done. I would gladly give my life now to undo it, but I can't. You are my brother and I only want to have you forgive me. It's all I have left."

"I'm sorry. I just don't know if I can give that to you right now."

Kale looked at him now, but there was great pain behind his eyes that Tiet partly wanted to see and partly wished he could relieve; but he just couldn't find it within himself.

Then Grod came into the room flanked by several warriors. They were still outfitted for battle.

"Grod, I'm glad you changed your mind about what we talked about," said Tiet.

"We can discuss that later," said Grod. "Right now, gentlemen, we have more pressing matters. Follow me."

He turned and led them out of the medical lab and down several corridors to another larger room full of data screens and all manner of technical equipment. Tiet immediately noticed a huge window on the far side of the room and walked past the general to see it.

He could see that it opened up beyond to a huge dome that looked increasingly familiar as he stared. It was the same room he had been brought into to fight, when he was captured by Grod months ago, but now it was full of various equipment and a huge gateway of some kind that seemed to lead to nowhere; only the other side of the dome could be seen beyond.

"General, this room looks familiar," he said accusingly.

"Your right, it is the same battle arena where you killed my teragore," said Grod matter-of-factly. "A very impressive display, young Master Soone," he continued without any note of remorse. "Come look at this information."

He joined Kale and Grod before the main tactical view screen in the room. They were surrounded by Horva warriors who were performing data retrieval and sorting.

"Here you can see what is left of your ships still in orbit as they battle the Baruk," said Grod as he pointed to the display. "We've been monitoring your progress for some time now and there are very few ships left. We noted that a number of them retreated at once while the remainder has taken to trying to attack the Baruk's main battle cruiser.

It appears that they were able to somehow get through the Baruk shields using a random frequency generator to fire your dispersion cannons; most ingenious, by the way. But you don't have the firepower to take out that ship, and it is essential that you do so.

We know that the Baruk are telepathically controlled by their leaders, known only as The Three. They will be aboard the flagship."

Kale listened carefully, but he did not volunteer what he knew about the Baruk leaders. The Three, were much more than just telepaths. Lucin himself was embodied in those men. It was the Wicked One who controlled the Baruk.

"Grod I don't have any more ships to throw at them," said Tiet. "If you have ships to aid us, then we would be happy to coordinate an attack, but otherwise…"

"I don't have any ships like that here, but I do have something else," said Grod as he looked to the window and the chamber beyond.

Kale and Tiet looked at each other puzzled as they followed Grod to the window.

"That apparatus down there is called a transgate."

"Is that how you appeared in Thalidi?" asked Kale.

"Exactly," said Grod. "We had been working on it to attack your people by surprise."

"Great," said Tiet with a roll of his eyes.

"But now we can use it to get a strike team into the Baruk flagship," said Grod.

"You mean that thing will transport us inside that ship, even through their shields?"

"Yes, but we have one problem: the transgate draws a huge amount of power and we can't send a large force without draining our power reserves past the safety point. We're already down from the mission inside Thalidi," said Grod.

"Well, I'm glad you did," said Kale. "What can we do now?"

"We have enough power to send two or three people through the gate. If we can get inside then perhaps we might stand some chance of destroying their leaders and cutting off the ground army from their coordinated mental control."

"Without their leaders, we have a real chance against the Baruk," said Tiet. "I'm in."

"I'll go with him, General," said Kale.

"I will also go. I may not be a Barudii, but I can still fight the Baruk. If you're ready to go, then we don't have any time to spare."

"We're ready. Just lead the way," said Tiet.

"I know my way around that ship," said Kale. "I should probably lead the way once we get onboard."

Tiet looked at Grod who nodded his own approval.

"Then let's go."

The three men made their way quickly down to the domed chamber. They each noted their own weaponry on hand as one of the Horva prepped the portal for power up. Grod was wearing one of the plasma glove weapons they had seen the Horva using during the rescue in Thalidi.

"What is that thing anyway?" asked Tiet.

"The glove channels plasma energy from this pack on my back and targets by way of this targeting laser located in my data-scope lens," said Grod. "They're good; we've worked hard on these weapons."

"Oh, we noticed," said Kale. "Your men fried those hurutai with no problem."

"The weapon is similar to throwing a bolt of lightening," said Grod.

"I'm glad you've decided to be on our side," said Tiet. "It sounds like you've been monitoring our every move lately."

"Well, it helps to stay informed, doesn't it?" said Grod jokingly.

The tech signaled a lock on the Baruk flagship when they were ready. "Sir, we can't get an exact scan on what you'll face up there," said one of the men operating the control panel at the gateway.

"We don't have time to waste, we'll just have to deal with whatever we find," said Grod. "Activate the transgate."

The gateway came alive with energy before them. An image began to coalesce as the transgate brought the chamber at Nagon-toth into direct contact with a location somewhere on the Baruk flagship.

"Gentlemen, it's time."

WYNN was watching the last of the pulse cannon fire emanating from Thalidi's defensive batteries. Tiet had been wise to set the front for this defense at ten miles out from Thalidi's perimeter.

The Baruk had been trying for nearly twenty minutes to use the city's cannons against them but the range was not great enough to reach. It appeared they were giving up on that tactic now and Wynn wondered if they might emerge soon for a face to face fight with his forces. He didn't have long to wait.

The sixth gate began to open on the defense wall as Wynn watched through his data-scope lens which magnified the image. They were coming on a fast march toward their position. From his grounded angle it was impossible to tell how many, but it looked like thousands. With all of their new recruits, Wynn still only had five thousand warriors to face the Baruk. It wouldn't be enough. The Baruk were strong runners and within an hour they would be locked in combat.

THERE were no warriors anywhere in sight when the trio stepped out of Nagon-Toth's domed chamber into the Baruk Flagship. Kale studied the location for a moment and recognized where they were.

"Tiet, we're near the core of the ship. That means we could easily access the power stream for the gravity bomb containment chamber."

"What in the world is that?"

"Gravity bombs are large super dense alloy spheres that produce a gravitational field powerful enough to crush a ship's hull like an egg. If we can disable the special containment field that prevents them from destroying this ship, then—"

"Then this ship will implode around them," said Grod quickly. "What do we have to do, Kale?"

"The coolant system would be the easiest to disable from where we are. If you and Grod could make your way down this corridor, you will come to an overlook for the containment chamber. You'll be able to see a series of yellow colored conduits running from above the chamber; these are the coolant conduits. I'm not sure how many there are, but if you can blow out at least two of them then the coolant pressure will rapidly fall to zero; after that it will take about ten minutes to lose the containment field altogether."

"What about you?" asked Tiet.

"I'm going after the Three. They'll need to be distracted or killed while you two attack the coolant conduits. That area is heavily guarded, but they can pull many more warriors to stop us if someone doesn't distract them."

Grod and Tiet eyed one another. "I think it's a good plan," said Grod. "Anyway, what else do we have? But if we are not back through the transgate before the ship implodes, the gravity could threaten Nagon-Toth—and of course, we won't survive either."

"Then we'll meet back here at the transgate," said Tiet.

Kale watched his brother and General Grod as they headed down the long corridor. He would have liked to agree on meeting back at the transgate, but he did not plan on leaving the ship.

Given the power of Lucin, he would have to remain to prevent him from escaping when the containment failure alert sounded all over the ship. If Lucin survived then this effort would be wasted and the war itself would likely carry on to the inevitable end with the Baruk dominating the entire planet. Kale was determined to give his brother the chance to be the king he could never have been himself.

XIV

KALE knew the ship well and made his way quickly and quietly toward the chamber of the Three; Lucin's mortal puppets. Kale encountered a number of warriors as he went, but evaded their notice. Soon he arrived at the chamber.

He guessed that Tiet and Grod would probably be close to the containment area by now and he had little time to distract Lucin before intruder alarms would sound and they would lose the slight advantage surprise gave them.

Kale removed two spicors from his uniform and stepped back enough to throw them into the chamber door. They flashed violently leaving a large hole through the alloy that comprised the door. Kale was through the door as soon as the energy dissipated.

He dived through and rolled to his feet drawing his blade as he stood. The dispersion field ignited and lit the dark room around him, but the Three were not immediately seen. He closed his eyes and relied upon his mind, and then he found them. "You can come out, I see you," said Kale.

Kale immediately formed a kinetic bubble within the hole he had made and blew out the door mechanism with a thought.

"Do you think we will run from you Kale?" asked one of the Three.

"Or are you ready to end your life by trapping yourself with us?" asked another.

"You'll try to run before I'm through with you Lucin," said Kale.

They laughed in unison. "Pride goeth before a fall, mortal. Do you really expect to defeat an angel?"

"You were an angel, Lucin; now you're an abomination."

They approached him from three sides, coming into the yellowish glow of his blade. Kale protected himself mentally as he felt them apply their own great mental faculties against him.

Lucin was putting tremendous pressure upon him as he searched for a weakness in Kale's defense, but he could find none.

Kale could feel the pressure continuing to build as Lucin sought to attack him mentally. He knew very well that he would have been easily overcome by the angel if he was not forced to split his attention and power in coordinating his warriors on the ground and with the ships still fighting the Vorn cruisers around the flagship.

Kale decided that he would have to try a counterattack soon or Lucin might break through his mental defense. Suddenly Kale lunged at one of them to strike with his blade. The symbyte swept out of the way fast toward one of the others like a hand being pulled back to its body.

A large piece of equipment flew at Kale from its place in the shadows as he attempted to correct his maneuver to hit his target. He struck the large metal object, cutting it in two pieces.

The Three came close to one another now and Baruk warriors could be heard outside the one door to the chamber, but they could not get through Kales kinetic bubble or open the doorway to help their masters.

"Have you already summoned help for yourself, Lucin?" he asked sarcastically.

Lucin did not answer him. The Three came together, touching, their forms beginning to change before Kale's eyes. The human forms melded with one another increasing their size to roughly three times their individual size. They congealed into a monstrous form.

"If it is a physical battle you desire, you shall have it, Barudii," scolded Lucin.

GROD and Tiet were able to see the massive containment chamber from their perch. They had climbed beyond the walkway toward the mechanism to avoid any Baruk warriors that might be happening by during the course of their duties. They climbed quietly along the structure toward the conduits above the chamber. The pipes were huge. It would take a throw of multiple spicor discs to get through those conduits without being instantly covered in the coolant flowing within. There appeared to be a minimum of personnel in the area at the moment. There was no time to waste.

Tiet removed three spicor discs from his vest. He and Grod moved to a catwalk that would give them an easier escape route. Tiet stood for the throw and targeted three separate conduit pipes to prevent any rerouting of coolant to the containment system, as Kale had suggested.

With deadly accuracy he sent the discs away to their targets. The discs exploded as they impacted the pipes, leaving huge holes in each one and bluish colored coolant vapor spewing forth from them.

An alarm immediately sounded throughout the ship, as they began to make their way down the structure again to escape through the transgate. Baruk began to clamor into the containment system area. Then they spotted the pair. "Saboteurs!!"

The Baruk began to fire upon them as they ran down the catwalk. Projectiles clattered around them like rain as Tiet tried to block them with a kinetic field. More warriors began to approach them from the other end of the catwalk.

Tiet drew his kemsticks as Grod targeted the group with his data-scope lens. Suddenly a strike of plasma energy burst over the kinetic shield arcing into the approaching Baruk. The warriors tumbled over the side of the catwalk as the energy hit them full fury.

More warriors were mobilizing already, but they didn't have time to draw out the fight; according to the wailing security alarms, this ship would be imploding in seven minutes.

KALE deflected several tentacles flying at him from the Lucin's symbyte form. The creature screeched as his blade vaporized some of its morphing tissue. Lucin couldn't get past Kale's defense. Then the ship's warning system went off.

"Evacuate ship, seven minutes to containment meltdown, evacuate ship," sounded the alarm.

The symbyte creature reeled back from the fight as Lucin realized the imminent destruction of the ship. He turned his attention to opening the door and breaching Kale's kinetic force field. Kale moved in to strike again trying to keep it occupied and imprisoned until the containment field collapsed completely.

The creature spun on Kale and sent him flying backward with a burst of mental energy. Kale wondered if Lucin had now stopped expending his power coordinating his troops to concentrate on saving himself. Kale regained his stance and flung his blade at the creature. The blade struck and rebounded under mental control to his hand.

Lucin howled at him and held Kale in a mental grip that instantly fixed him frozen to the floor.

He knew that he would not get through the force field until Kale removed it. Lucin's monstrous form came at Kale and smashed a hardened appendage across his body that sent him into the ground and his blade spinning out of his hand across the floor.

Kale could hear the warning system stating that only four minutes remained before containment meltdown as the creature stood over him and began to pound away at his body. He could feel his bones shattering as Lucin desperately tried to remove Kale's mental focus on the shield that prevented his escape from the room and the doomed ship.

Kale was in terrible pain, but he blocked it out as much as possible as he continued to focus on keeping the field up across the chamber door until the last possible moment. Blow after blow pounded across his battered and bleeding body.

Kale could barely hear over the ringing in his ears. The warning system sounded a muffled cry of three minutes. Kale felt like his life was beginning to slip away and his body was numb; yet he continued to focus all energy on the field.

GROD and Tiet leapt away from the catwalk and landed where they had ventured out of the corridor leading to the transgate. Several Baruk warriors met them as Grod blasted them with plasma energy on their way through.

They ran hard for the transgate and did not encounter any other warriors along the way. The ship's warning system sounded out again at four minutes to meltdown as they reached the transgate and ran through. When they came into the domed chamber at Nagon-Toth, Tiet immediately asked the technician monitoring the gate, if Kale had already come through.

"No. You are the only ones to return," said the technician.

Tiet turned back to the gate as Grod caught his arm to prevent him. "Don't go back, Tiet."

"He's my brother!" snapped Tiet. "I have to go back!"

Grod looked at him urgently, showing concern in his eyes.

"Keep the gate open as long as you can," he said and Grod released his grip on the young man's arm. He ran back through the gate and was immediately within the flagship again. He had no other way to find Kale except his mind.

Tiet felt for him and found him nearby. Several Baruk were working on a damaged door to the chamber; he could feel Kale inside and in horrible pain. He blasted the Baruk warriors with his mind before they even realized he was upon them.

He sent them into the wall with such force that none of them moved after they hit the ground. He could sense a force field that Kale held over the chamber door and the screeching of some animal was heard from within.

Tiet pulled a hand full of spicors and flung them into the wall, blasting a hole to access the chamber. As he entered the room a monster peered up at him. It was a horrific-looking creature and Kale's bloody beaten body was lying beneath it. The creature tried to attack him mentally as he flung a handful of spicors at it.

He was knocked down by the attack as the spicors sailed into their intended target and erupted all over the creature's large body. The symbyte flailed backwards away from Kale and writhed upon the floor trying to reorganize its form.

He took the opportunity and grabbed Kales battered body up in his arms; supporting his limp form mentally as he made his way back out of the chamber to the transgate. The warning system sounded again, "One minute to containment breech..."

ESTALL shifted in his captain's chair as new information began to come across the view screen. "Sir, there appear to be a large number of escape pods jettisoning from the flag ship," said one of the scan techs.

"Ranul, what's going on?"

He ran more specialized scans of the vessel. "I'm picking up some sort of gravitational flux onboard. It's difficult to pinpoint behind their shields, but there is something else odd about it."

"What?"

"The other ships are beginning to drift from their protective positions around the flagship."

"Are they running?"

"No, it just looks like they've stopped calibrating their position, like someone is asleep at the wheel. Wait a minute! The waveform I've been monitoring has discontinued."

"Can we break through?"

"I would caution against it, the gravitational disturbance is building in intensity. If it keeps up it will destroy their ship and pull in anything within a range of one thousand kilometers."

"Gunner, continue trying to punch through. Maybe we can help them on their way," said Estall.

WYNN could clearly make out the forms of the Baruk warriors as they began their charge across the battlefield toward their position.

"Ready your guns!!" shouted Wynn to his troops through his com-link.

The Baruk were running hard at them now, shouting a war cry as they advanced. And then suddenly, many began to slow and stop.

"What's happening?!" He asked as he peered through his data-scope lens.

Suddenly a number of monstrous worm-like beasts broke through the ground from within the group of Baruk warriors and began to attack them.

"Sonders!"

"Yes, sir," said the soldier as he ran to Wynn's side.

"Aren't those the same creatures that were spotted entering the city before the attack on Tiet's group?"

"Yes, sir, the same. But why are they attacking the Baruk?"

"I don't know but their group is within the range of our guns.... Fire!!"

The Baruk warriors were caught in between their own creatures attacking them as the mental domination of the Lucin was released, and the rain of fire coming against them from the Castillian army. Many of the warriors ran in various directions to escape, while others tried to kill the Hurutai that were trying to kill anything within their reach and others tried to fire back at Wynn's forces.

"Should we charge them, sir?" asked Sonders.

"No, not yet.... Let's allow those creatures to finish off as many as they will first. Something is finally going our way in this fight. Let's not give up the advantage we've been given."

TIET'S steps were beginning to get heavier and heavier as he ran toward the place where he hoped the transgate would still be open to escape through. The Baruk ship's computer was counting down the last minute. Tiet was still supporting the weight of Kale's body with his mind but he was struggling as the gravitational forces began to build aboard the doomed vessel.

Lucin's symbyte form began to recover itself from the spicor disc explosions. Pain coursed through his body, but that only fueled his anger and desire to escape the ship that much more. The Barudii had seized Kale's body but had left the chamber open as well.

With only precious moments to escape, Lucin's monstrous form moved quickly through the opening in the chamber door.

The computer was counting down and there was no time to reach any of the escape pods. Then he saw a trailing glimpse of a man with another across his shoulders running from the area; blood trailed behind them on the floor. However they got on the ship, there must be a way they were planning on leaving.

The gravity was causing intense pain in Tiet's legs as he tried to continue his pace toward the transgate, which he could now see up ahead. Nagon-Toth looked like home sweet home in comparison to this place now. Then he heard something approaching fast from behind.

He could sense the same creature that was trying to kill Kale back in the chamber. It was coming up fast on him, but there was no time for a fight; only seconds remained before a complete collapse of the containment field surrounding those gravity weapons.

The symbyte gained rapidly on Tiet as he continued to run. Lucin moved quickly, contorting his terrifying symbyte body to reach for anything he could and pull himself along the corridor. His morphing appendages sprang outward, several at a time, to find anchors with which to pull his body along at a swift pace. He could now see the same portal that Kale's rescuer was running for and his pace quickened as the computer counted down the last ten seconds.

The portal was within reach now. Tiet ran through with Kale still across his back. His brother's blood could be felt across his bare neck and was beginning to soak through his own uniform; but he was still breathing, still alive. As he ran through the portal he saw Grod waiting.

"Close the gate!!" he shouted as they ran through.

The technician punched the button as the symbyte monstrosity reached the field and began to come through. The transgate snapped shut like a light going out. A piece of the symbyte creature burst away as the field separated it from the rest of the body still aboard the Baruk flagship. The lump of tissue landed on the floor smoldering, but did not move.

THE Baruk flagship began to crumple inward upon itself as the containment field fully collapsed around the store of massive gravity weapons within its core. Ranul and Estall watched with their bridge crew as the whole superstructure caved inward.

The numerous escape pods trying to jettison into open space were quickly succumbing to the gravitational pull and being cast back upon their mother ship to join the imploding mass.

The other Baruk ships, many of which were already drifting or damaged were now pull toward the implosion. Then, without warning it burst outward again destroying or damaging nearly all of those ships being pulled to it.

The bridge crew of the *Esyia* howled their approval as the whole conflagration went up before their eyes. Only three ships of the Castillian army remained and they were nearly out of shield power, but the fight appeared to be over; they had won against the odds.

"**GET** the medics in here!" shouted Grod to those monitoring from the control room.

Tiet laid his brother to the floor as gently as he could. Kale's expression was fixed on his face. His face was a mask of blood as he tried to speak to Tiet.

"Forgive?" he asked through the pain.

Tears welled up in Tiet's eyes as he watched the brother he had only recently known, dying before him. He could not hold them back as they fell upon the damaged body.

"Forgive?" Kale strained again.

"Kale, I forgive you all, my brother," he said through the lump in his throat.

And with that, Kale's expression turned from anguish to peace. He stopped his struggle and laid his head back to the floor and was dead.

The Horva medics rushed into the chamber but Grod bade them to hold with a wave of his hand. The Barudii warrior was dead and they could not have saved him.

Tiet moved away from his body as the Horva prepared to remove him.

"I am sorry for your loss," Grod said genuinely.

He only looked at the General. He had no words now.

"My men will show you where you can rest awhile. I will contact your people in Baeth Periege and we will arrange transport for you back to the city."

Tiet nodded as he choked back his emotions. He followed one of the warriors out of the room as the medics loaded Kale's body onto a carrier.

"What do you want to do with this tissue that came through the portal?" asked the transgate tech.

"Have it taken to the incinerator, that way it will be completely destroyed," said Grod as he followed the medics out of the room.

The transgate technician left his controls after shutting down the control board and went to find a suitable container to remove the tissue. He found an old metal box and scooped the symbyte flesh into it. With the lid shut he headed for the incinerator to dispose of the specimen.

THE trip back to Baeth Periege was lengthy but uneventful. Tiet did not speak to anyone and no one attempted conversation with him. General Grod sat behind him on the shuttle flight along with a contingent of his warriors; a proper escort for the Barudii king.

When they arrived within the city, Wynn was there to meet him at the port, along with seemingly thousands of people both warrior and civilian from among the Castillian and Vorn races. Tiet followed the casement carrying Kale's body as the Horva warriors carried it from the shuttle toward the main port building.

The crowd clapped and cheered for their young king as he passed through them on the walkway. He tried to be as cheerful as possible; waving several times to the people who had come to see him home, but the pain of losing his brother after so short a time of knowing him ate at him.

He was reminded of his other loved ones who had died around him in so short a time. He never doubted the purposes of God in all things, but it seemed so senseless to him.

When he entered the main port building, Mirah was there to meet him.

"I thought we had lost you," said Mirah.

Wynn was relieved to see him safe. Tiet would grieve for Kale, but he would certainly bounce back, in time.

They remained in the south gate only minutes longer before going on to the medical complex where he could get treatment for any lingering effects of the neurotoxin he had been subjected to and dress his wounds.

WHEN they arrived he followed Mirah on into the treatment bay. He seemed to be bruised all over. Mirah noticed fresh blood trickling down his arm, the same that had been previously broken and repaired. She cut away the sleeve of his uniform to examine it.

Mirah wasn't exactly sure what to say as she tried to concentrate on her medical duties. She liked Tiet, but they had never been anything more than friends. She had wondered if they might ever be more. He had lost some of the brashness he possessed when he had rescued her from the Vorn prison back on Castai's twin across the Rift. Now he was quiet and kind and very respectful of her as a professional.

Mirah remembered that he had promised her they would sit down and talk soon. As she dressed his wounds, she decided she was going to hold him to that. When the time was right, they would have a very serious talk about the true nature of their relationship and an honest discussion of how they felt about one another.

RESNOIR watched the alarm on the transgate with frustration.

"Where did Merin go? He's been gone for hours and he's the only one trained on the shutdown procedures for the transgate until Orikel comes on tonight."

"I think the General had him running some errand to the incinerator," said one of the other techs in the control room. "But that was hours ago."

"Well someone needs to take care of shutting that thing down and I'm not messing around with it. I'm going to see if I can find him."

Resnior got up from his station and headed out of the control room and found the lift to take him down to the incinerator.

When he came down the main corridor he could see the main debris port was open. There was a metal container on the floor next to the port, but no Merin. He walked over to the container, which was open and laying on its side. On the ground was some sort of liquid residue. Resnior bent down to examine it. He noticed that there was also blood mingled with it.

When he stood and turned to return to the lift, Merin was standing there almost on top of him. Resnoir only had a moment before Merin caught his head with his hands and quickly turned it hard to snap his neck. The body fell to the ground dead.

Merin tapped the switch to open the disposal chamber with his elbow and pushed the body inside. He picked up the metal container from the floor that he had carried the symbyte tissue down in and threw the empty casing inside with Resnior's body.

After shutting the chamber door again he switched the incinerator on and turned to leave. He reached down on his abdomen and began to close the uniform shirt he wore. Underneath it, fluid from the symbyte tissue began to bleed through the cloth. He covered it up with his vestment and walked to the lift, letting the doors close behind him.

A Horva wasn't a hospitable body for Lucin to inhabit. Another would have to be found before the man's natural defenses could respond. Fortunately this planet had many to offer.

XV

DATE: The Year 9042 (Planet Castai-Rex)

THERE was a steady wind blowing across the plains that night that caused Wynn to stoke up the fire that burned inside the custom pit within his living room. The whole space was very open and he liked it that way. The whole back wall was capable of opening up onto the courtyard beyond where he liked to train and teach his personal students.

Many of the soldiers in the Castillian army had decided to extend their training into the Barudii warrior arts, well beyond the normal military regimen. The war had been over for fifteen years now and the military had been on stand down since two years after the last of the Baruk were disposed of. The soldiers reported for regular training but were otherwise free to conduct their own personal lives.

An increasing number of the soldiers had become interested in knowing more about the concepts and tactics used by the Barudii of long ago and began to come to Wynn for the training. He had been reluctant at first, but as his duties lightened with the end of the war and more people turned to him for additional training, he had decided to begin his own formal program. It brought him a nice income and provided him another means of keeping his own skills up while contributing to the overall well-being of the people.

Wynn sat at his desk near the screened wall leading to the courtyard, which was bathed in moonlight. He liked the feel of nature and tried to keep his home as free from overt technology as was convenient. He wrote upon paper to complete the idea as he formed his lessons to give to his students. Only one of them possessed Barudii psychokinetic abilities, but still they were mastering the ancient fighting techniques that predated the kinesis.

The fire flickered with the wind as he continued his writings in preparation for tomorrow's class with his students. He began to sense something around the edges of his consciousness, and the feeling something or someone was approaching. He stopped his writing but did not move otherwise. His eyes closed as he tried to fix his mind on what was nearby. Then he had it; a brutish form of the Horva was within the confines of his perimeter wall around the courtyard.

This dangerous form of Horva had managed somehow to survive in the wilds of the planet and only rarely did they venture into populated areas when their food shortages ran low. It appeared one was hunting for food on his property now and likely he was the intended meal.

Wynn stood looking out into the courtyard and with his mind he cut the lights around him leaving only the firelight flickering behind him. His eyes quickly began to adapt to the moonlight beyond in the courtyard. He could not see anything moving yet with his eyes, but his mind was focusing in on a life form; definitely one of the feral Horva.

His blade leapt off of a wall mount across the room into his outstretched hand as he opened the courtyard access door mentally. Wynn moved quickly and silently into the courtyard toward the figure hiding in the foliage beyond. Suddenly he sensed the creature coming down fast on him from behind. He whirled with his blade, igniting it in mid-swing. He sliced the air behind him but there was no attacker. He searched quickly with his mind but could not sense anyone else at all now.

Wynn was completely perplexed. He had been quite sure of his senses and now he was out here cutting air in the dark like a fool. Suddenly he sensed something again, but it was a different form. He could clearly sense a bathosphore coming up behind him. He whirled again, expecting to find it there, but again there was nothing.

"What's going on here?" he muttered.

Then he heard something approaching, rolling across the ground. He looked to see a wooden ball twice the size of his fist rolling toward him. Simultaneously there were six others coming from directions all round him. He could sense that they were nothing more than wood and yet they were under some control. He realized what was going on just as the balls leapt off the ground to attack him.

He brought his blade to bear as he dodged several of the fast moving objects that began to swirl about him. As they came at him he struck them each in turn, disintegrating them until only one was left. As it came at him again, he seized it with his own mind, halting its advance.

"Alright, Kale, where are you?"

Then he sensed someone coming from behind to attack and he turned to find nothing again. Realizing another trick he turned back in time to meet the real attacker's ignited kemsticks. The dark clad figure was furiously flourishing double sticks at him. He tried to meet the strikes, but they were so fast the light blurred together like a wall of neon in the dark. How had his attacker masked his presence so well and made Orin sense other creatures instead?

Wynn was beginning to lose ground in the fight and pushed out with his mind against the attacker. The figure sailed backward through the air, flipped over under control and landed on his feet again. Then he linked the ends of the kemsticks together, forming a staff with kemblades at either end.

The attacker sent the staff spinning at Wynn's head. He ducked below as it passed inches over his head and thrust the tip of his blade upward to slice both of the linked hilts. The weapon fell into pieces as the dispersion fields shut down and it spun off to the ground. Wynn looked back to find Kale was gone.

"So, trying to get a little surprise practice in, hmm?" he said to himself as he extinguished his blade with a sly smile and walked back into his house. He was amazed by the young man's ability to disguise his presence and trick Wynn's senses so effectively. *I think the trials tomorrow will be very interesting indeed.*

WHEN Mirah had prepared the morning meal she called for Tiet, then she walked to their son's room to call him. The door opened, and beyond, in the large room that contained a bed, some personal effects and room enough for personal training—sat her thirteen year old son, Kale, polishing up his personal set of kemsticks. He didn't look up as she came in.

"Good morning, Mother."

"Are you hungry Sweetheart?"

"In a minute. I have to finish prepping for the trials."

"Today's the day, are you excited?"

He looked back and smiled then. "Is Father eating a big breakfast? He's going to need it today!"

"I think your father has been ready for this day since the day you were born."

"He won't go easy on me, will he?"

"He loves you more than just about anyone. Knowing how much this means, he won't let up at all."

"Good."

Mirah turned and walked back to the dining room, leaving Kale to finish his preparations. This day was the biggest day in a young Barudii's life; the trials confirmed one as a man and a warrior, worthy to fight in real combat if necessary.

He had eagerly awaited the coming of this day, his thirteenth birthday, for several years now as he trained side by side with his father and Wynn Gareth. Though they were the only three Barudii known to be living, the tradition of training and trials to manhood continued.

He was looking forward to this. He was required by tradition to fight a group of elder warriors and since Wynn and his father were the only ones available they would be the ones to fight. According to archives on the trials, very few of the young warriors facing the test ever defeated the elders testing them. They only were expected to show their abilities as young men. But Kale had no such expectation; he planned to surprise his elders today.

COMMANDER Zurig looked at himself in the mirrored door of the lift as he ascended to his private meeting with the Vice Commander of Armed Services, Estall of the Aolene clan. He opened his mouth and examined the inner lining of his mouth and teeth which shifted tones quickly to pink flesh from a greenish hue that was not human. His eyes glared, then settled to the appearance of the man Zurig had once been when he was still completely human—that had not been so long ago.

The lift stopped at the appropriate floor of the auspicious Gladstone tower where the Vice Commander had his residence. Zurig was one of the few men able to gain such a meeting with Estall and that was very important. It was exactly the reason Lucin had chosen to use his form for the task. He had told Estall that the meeting was necessary because of dissension that was building within the Council of Twelve and the Vorn constituents under them concerning the rule of King Tiet.

And while there was truly a dissension building among the council, Lucin knew exactly what forces were at work to cause it and was glad for it. Now it was necessary to add another piece of the puzzle for gaining the power he wanted. Everything was going according to his plan.

He walked out of the lift and found the door to Estall's quarters which just happened to take up the entire twentieth floor of the tower. Two guards were in place at the entrance, but they quickly stepped aside when they recognized Zurig. After all he was their commanding officer. One of them entered the proper code and the foyer door slid open allowing him to enter. The door beyond was partially of glass and Estall himself answered it.

He motioned for Zurig to come inside as he greeted him in civilian attire.

"How are you doing, my friend?"

"Well, as you know, things are disturbing of late."

"Yes, I know."

"I fear things may turn worse than we've expected. The council has all been challenging the king's decisions regarding the rule of the Vorn. And the rift between the Castillian population and the Vorn population has been growing as well. The word on the street among the Vorn civilians is that they should have someone from among their own race ruling over them."

Estall listened, his expression grim.

"I don't know how long it will be before the council makes an out-right move to disassociate their selves from Tiet's leadership and elect their own."

"It still doesn't seem hopeless to me," said Estall. "The Vorn warriors within the military are still loyal to the king. That has to have a positive influence on the whole situation."

"I'm not sure that will do it; you may be a bit detached from the men as the Vice Commander. My own observations have been more telling. Behind closed doors many of the Vorn warriors are changing their views about Tiet and that's probably due to their civilian loved ones and loyalty to the all Vorn council."

"I had no idea it had gotten so far even among my warriors. What can we do, Zurig?"

"Perhaps we can maintain some control over the situation if Tiet were persuaded to make some of the concessions the council has been asking him for."

"He'll never give in to those demands!" said Estall. "Frankly, they're ridiculous."

"I understand what you're saying, but if he doesn't compromise with them, we could be looking at best at a break between our races again and at worst a civil war."

"Do you really think they would take it that far?"

"If they feel as strongly about the issues as they're presenting to the public then who knows what they'll do."

"They've already created a rift between themselves and the Horva; all the Horva took their families and settled back near Nagon-Toth because of it. It's just racial hatred, pure and simple, and there was never a good reason for it. The Horva made peace with us and they would never attack us."

"That may be so, but the Vorn still perceive a threat and they're acting on their beliefs; right or wrong," said Zurig. "And with Tiet unwilling to break his affiliations with Grod and the Horva, what else can we expect?"

Estall still looked grim as he got up. "Excuse me a moment."

He went to the restroom down the hall, leaving Zurig there on the sofa. But he did not remain there. When Estall opened the door of the restroom, Zurig was there glaring at him. Before he could ask the man what he wanted, Zurig's hand smashed into his face.

He proceeded to push him back into the restroom and the door shut behind him. His hand covered Estall's mouth as he shoved his head back into the mirror on the wall; cracking it upon its mount. Zurig's hand then proceeded to morph and push further into his throat. Estall struggled but his old friend had overwhelming strength to subdue him. A lack of oxygen soon claimed him as consciousness faded and all went black.

THE intercom on Daooth's shuttle came to life with an incoming message. He tapped the panel and a video image of Ultis Thau, the council delegate for the city of Onnith, appeared on the panel.

"Daooth, we are convening an emergency session of the council in two hours. Your presence is required."

Daooth showed a look of disapproval on is face. "Councilman, I have a previous meeting that I must attend during that time, is there any way that I could be excused and briefed later?"

"No."

Daooth looked put-off by the lack of flexibility being shown.

"I would remind you that as a representative of the council your first duty is to us—"

"I was under the impression I dwelt under the authority of the King first and foremost, as does the council," he interrupted.

"Your duty should be to your people first!" shot back Ultis. "As for the king's authority over this council, that is entirely questionable. You will report to the council in two hours."

"I'm sorry, Councilman, your transmission is breaking up..."

"Daooth, we—" He cut the transmission off. He still did not understand the radical change of view spreading through the Council of Twelve toward Tiet's rule. Gradually more and more council members had come to view the Horva under Grod's command as a threat.

There had been no reason at all for the change of mind; it had come about mysteriously. Once the council subscribed to it, the civilian population of the Vorn began to be swayed by it as well. Having been unwilling to sever the peace between himself and the Horva, Tiet was quickly branded as a traitor to the Vorn and his leadership had become the target of constant scrutiny of late. It didn't take much insight to see that the council would soon move to remove Tiet's title. The threat of civil war was even floating around, and it was becoming dangerous to be caught between sides—as Daooth was in his position as Council representative to the king.

In his own mind he believed Tiet was right to hold fast to the peace. Grod, whatever he may have been before the Baruk war, was certainly no threat to the Vorn now.

He had actually taken the whole situation quite well and caused his warriors to return to the lands near Nagon-Toth rather than stir the pot of conflict. Many of the warriors, including Grod, had taken wives from among the Vorn and started families in the time after the war. When they pulled out they had taken their families with them and had not made any effort to reintegrate back into society.

Castillian and Vorn relations had certainly suffered because of the situation, with the Vorn generally following the council and the Castillians unanimously holding Tiet's position of reconciliation. The situation was growing more volatile by the hour.

Daooth's shuttle careened around an outcropping of rocks and the fortress of Nagon-Toth came into view. Grod had agreed to provide a place for the trials to be held today. It was hard to believe thirteen years had already passed since the birth of Tiet and Mirah's son.

Kale was certainly proving to be a child to be proud of; following in his father's footsteps. It would be nice to one day see the young man lead—if there remained a people to lead, anyway.

He landed the shuttle on a landing pad at Nagon-Toth and upon exiting was greeted by General Grod himself.

"General how are you?"

"I'm well, my friend, and you?"

"Things have been better."

"Ah, the council still vilifies us—as usual?"

Daooth only smiled through his sarcastic expression.

"Don't worry, Daooth; we'll manage to get through all of this. I've seen Tiet handle more dangerous situations than these."

"Yes, but public opinion can be a sly enemy to defeat."

"True. Anyway today is a happy day. Let's try to put those matters away for today and enjoy it for the family's sake."

They walked on toward the site chosen for the trials of Kale Soone which lay beyond the fortress' perimeter wall. The area was a nearby crater site that allowed those assembled as spectators to line the rim for a fantastic view of the action a hundred feet below in the hollow.

TIET and Wynn were standing at one end where they prepared for their attack against Kale, who remained at the opposite end of the crater floor. Between them were large hunks of rock that had collapsed out of the crater wall and remained where they fell.

Kale was feeling very confident. He could sense his father and Wynn at the opposite end of the crater talking with one another. He could sense their awareness of him as well; their minds as they took in the surroundings in detail. He did not perform any physical exercises to prepare, but his mind was alive with activity, taking in every inch of the battlefield available to him, even the weather around him. It was of particular interest to him at the moment. He looked up to the overcast sky that was the prelude to a coming storm. No matter the rain, if it came they would not stop the trials. One must be ready for any situation and use every opportunity afforded by it. Wynn had mentioned that to him on many occasions and Kale was a very good student.

Kale watched the dark clouds hanging overhead as heat lightening flashed through them. Excellent, he thought as he pulled two of his four kemsticks to his hands. Then he began to walk out into the floor of the crater toward his adversaries.

Tiet and Wynn talked strategy a little, but mostly they bubbled over Kale's progress and it was easy to see their mutual pride in the young man.

"I have to warn you that Kale came by last night and pulled an interesting stunt on me."

"What do you mean?"

"Somehow he was able to persuade my senses that a feral Horva was coming through the courtyard and he completely masked his own presence from me."

"Are you kidding, you!?"

"If I hadn't figured out what he was doing just in time I could have been in the infirmary today instead of here with you."

They both grinned delightfully, and then they turned toward Kale's position across the crater.

"He's moving," said Wynn.

"Shall we?"

The two warriors moved out into the crater floor. Tiet took to the air and landed upon one of the huge pieces of rock covering the ground. Wynn stayed to the ground and began to weave between the rocks toward their prey.

As Tiet crossed part of an outcropping he suddenly lost sense of Kale; as though he had simply vanished. He looked over the rock protruding in front of him and could not see him.

"Wynn, I've lost him! I can't sense him!"

"Be careful," said Wynn from below Tiet's position. "I told you, he's gotten sneaky."

Tiet brought his blade to bear. He was grinning the whole time. As the proud father of this warrior coming of age, he couldn't help it. He could sense the worry from Mirah on the crater rim above them. She doted on the boy as much as any mother could, and as a concerned parent, the trials worried her. Kale was growing up, and it required him to develop more and more independence especially after today.

Thinking on Mirah above them, Tiet almost didn't see the piece of rock skimming low across the surface of his perch. Quickly, he found a piece of his own and hurtled it mentally into the path of the projectile; smashing them both to rubble. Now, where had it come from?

LUCIN looked at his own reflection in a mirror on his shuttle's restroom wall. A greenish tint faded to fleshy white across his conjunctiva. He opened his mouth to examine his mucus membranes. The greenish tint faded to pink as Lucin looked over his form as the Vice Commander Estall one last time while the shuttle landed at Nagon-Toth.

He was late for the trials. They had evidently already begun. Lucin could see beyond to the trial site at the nearby crater specified in his invitation. Castillians and Horva warriors alike lined the crater rim. The trials were scheduled to take place on the crater floor.

Lucin hurried on toward the crater site. If all went well, his *friend* the king would not ask too many questions about his late arrival. He hoped they might have a private meeting sometime after the post trial celebration. Tiet was the key to accomplishing the goal Lucin strove for; control of the planet and its population. Fifteen years of continuous work infiltrating human society, it was all proceeding according to his plan.

MIRAH searched along the crater floor for her son. He had disappeared somewhere among the huge boulders strewn along the ground below. Ranul patted his worried daughter's shoulder in support. She could see Tiet atop one of the rocks brandishing his blade. Don't hurt him, Tiet, she thought. Wynn was nowhere in sight. He too had disappeared among the rocks.

Tiet came down from his position. He could sense his son below and moved in for the attack. Silently and swiftly he came around one of the large boulders. Kale was approaching from the other side. Tiet raised his blade and ignited it as he came upon Kale rounding the boulder. He struck out at the young man and met Wynn's blade instead. The two looked at each other puzzled for a millisecond; realizing what their opponent had just pulled off. They had each thought the other was Kale. Tiet laughed lightly at the trick.

Wynn spotted their attacker just before he struck. Kale moved as a blur, bouncing off of the side of one of the boulders towering around them. Two kemsticks flared to life in his hands as he flew into them full force. They weren't quite expecting what Kale did next. Instead of landing in front of them, he brought his feet up to land against the rock wall between them. He crossed both arms across himself so that a kemstick was brought to defend on either side of his body as Tiet and Kale both struck at him. He forced back with simultaneous counterstrikes as he unfolded his arms and leapt back away from the rock wall between them, tumbling over back to his feet all within two seconds time.

Tiet came at him fast trying not to allow him to get his guard back up. He struck multiple times with his kemstick while Kale blocked each strike. Wynn was just behind him looking for an opening to get in the action, but Kale was moving to keep Tiet in between himself and Wynn; a tactic he had taught the boy himself. It was a flashy move he had just pulled off, jumping right into the middle of them. He had greatness within him, thought Wynn.

Wynn leapt over the two warriors to come down behind Kale and immediately began his own barrage of strikes. Now the boy had to defend against both attackers. His kemsticks whirled around furiously defending the warrior within from every strike. They were trying to push at him mentally as well, to expose a weakness but he was already there waiting for them and pushing back.

His mind was somewhere else as well. The clouds above continued to flash periodically with lightening. He had practiced the technique only twice and had been successful only once, but it was time. Kale put his mind to raising a streamer off of the rock towering above them.

He maintained it mentally and hoped for a bite from the clouds above but none came and the fight continued on until Wynn and his father began to overcome his defense. Why wasn't it working?

Kale abandoned the current position and leapt away from the both of them to regain his stance, but neither of his elders was going to let up on him that easy. They leapt in turn to follow and stay on him. Still it was enough for him to change strategy.

As they came back at him, Kale launched first one then the other kemstick at his opponents while the other pair he carried leapt to his hands and no sooner touched his palms before they were thrown away as well toward the attackers. They blocked the sticks as they flew at them and the sticks in turn rebounded back to Kale, one after the other striking then rebounding and back to strike with a pair per hand striking at each opponent like some mad juggler had been unleashed upon them.

Wynn had never seen such a fighting technique used by any Barudii. It was amazing to him how well the boy was controlling the weapons; all four of them in coordinated attack. Wynn dodged as he blocked trying to keep from getting hit. Even though they were only ignited with fields strong enough to stun, he didn't want to lose, but they were getting battered hard now and without hands to guide them the flying strikes were less predictable to counter. Then it happened as one got past and struck him in the thigh, the stunning current sent him to his knees and out of the fight.

Kale knew he had won as Wynn went down and he immediately concentrated all four flying kemsticks at striking his father. Tiet had already pulled his second kemstick into his defense and was furiously countering everything Kale was throwing at him.

Then somehow he was able to counterstrike at the handles of one pair coming at him, deactivating them. They fell to the ground as Kale quickly pulled back the other pair to his hands. Now the fight was on between him and his father. No more private sparring for fun and practice. Play time was over and Kale was determined to win in the trials today.

He had been maintaining a streamer now throughout the fight and had almost put it in the back of his mind when the weather decided to engage the bait. A lightening strike burst into the crater battlefield before anyone could react. It struck the rock nearby but the current coming off of it managed to knock down both fighters. Kale returned to his feet quickly but he saw Wynn next to his father, who was not moving. He checked his vitals for breathing and heartbeat then a look of relief came over his face. He was still alive.

Kale was at his side in an instant and scared to death as he tried to help Wynn wake up his father.

"Wake up, Father, I didn't mean to—"

The boy was in a panic.

"Kale, I think he will be alright, but we need to get him to a med lab to make sure," said Wynn.

People had begun to come down onto the arena after the lightening strike. Within moments Mirah was next to Tiet who was trying to regain consciousness now but was still very weak from the electrical shock. Grod and Daooth along with Estall were all around them now as Grod instructed some of his warriors to get Tiet back to the med-lab within the compound.

"Wynn, I'm sorry I didn't mean to, it wasn't supposed to come so close."

"Are you trying to tell me you caused that strike?"

"It wasn't supposed to be like that! I threw up a streamer just hoping to…"

But Wynn was only half listening now. As he watched the Horva escorting Tiet to the med-lab he couldn't believe the inventive ability of his pupil. This was certainly not something he had taught him, neither the use of two pairs of kemsticks simultaneously or the ability to mask his presence while presenting others as decoys.

Kale was extremely powerful, perhaps the most powerful Barudii he had ever known. He watched him as his mother took him with her to go after her husband to the medical lab—and another being watched as well.

LUCIN watched the boy through Estall's eyes as the mother led him away. He walked over to examine the strike point of the lightning, while people milled about on the crater floor. The boy was more valuable than Tiet, he thought. To gain him as a host would mean the ability to conquer even the king.

Lucin made his way quickly out of the crowd and onto his shuttle. It was time to get back to Baeth Periege and set a trap that would give him the boy.

MIRAH checked over her husband who was now conscious but slightly dazed.

"I'm fine, I'm fine. Mirah, I'm okay," protested Tiet.

"How many times have I told you not to argue with the doctor?"

Tiet gave up and allowed her to finish her examination.

"Well, you do seem alright," she said finally.

"I just can't believe Kale actually caused that strike. It's amazing!"

"I don't think he sees it that way. Kale was terrified while you were unconscious. He thought he might have killed you."

"Yes, but the fact that he could even have come up with it. That's great."

When Tiet was dressed again after finishing the exam he made his way with Mirah out to the waiting area where Wynn, Kale, Grod, his son Emil and Daooth were all anxious to see how he was doing.

"Well, you appear well enough," said Wynn.

Kale didn't look directly at him. He was ashamed of his actions and the danger he had put his father in.

"It just took the wind out of me. I've been given a clean bill of health by the doc here," he said smiling at Mirah.

Kale stepped to his father now, "Father I'm really very sorry for hurting you, it really was an accident...I didn't mean for it to strike so near, just to draw your attention and distract you."

Tiet smiled full of parental pride. Then he looked back to Wynn.

"Wynn, what do you think? What is your judgment of this candidate's performance in the trials—should he progress or regress for further training?"

"I would most definitely recommend that this candidate progress to the status of Barudii Warrior," said Wynn with a delighted grin.

Kale smiled noticeably from his downcast face and cast a gleeful look back to his friend Emil at his own father's side. Tiet laid his hand on Kale's shoulder.

"Son, I'm very proud of you. Don't think you'll be perfect and never make a mistake. Mistakes are to be learned from; you'll always be my son and I'll never stop loving you."

Kale grinned openly then hugged his father as hard as he could; which Tiet noticed was pretty hard. His boy was no longer a boy, at least not by Barudii standards; he was now setting out as a man.

"Well, Mirah are you sure you still want to put up with Emil for a week?" asked Grod.

"Of course! We're just beginning to celebrate. How could Kale ever enjoy it without Emil around?"

The two young men grinned at each other again.

"You two go on ahead and get Emil's things. We'll meet you at the transport."

"Yes, Mother."

Emil looked to Grod who nodded his approval then he went off with Kale to the boy's quarters to fetch his things. This was a time of celebration and it was customary for the boys to go out on their own for an outing after the trials were passed, and they were eager to get going. They were planning another surprise upon their return and they needed just a little more time for their final preparations before unveiling it.

XVI

THERE was no need to chime the door when Lucin arrived, in Estall's form, at the Councilman's home; he was already waiting for him. Licoure opened the door and allowed him in. No need for introductions, they knew each other all too well. Licoure was already a part of Lucin's assimilated slaves.

"You have it, then?" asked Licoure as he motioned to the object Lucin was carrying wrapped in a black cloth.

"Of course, Councilman. After all, I'm a friend of the family and trusted," Lucin said deviously through his form as the human Estall.

"Then let's proceed."

Lucin removed the cloth to reveal a Barudii blade of particular ownership.

"This action should provide enough doubt among the Castillians and Horva to allow us to remove Tiet from the equation and gain the boy," said Lucin.

"The boy is most valuable. He will provide a fitting body for you, master."

Lucin nodded and then raised the blade to set his mark and drove it straight into the chest of the councilman. The Vorn man jerked and cried out from the pain then fell dead to the floor; his life pouring through the wound and out on to the floor around his body. Lucin left the blade inside the man and walked back out the door.

There were no guards present at the time. Licoure had given them some time off, telling them he had a meeting planned with the king. Everything was progressing perfectly and soon he would have he boy and complete conquest of this planet would be his.

TIET didn't even bother to return home after the trials at Nagon-Toth. He had a little time to shop in Baeth Periege at the downtown district before getting to his meeting with Licoure. The councilman probably wanted to threaten him again concerning his willingness to keep associations with the Horva. Doubtless the councilman was aware of the trials having been held at Grod's compound and was fuming about it.

He left his transport in the basement garage of the tower complex where Licoure had his residence and ascended in the lift to the councilman's private floor. When the lift doors opened Tiet was met by armed Vorn soldiers.

"So you've returned to the scene of the crime! Guard him, men," said Councilman Teman.

The soldier's trained there weapons on the king.

"What's going on!?" asked Tiet urgently as the group of soldiers encircled him with looks of hatred on their faces. Men that he had trained and fought with suddenly looked like they would enjoy pulling the trigger on him.

"You have killed the chairmen of the high council and you dare to come back here and feign ignorance? Maybe you've returned for this!" said Teman as he pointed back to Estall who was behind him holding a very familiar item; his own father's Barudii blade. The weapon was covered in the coagulated blood of Licoure. Tiet couldn't believe what he was seeing.

"Was the councilman's request of you so harsh that you had to kill him?" asked Estall with astonishment on his face.

"Surely you don't think I did this!"

But the look on his face was not reassuring.

"It is your blade and you were scheduled for a meeting with the councilman today, which you're an hour late for..."

"I'm not late; the meeting was set to begin in another ten minutes."

"Not according to Licoure's schedule!" said Estall. "Do you happen to have a transcript of the message Licoure sent to you concerning your meeting?"

"No, why would I bother to—"

"Perhaps you would have us believe the chairman gave you a different time and then he conveniently crept into your secure residence and stole your own weapon so that he could creep back here and drive it through his own chest to kill himself!" said Councilman Teman with as much malice in his tone as he could muster.

"Councilman, honestly I don't know what's going on here, please just allow me to prove my innocence."

"You may do that in our court of law; that is, if you are willing to surrender yourself to our authority?"

Tiet was about to answer when Estall interrupted. "I'm sure, Councilman that the king would be all too willing to cooperate in this matter—after all, an innocent man has nothing to fear from the law."

It wasn't exactly what he was thinking to say, especially with public Vorn opinion going against his leadership right now. He might very well end up as a scapegoat in such a situation, and who but the Castillians would oppose it with a Vorn councilman dead and Tiet's own blade apparently the murder weapon. But with Estall and Teman staring at him waiting for his response, what else could he do?

If he resisted, he would only worsen his public image putting himself above the law and with these armed soldiers around it would be a fight to leave anyway. He could probably get away from them, even unarmed, but at what cost? Civil war would certainly erupt and it would only be the grace of God that would prevent it now anyway. "Of course I will comply with the law, Councilman; I only ask a fair hearing."

"You will have what the law provides as with any other suspect. Men, arrest this man."

Two of the armed Vorn men moved to place restraints on him while the others stood their ground with their rifles still trained on him. Tiet did not offer any resistance to their efforts. Lucin, in the form of Estall, watched without suspicion as Tiet was led away by the soldiers.

A secure facility was already awaiting his arrival. Lucin had taken great care to see that every possible measure was in place to secure him. He looked at Teman as Tiet was escorted off of the floor by way of the lift.

Teman was not of his mind, at least not yet. But he was a willing participant nonetheless; even if he didn't realize that the prisoner was actually innocent of the crime. He was all too ready to believe that the king was capable of such a crime and was poised to make the most of the entire situation.

"I suppose you will need to assume control of the council in Licoure's absence, sir," suggested Lucin with devious intent.

"It's unfortunate that this has all happened, but I'm ready to do my duty to the Council as the alternate for the chair," said Teman.

"If it's all right, Mr. Chairman, I will accompany the prisoner to our detention facility and see that he is secured properly."

"I know you and Tiet have been good friends, Estall. I hope you realize that he must stand trial; I want to know you won't attempt to help him escape the law. It would cause a civil war."

"Sir, I assure you, I couldn't have any thought further from my mind."

Teman looked pleased by the response and Lucin, in his guise as the man Estall, turned to go into the lift. A sly smile crossed his lips at the thought of trying to let Tiet go after all the effort to frame him. After years and years of covertly assimilating a large portion of the population in the twelve cities, the time had finally come. The populous was his to command; an angel severed from the gates of heaven, but still commanding his own destiny.

There wouldn't be enough time to have any sort of legal proceedings. Everyone would soon be under his control and come to be joined within the symbyte collective as the Baruk once had been. With the king out of the way, and the boy within his grasp, the time to act was now. The lift doors closed in behind him as Licoure's body was being removed from his residence; all according to plan.

EMIL steadied himself as he awaited the attack. Kale stood across the large training room that doubled for his bedroom. From a rack of weapons, he picked up a vest with spicors stuffed in it and put it on as he looked at Emil, who stood with only a wooden bow to fight with. The spicors were not armed of course, as that would certainly bring his parents screaming into his bedroom if any were to go off.

Kale started toward Emil with his array of weaponry located all over his uniform.

"Now concentrate, Emil. Remember to let go of your physical senses to some extent and allow them to be heightened and helped by the kinesis."

"Sometimes if I concentrate too hard I lose it altogether."

"Just try to let it flow naturally. You'll get that feeling of being inside and part of an energy field, as though it were an extension of your own body and mind; transmitting information to you and obeying your commands. Don't fight it. Embrace it. After all, you have the ability; you just need to hone it."

"My father will be so excited when we surprise everybody; I can't wait until we get back from the outing!"

"Well let's get to work so you can really show him something."

Kale brought up a handful of spicors and began to hurl them at Emil. He dodged the first which was meant to bring him into the path of the second. He brought his bow to bear as the disc embedded into the wood in front of his face. The remaining discs came quickly as he dodged about, allowing some to pass into the wall behind him and others he deflected away as he brought the bow spinning elegantly around himself.

"Very good."

Kale pulled his sticks from their magnetic clips and extended the emitter posts. He flew into an attack against the youth, who brought the bow staff into play to counter the strikes. Emil quickly moved to the offensive and spun down low with his body underneath Kale's strikes swinging the whirling bow at his friend's lower legs. He very nearly caught him with the effort, but Kale flipped forward over him instead and returned an extended kemstick back at Emil as he landed.

The boy was already there with his staff to block the strike and moved again to try and push back at Kale. In mid-swing Kale ignited the kemsticks and one of them cut right through the middle of Emil's wooden bow staff. He quickly threw the pieces at Kale as he searched with his senses for another weapon.

He found them on his attacker's legs. As Kale deflected the bow staff pieces thrown at him he felt his other pair of kemsticks leaping to Emil's waiting hands. They ignited and he traded blows with Kale.

They had made the discovery of his power two years before while Kale was training under Wynn. While practicing various exercises in his bedroom training room with Emil, the young Horva had followed him through one of the mental exercises and actually produced some result. With more experimentation, they had discovered his power and Kale had taken it upon himself to pass on everything Wynn was teaching him; but secretly.

They had no idea how he could have come to have the kinesis in the first place, until the two had heard from Tiet, whilst he was in a reminiscing mood, about how Grod had once been his enemy and captured him for the purpose of using his DNA for an experiment to rejuvenate his own chromosomes with the Barudii power. But the experiment had failed to produce any such power in Grod, and was never dwelt on further by either of them. The boys assumed that what had not manifested in Grod was now showing up in his son.

The boys traded further blows playfully as Emil used the kinesis to carry his body elegantly through dodges and flips as the two fought. The power was a wonderful feeling. So much freedom and his mind and senses had never felt so alive. He thought of how proud his father would be when he learned what he had unknowingly passed on to his son.

Suddenly Kale felt something else; something besides their sparring. He stopped his attack and dodged away leaving Emil looking puzzled by his friend's sudden withdraw.

"What is it?"

"Something's wrong. Something is approaching."

LUCIN'S intercom link beeped to life. "Yes?"

"Sir, the squads are positioned outside the king's residence and Commander Gareth's."

"Very good, Lieutenant. I will contact you momentarily with an order to secure the premises and capture everyone on the grounds at the king's residence. Wynn Gareth, I want killed on sight; understood?"

"Understood, sir. We're standing by."

Lucin watched as the containment field charged up around Tiet inside the special chamber that was prepared to hold him. The last of the guards left the chamber as Lucin entered in the form of Estall and faced Tiet.

"Estall, you know I couldn't have done this, don't you?"

"I am very confident you did not."

"But can you help me to prove it?"

At that, Lucin began to pace around the bubble of the containment field.

"I don't think that would be possible."

"I don't want you to break the law, just see that I receive a fair trial," said Tiet

Lucin stopped his pacing and chuckled at the comment. "I don't think a trial is in your future."

"What do you mean?" asked Tiet with a puzzled look on his face.

Lucin faced him and stared into his eyes. "It is no longer necessary to prolong this charade. You have walked into a trap and you will die here in this room before long."

"Estall, what are you talking about!? What's going on?" he asked as he noticed a look on his face he had never seen on him before. "Who are you?"

"Did you really think you could destroy me by wiping out the Baruk?"

Realization washed over Tiet like a wave of doom. Estall was dead; the same creature that had held control of the Baruk was inside him now. "Why imprison me, if you're so powerful why not face me openly?!"

"Do you think revenge on you is my plan? You are vain. It is complete control I will soon have; and a new young body to rule with." He laughed, "God may have cursed me to these physical forms and favored man, but I'm not through fighting yet."

Tiet was trying to take in what he was hearing, but it wasn't all registering.

Lucin spoke into his intercom link. "Lieutenant…"

"Yes, sir."

"Sweep the residence and be sure the boy is kept alive. Kill Commander Gareth."

"Yes, sir. It will be done."

"Kale?!"

"Oh, yes, old *friend*. Your son will make a fitting body for me to rule this planet and those that will follow."

"I'll kill you!"

"That would be a neat trick. This bubble was engineered by your own scientists to hold even a Barudii."

Tiet was fuming with rage, but the containment field prevented him from using his power to break free or affect anything beyond it.

"Enjoy your stay Tiet; I have a meeting with your son."

"Take me instead...wait!!"

But the possessed body of Estall did not wait. He turned with a devilish grin on his face and left the chamber. Tiet pounded a fist into the containment field which repelled him, but his rage kept him from collapsing. He felt like exploding, but he knew it would be useless. He needed to get out of here and quickly. That creature would kill everyone he cared about if he didn't do something; but he had no idea what.

The containment field kept his powers nullified and the chamber looked extremely dense and capable of keeping him from breaking out even with the use of his kinesis. What could he do, but wait. Wait for them to come to kill him; wait while his family was taken the way that thing had taken Estall and possessed his body. He wanted to scream, to cry out, but he could only sit on the ground and pray as Orin had taught him to do in times of seeming helplessness; just to sit and think and pray God would give him an answer to the dilemma. It was all he could do.

WYNN sat at his table eating dinner. He was still feeling tired from the trials. He finished the plate of food, and felt...a disturbance, as he got up. Someone was here. It was not the same as Vorn or human. Something else vaguely familiar, but he couldn't place it. They were coming now, he could sense it. He moved toward the main room where he kept his weapons mounted on the walls.

The entire side wall exploded inward, covering him with rubble. He thought he might have lost consciousness for a moment. When he opened his eyes he could see and sense soldiers all around walking across the wreckage they had made of his house. They were looking for him.

He remained as motionless beneath the wreckage as possible. He concentrated, his mind taking in the entire area. The soldiers were mostly Vorn, yet they weren't. Something was alien about them and the Castillian soldiers with them. It was like the body was proper but the mind controlling them was joined one to another like one mind controlling them all in a way.

Then it hit him. It was the same sense he had of the Baruk. The creatures that inhabited them were still alive. He felt for a weapon and found one two feet away under some of the wreckage. *Time to act.*

With his mind he raised the entire room full of wreckage, in a massive burst of motion, along with the soldiers standing on top of it. Wynn stood up as he called the kemstick to his hand and ignited the extended post.

The soldiers were returning to the ground along with the rubble as he began to whirl through the rainstorm of dust and debris cutting through the symbyte possessed soldiers. Others were approaching fast from outside of his demolished home. He deflected several blasts then retreated into another portion of the home that was still standing. The symbyte soldiers pursued him hard, like hounds on the hunt. They reached the innermost portion of the room as he escaped through a window. He returned a mental command that blew out the supports that remained and dropped the rest of the house on his pursuers; more were on the way.

He could head right into them and try to kill as many as possible or try to escape and reach Tiet's home. These things would certainly be on the attack at the king's residence if they were going all out here.

His estate was near the airway and overlooked it to the east. He ran for it as the soldiers began to come beyond the wreckage of his home after him. The hill had a wall across it that prevented someone from falling over the edge into the airway lanes below. He jumped up to it and down on the narrow ledge on the other side as laser fire blasted into the wall near his position. Below him, shuttles and transports of every sort sped along the airway lanes in two directions.

The chances of successfully landing on one of the small transports without serious injury were not very good. Then he spotted a large bus transport. It was still moving pretty fast but the margin for error was more acceptable. Laser fire was eating away at the wall as the soldiers approached; they weren't taking any chances. Wynn leapt away and guided himself over to the bus. The transport's speed jerked his feet out from under him and he rolled backward and landed hard, but he was still onboard.

The soldiers came to the top of the wall looking for him, but he wasn't sure whether or not they actually spotted him on top of the transport. It was going the right direction to get him to Tiet's home, but it would take about ten minutes. He hoped it would get him there in time to help them.

"**WHAT** is it?" asked Emil.

"Don't you feel it?"

"No."

"Don't worry, that will come in time. Grab some real weapons and follow me."

Kale headed for the main room of the house with Emil in tow close behind.

Mirah went to the door to answer the chime. When she opened it soldiers were all over the place. They raised their weapons as she turned to run for cover. The blasts caught her full force and sent her flying across the floor under her own momentum. The soldiers at the door poured into the room after her.

"How is she?" asked one of the soldiers as another knelt to check her.

"She's alive."

"Alright. Let's retrieve the boy. All weapons on stun, men. The boy is not to be harmed."

The soldier kneeling beside Mirah stood to his feet again and went to raise his weapon. A flash of light severed half of the rifle from the rest and took off his head. Kale was a blur. His thoughts brought the door slamming shut on the soldier standing in the doorway. He slumped down the wall with cracked ribs and sternum as the door released him again. Soldiers from behind kicked it back open and rushed in with their rifles blazing. They ran into the room but couldn't find anyone.

Kale looked down on them from his suspended position against the ceiling. He dropped right into the middle of them with twin sticks blazing. He cut down several before they could fire a shot. But more were rushing in as they saw him engage the others. They fired their rifles right into the crowd taking down their own men in an attempt to get him. He used the soldiers still standing around him as a shield to get away.

More soldiers began to file through the door. Then a number of live spicors flew at them from Emil's hand on another side of the main room. The discs exploded, cutting down most of the soldiers coming through the doorway.

Kale used Emil's attack to use the opportunity to scoop up his mother. He hoisted her to his shoulder and headed back toward his own training room with Emil coming through the room to follow. They shut the door behind them.

"What's going on? Those are our soldiers out there."

"I don't know. Something doesn't feel right about them. Maybe the Vorn council has decided to stage a coupe against Father."

"Too bad he's not here now."

"Maybe there's a reason for that. Right now we better get Mother out of here. I think they've only stunned her; they must mean to capture us."

"The transport!"

"Let's go. You drive."

"Right."

They headed out of the other side of the room into a garage area that housed the transports. Emil raised the canopy on the transport they had planned on using to go on their post-trial outing.

"Hey, look," said Emil pointing to another ship across the hangar.

"The *Whiplash*! We'll take that instead."

"Do you have access codes for your father's ship?"

"Are you kidding? Father had me flying this thing as soon as I could reach all of the controls."

Kale opened up a hatch behind the navigation area of the two man cockpit and slid his mother inside. The compartment was used to carry a wounded person and have them better protected beneath the ships thicker armor plates. He closed the compartment and keyed in the code to raise the canopy. He and Emil jumped inside.

"I'll fly this one," said Kale.

"I thought you might say that."

"You take the weapons console up front."

"Aye, Captain."

The canopy came back down again as Kale fired up the engines and other systems came on line. Emil placed the targeting lens on his head and adjusted it to his eye. The targeting icon blinked to life as the forward cannons began to track his head movements.

"Here they come," said Kale looking toward the access door from the house.

Soldiers began to file through it with their weapons trained on the ship.

Emil activated one of the wing turrets which immediately tracked with the lens toward the soldiers. The cannon blazed to life with fast repeating laser blasts from the rotating barrel assembly, cutting the soldiers down in a moment.

"Let's get out of here," said Kale as he raised the ship off of the platform and began to move it toward the hangar opening ahead. A Vorn troop transport came into view ahead of them, trying to come into the garage bay.

"Shred it!"

"I'm on it!" said Emil as he activated the forward cannons.

Rapid laser fire filled the troop transport's cockpit causing it to burst outward. The transport dropped out of the way as Kale moved the *Whiplash* out of the garage bay and punched it—they sprang away from the area fast.

"Where do we go now?" asked Emil.

"We'll head for Wynn's and see if he knows where Father is and what's going on."

WYNN heard a familiar engine sound as the airbus continued to carry him toward the Soone home. He could see Tiet's ship blasting away from their home fast. The *Whiplash* came around hard and sailed by overhead as Wynn flailed his arms to flag them down. Apparently they did not see him.

The airbus brought him into view of the hill where the Soone home was and he could see smoke billowing off of a smoldering pile of wreckage just outside of the garage bay entrance. It appeared to be a troop transport or what was left of it. Must have got here too late, he thought.

It was likely that Tiet was coming to see if his home had come under attack as well. He needed to get back and meet up with him and find out if he knew what was going on.

Wynn sent a thought to open the bus door as he grabbed the ledge along the roof and swung down and inside. The driver looked surprised as Wynn adjusted his garments and produced a transit card to slide along the reader.

"Sir, this bus has been commandeered by the military," said the driver meekly.

"What?"

He turned to see a group of soldiers, both Vorn and Castillian, beginning to rise with their weapons drawn as they realized who he was.

"Oh, you've got to be kidding."

Laser flashes erupted between the soldiers and Wynn as he intercepted several blasts with his kemstick. With a thought he sent all of the soldiers crashing out through the airbus windows. They fell a hundred feet down to the pavement below the airway lanes; leaving only Wynn and the shocked bus driver onboard.

"Alright, turn this bus around and head back to these coordinates," said Wynn punching them into the driver's navigation system.

"Y-yes sir."

Wynn sat down in one of the chairs as the driver brought the large vehicle around and headed back toward his home.

DAOOTH waited as the intercom chimed for Teman's reply to his message.

"Yes?"

"Councilman, I was informed something has happened to Councilman Licoure; what's going on?!"

"Your king killed him. I told you he was no good, but you wouldn't listen. We'll be lucky if he's not already organized the Horva against us."

"That's absurd!"

"And yet Licoure is dead; killed with Tiet's own blade."

"I can't believe it, there must be another explanation."

"Believe it, Daooth. Estall has arrested him and put him into a special containment chamber. He's not going anywhere until he is tried by the council."

"When is that taking place?"

"The council will be meeting in emergency session in several hours to decide what action to take."

"May I be present at that meeting, sir?"

"If you want. But don't expect to sway our decision by your love for the man. We will have justice in the matter. Be at the council chamber in two hours; the meeting will be a closed session."

The transmission was cut by Teman before he could reply further. He immediately punched in the transmission code for Wynn's home. The screen returned a "No Reply" signal. That was odd. He knew that Wynn was supposed to be at home this evening and he hadn't said anything about Tiet's involvement in the murder when he had talked to him hours before. He tried the secure band that fed to Wynn's personal com-link.

ONBOARD the airbus, Wynn's com-link beeped at him from his collar pin.

"Wynn here."

"Wynn have you heard what's happened to Tiet?!"

"I know our troops have turned on us. I was just attacked by a full squad at my home."

"Councilman Teman told me that Tiet has killed High Councilman Licoure, but I don't believe it."

"Of course he didn't, but where is he now?"

"Teman said that Estall has arrested him and placed him in a special containment chamber of some sort, but I'm not sure where."

"I know where it is. But why did the council order the attack on me?"

"I'm not sure; Teman didn't mention anything about you at all. Something is happening, Wynn, something behind the scenes."

"When I was under attack I sensed what I believe was the presence of the symbiotic creature that inhabited the Baruk years ago. I wouldn't trust anyone at this point. Anyone associated with the council or Estall and the military should not be trusted; in fact I think we should meet up at Nagon-Toth until we can decide what to do."

"How could those things have survived? I thought we wiped out the Baruk?"

"I don't know; it just doesn't make any sense."

"I have a meeting with the council in two hours they say they're going to decide what to do with Tiet."

"Skip it. It's not safe to be around them now. It could be a trap. They know you are affiliated with Tiet. Just meet me at Grod's compound as soon as you can."

"Alright, Daooth out."

Wynn wasn't going to the detention facility now. He had no chance of breaking in or out of it with the military guarding Tiet and looking for him. He needed Grod's help. He had one device that could get them in and out without a problem.

"Driver, change course. I want you to head for the compound at Na-gon-Toth."

"But that's where the Horva are!"

"It wasn't a request," said Wynn leaning to the ear of the driver.

"Yes, sir."

XVII

THE *Whiplash* skimmed above the highest airway lane alone. It was only moments before they had reached the hill where Wynn's home was located. All that remained of it was a large heap of smoldering debris and one retaining wall. Kale could see the military presence all around it. They had already attacked, but they were still dispersed around the area like they were looking for something.

Kale hovered at a distance but the word must have already gone out to look for them. An armored carrier lifted off and was headed in their direction.

"What do we do?" asked Emil.

"What else, blow it out of the sky!"

Emil locked all guns and fired on the carrier. Sparks and fire billowed across its surface as it continued to come at them.

"It's still coming!!"

"Armor's too tough. Hold on!"

Kale brought the *Whiplash* around and fired the thrusters. The ship gunned away toward the city with the carrier lumbering on behind them. On the scanner several targets came into view.

"We've got company!"

Several faster ships took up pursuit as the *Whiplash* shot into the maze of tall skyscrapers. Kale buzzed around one of the buildings and full throttle came around on one of the pursuing ships. Emil took the initiative and blasted away at the military viper fighter, shredding its rear and midsection. The other three vipers reorganized and took up the pursuit again as the *Whiplash* spun away from the kill.

A symbyte controlled pilot locked on the *Whiplash* and fired a homing beacon. It attached to the hull undetected. Their orders were not to engage the ship, just place the homing beacon. The remaining fighters disengaged and the *Whiplash* burst away from the city toward the wilds beyond.

Normally it would have been a good place to hide with all of the huge trees and jungle area; it was easy to lose a ship in all of it. Most people were lucky to get out alive because of the vicious wildlife that dwelt there, including a large number of the feral Horva. But the tracking device would allow them to find that ship no matter where it went on the planet.

WHEN the airbus arrived at Nagon-Toth, Grod was already waiting on the platform.

"You might as well stay for a while," said Wynn to the driver.

He nodded nervously as he looked from Wynn to the gathering entourage of Horva on the platform.

The door opened and he descended to his old friend.

"My friend, Daooth has already briefed me on the situation with Tiet. I'm confident you have a rescue in mind, yes?"

"Absolutely. We'll need the best team you can put together,"

"Of course,"

"And we'll need to use the transgate to get inside the compound where Tiet is being held."

"At your disposal, anything you need to set him free," said Grod. "Daooth told me about some setup for murder."

"It's not so much about that, Grod. It's those symbiotic creatures that controlled the Baruk. They've survived somehow all this time since the war; apparently taking up host among our people. They're behind this plot. I was attacked at my home by scores of soldiers, some under their control and others who have been caught up in this plot unknowingly."

"What about Mirah and the boys?"

"I'm not sure yet, but I did see the *Whiplash* running and gunning toward the outskirts of the city, and Kale is the most likely to be flying it."

"You're probably right. We'll concentrate on the Tiet and hope for the best."

"Grod, the boys are well-trained, both of them. They'll be alright."

He smiled through the obvious worry he was feeling. "I'm sure you're right. Now let's get to work."

LUCIN walked into the monstrous hangar bay of the main city complex in the form of Estall. Assembled before him was a huge mass of symbyte-controlled soldiers and civilians; at least one hundred thousand of them; all under the influence of his angelic mind.

In all of the twelve cities, groups of symbyte-controlled soldiers and civilians from among both the Castillian and Vorn population were assembled. Lucin spoke to the assembled masses in every city through video feeds and satellite uplink.

"Now is the time. We are ready to ascend to complete power. It is time to assimilate all of those who are not part of my body. Arm yourselves and use stun on our prey if possible. Dead people are of no use to us. However if the warrior Wynn Gareth is found or any of the Horva who might come to his aid, they must be eliminated immediately. The special legion of warriors I have chosen will be with me as we follow the tracking signal and search the wilds for the boy, Kale Soone. Once we have him added to us we will be ready to move beyond this planet and conquer again. Our special envoy is to remain at the detention center guarding the king. He will serve as the bait to lure the Horva into a rescue attempt. Then we will end them. Go now and add to my body."

The legions in every city moved on command and prepared for the night of conquest to come. Every symbyte-controlled man, woman and child headed out into the cities armed for capture or kill. No one would be spared. All would be liberated from their miserable individual existences to the serenity and power of Lucin's collective body. What was taken from the Baruk would be restored more gloriously in these peoples and Lucin would rule again. The boy was the key. The people were obedient at this point but somewhat disconnected. Kale's powerful mind was what Lucin still needed to connect the people to one another and to him; then they would truly be one.

WYNN watched as the schematics for the detention center scrolled by, until he found the one he wanted. He motioned to the transgate technician to highlight one spot in particular.

"I think this would be a good location to get our team in," said Wynn. "It's a large hall that's behind most of the security barriers and should give us pretty easy access to the chamber where Tiet is being kept."

"What about going into the chamber itself?" asked the technician.

"If Tiet can't get out of there from the inside then we won't be able to either," said Grod. "What about the shield controls for the chamber?"

"We'll have access from the panel in this room," said Wynn as he pointed to a place on the schematic.

"Alright then, load up the destination and prepare to activate the gate."

Grod and Wynn left the console and returned to the jump area. The rest of the strike team was already assembled in the designated area on the chamber floor. There were twenty top notch warriors from among Grod's elite guard fully outfitted with plasma weapons, blasters, spicors and E.M. shields. The best of the best to rescue the one man they all still considered to be their king.

Wynn and Grod took up positions in the front as the transgate hummed to life. The technician locked the coordinates and punched the controls to establish the gateway. Before them, a wall of light snapped into place between the gate posts. The team all readied their weapons as the light faded and the destination came into view.

"Lets go get our king back!" shouted Grod to the team as he ran through the field with the others following.

WITHIN the assembly hall of the detention center at Baeth Periege a wall of light snapped into existence. The two guards looking on readied their weapons. Two kemsticks whirled out of the energy portal into the sym-byte guards before they could make a sound or fire a shot. The kemsticks flashed shut and then rebounded back to Wynn's thigh clips as he ran through the portal. The bodies fell as the team began to come through behind Wynn and Grod.

"Those were the only two guarding this room?" asked Grod.

"Apparently," replied Wynn. "We'll need to follow this walkway over here."

They moved through the door, which—surprisingly—opened up without any access code.

Wynn might have thought it odd if he hadn't been so intent on Tiet's rescue. He looked at the schematic on his wrist-bound display as they proceeded toward the control room and Tiet's holding chamber. They had designed the chamber to be impregnable and Wynn himself had been the candidate to test it out. He had never supposed they might actually imprison a Barudii inside of it.

When the last of the Horva soldiers had exited the assembly hall and the door had closed again, another door opened and a lone symbyte-controlled Vorn soldier entered the room. He briefly examined the trans-gate portal before him and then he reached to a small pack on his back and flipped the arming switch on the fusion bomb he carried, then he ran through the portal.

Within the transgate chamber at Nagon-Toth, a group of special commandos caught the target coming through the portal. The symbyte soldier could only make it a few feet within the chamber before he was cut down by the Horva. But it was enough.

The fusion bomb detonated as they continued to fire on the symbyte soldier. They never felt a thing.

Back within the assembly hall of the detention center, the transgate portal flashed then disappeared.

Wynn and Grod's team continued on toward the control room and encountered minimal resistance getting in. The chamber was completely sealed so that no one could see inside. On the control panel a video feed showed Tiet inside sitting on the floor within a containment field able to dampen the exerted neural energy of his Barudii kinesis.

Wynn punched in his own access code; it was denied as expected. Without further delay he concentrated on the physical controls to the chamber door and began to manipulate them mentally. In moments the locking mechanism gave way. He located the power conduits feeding into the wall of the chamber that controlled the containment field and sliced his blade through them.

Grod opened the chamber door as the field went down around Tiet. He was already up on his feet heading for the door when he spotted Grod. As he joined them in the control room, Wynn tossed him a pair of kemsticks.

"What took you so long?" he asked with a grin on his face.

"Sorry, I got caught up in a game of tag with the military," replied Wynn slyly. "I think the creature that was in control of the Baruk is responsible for all of this."

"Absolutely. Estall, or what used to be Estall, confronted me in the chamber. They set me up for murder to get a clear shot at Kale; they want to use his power for themselves."

"They've already been by your home; I saw the *Whiplash* gunning toward the outskirts of the city."

"It had to be Kale. I can track the ship's location," he said as he made his way to a control panel keyboard.

"You'd better hurry, the symbytes will no doubt have realized we are here by now," said Grod as he scanned the video displays monitoring the different hallways and rooms in the detention center. He couldn't spot anyone on the monitors; no one at all.

"I don't think it's a coincidence that these monitors are showing no one in the building but us. They've got to be nearby waiting to ambush us."

"I've got it; the *Whiplash* is currently in an area of the wilds."

"The boys' campsite?" asked Grod.

"I think that's a good guess. Let's go."

The group began to make their way cautiously back to the transgate portal. Several of the commando leaders took up the point position on the way back. At each open doorway they flashed three fingers skyward to signal a clear room or hall.

"I don't like this," said Grod over again. "It's a trap."

"Yeah, but all we have to do is get to the portal and it won't matter," said Wynn as they continued through the corridors.

Finally they reached the main assembly hall door and watched it open. The point man's fingers once again went skyward then he paused and looked at the other soldier next to him in disbelief then back to Grod.

"Sir, the portal is gone!" he whispered harshly.

"What!?"

Grod, Wynn and Tiet ran to the doorway and peered in. The portal was simply not there; no symbytes, no nothing.

"Grod, could they have blocked the portal somehow; jammed the transmission?" asked Tiet.

"I don't think so, but I'm not sure."

Then a sound rang overhead, like a speaker coming on somewhere.

"Hello, General Grod, I assume you have Tiet with you and perhaps even the clever Wynn Gareth? No matter, this is not a social call."

"It's that thing that's taken over Estall," said Tiet.

"You may have noticed that your escape route back to Nagon-Toth is missing. That is, Nagon-Toth is missing now. And in a few seconds you will join them. Where can you run when your world goes boom?"

"A bomb!" said Wynn and Tiet looking at each other.

"We'll never get out of here in time," said one of the soldiers.

"The chamber where they kept Tiet; is it strong enough?" asked Grod quickly.

"Only one way to find out."

LUCIN was still speaking through the voice of Estall, but they were too busy running to listen. On board his transport he watched the monitor and the group of soldiers that were running back out of the room. He reached for the control panel and keyed in a code for the device he had left in the detention center. It wasn't as powerful as what was sent through the portal to take out Nagon-Toth, but it would be sufficient to destroy the detention center. He pressed the button to detonate. The monitor went blank as he looked out the window at the jungle terrain of the wilds passing below. *That's one problem solved; now to find the boy.*

WHEN the door to the detention chamber opened again, the control room beyond was gone; only fire remained. As the team looked out of their hold, they could see that most of the buildings superstructure had been blown away by the bomb that had been planted; but they were still alive.

They emerged quickly and found a trail through the rubble and fiery debris. As they came beyond the building's perimeter it became apparent that the buildings around were damaged from the blast as well. Several of them looked structurally unsound.

They reformed their group as screams came to their ears. People were being attacked; maybe hundreds of them. The blast site was clear of people all around, but when the team rounded the corner of a nearby building they could see hundreds of people being stunned and attacked by thousands upon thousands of the symbyte-controlled citizens.

They stayed in the shadows watching as mobs of the creatures that had formerly been normal people ravaged through the streets attacking any non-symbyte they could find. Once they had someone, their hands burst into spiny tentacles that were plunged down the throats of their victims delivering the seed of the creature into its host. Tiet, Wynn and Grod watched in horror as the victims were left on the ground gasping only to rise again within minutes under the control of the beast within.

"There are too many to fight," said Grod.

"He's right," said Tiet, "We've got to withdraw. We need a ship to get to the wilds and help Mirah and the boys."

"Are you sure Mirah is with them?" asked Grod.

"I just sense it. They're safe for the moment but Kale must know he's being followed."

"We could probably make it to the West Quarter Hangar without too much trouble," suggested Wynn.

"Wait...look," said one of the team members.

When they looked behind their position they could see a young Castillian girl, probably no more than four years old, staring at them with a blank expression on her face from an alley way. She looked like she had been through a rough time and her clothes were tattered and torn with several blood stains visible.

"Come here, little girl," said one of the team members.

The little girl waited until a large group of symbytes were coming down the alley behind her.

"Come on, hurry!" shouted the team member again to the little girl.

Then the girl pointed her finger at the team and hissed loudly as the symbytes passed on by her and began to fire at the team.

"She's one of them!" shouted Grod as he began to fire his plasma weapon into the approaching crowd.

"They're coming from over here too!" said Tiet as he ignited a kemstick and began to repel incoming blaster fire.

"They're mentally linked to one another," said Wynn. "We've got to get out of here fast or they'll be on us from every direction!"

The group began to run as fast as they could toward the West Quarter Hangar almost a mile away from their position. They returned fire as they ran from the growing mob of symbytes. Some were armed and others, probably recently assimilated to the organism, were not. The blasters they were using were set to the maximum setting. They definitely weren't trying to capture and assimilate Tiet's team.

The Horva soldiers were returning fire using their plasma gloves. But the laser-fire coming from the symbytes was beginning to overwhelm the small team. Some of the Horva were shot and killed. As the team passed another alleyway, some of the Horva toward the rear were cut off as the symbytes poured out of the alley, attacking them.

"They're everywhere!" shouted Grod as blaster shots rang into his E.M. shield.

Tiet and Wynn rebounded incoming shots with their kemsticks and shielded themselves kinetically, but the onslaught was becoming more than they could handle. The sheer number of symbytes pursuing them was unbelievable. It appeared the whole city was now a part of these organisms.

Finally the hangar came into view, but the streets were filled with symbytes coming from all directions.

"We're cut off!!" shouted Wynn above the sounds of the mobs footsteps and gunfire.

"Into the building!!" shouted Tiet as he ran for the entrance to the building adjacent to the hangar complex.

"We'll be pinned in!" said Grod as he reluctantly followed.

"Too late for that now," said Wynn at his side.

Once inside, Tiet headed for the stairs and ran up as fast as he could with the others following.

"Where are we going?" asked one of the soldiers.

"The roof!" said Tiet from way up ahead.

Only ten people remained of their group now. The others were gunned down or torn apart by the symbyte mob. They encountered only minimal resistance on the way toward the roof. Those who came at them from within the mostly empty building were quickly dispatched by Tiet up ahead of the rest of the surviving team members.

When they reached the roof, Tiet was already at the western side looking out over the distance between them and the eastern launch platform of the hangar complex.

"We can make it!" shouted Tiet.

"Sure, we can, but what about the others?" said Wynn coming up beside him.

"We'll get to a ship and bring it back over here."

"Those things are already coming through the building after us. There isn't time; there must be another way," said Wynn.

"No! There is no other way," said Grod as he joined them.

"But, Grod, we—."

"No, my friend. This is the only way. Go! We'll do our best to hold our own here."

Wynn knew they were right. He clipped his kemstick and then he and Tiet took a short run to the ledge and jumped. They carried themselves across the entire expanse kinetically and soft landed on the eastern platform. Without stopping, they ran into the hangar area out of Grod's sight, as they went looking for a ship to take.

The building was tall but not very wide. It only had a few access doors to the roof and Grod stationed himself and the other Horva soldiers in positions to defend those exits. At least, he thought, they can only file through the doors a couple at a time.

Wynn and Tiet broke into the first sizeable troop transport they could find.

"I don't have the right access code," said Wynn as he punched the keys on the panel with frustration.

Tiet didn't answer. He turned to find him concentrating on the controls mentally. Wynn heard a beeping from the display and the engines fired up immediately.

"Excellent!"

"I had a good teacher," replied Tiet with a grin as he jumped into the pilot's seat and took over the controls.

The transport lifted off of the platform and headed for the bay entrance.

When the transport climbed to the level of the roof on the adjacent building they could see the remainder of the team blasting away furiously at the symbytes pouring through the roof access doors. As one person was being hit by the plasma weapons the others would jump through over top of them. The roof was quickly becoming overrun.

Tiet brought the transport down near the few team members who were left; five more had been overrun by symbytes and had been pummeled by the crowd or thrown over the side of the building to their deaths. Grod and the others ran for the transport with symbytes hot on their trail firing with blasters.

Wynn took the controls of the mounted gun turret through an access panel behind the pilot's chair and began to fire into the crowd of symbytes chasing after the Horva. He mowed them down as Grod and two others jumped into the transport.

Tiet wasted no time lifting away from the roof. Several of the symbytes tried to jump and cling onto the transport but they quickly fell off over the city as Tiet brought the engines to full power.

"We've got to get to the wilds before they catch Mirah and the boys," he said plotting the navigation data into the computer.

"I only hope we're in time," said Grod.

KALE adjusted the controls slightly to keep on course for the campsite that he and Emil had previously scouted out for their post trial outing. It was located deep in the wilds. They had relished the idea of a rigorous survival trip, but had never intended on this.

The *Whiplash* glided just above the massive treetops as the sun began to set. Electronic eyes watched from orbit above the planet. A skynet satellite locked onto the fast-moving target. The satellite network had been intended to help repel invaders, but was now under the control of the symbytes.

The satellite's laser focused to a tight beam as the guidance system compensated for the speed of the target. A precise pinpoint shot was needed to bring the ship down in a controllable fashion.

The satellite fired from the silence of space. Onboard the *Whiplash*, the fighter rocked with the blast that took out its engine cooling system.

"We've lost the coolant system, something hit us, but I can't find it on the scope."

"The temperature will go up fast if I don't bring her down. How far to the campsite?"

"We're still twenty minutes out."

"That's too far. I've got to find a place to land now."

"I'm scanning the terrain…I've got something…I'm loading the coordinates."

Kale changed his course to reflect the new landing zone on his display. Smoke billowed from the laser burn on the hull as the engine began to heat up rapidly. He slowed the speed and spotted the clearing among the massive trees as he began to land the ship before it exploded.

"Kale?! Kale?! What's going on, where are we?"

"Hold on, Mother, we're on landing approach."

He continued the landing and got the ship safely on the ground. Smoke still billowed out of the laser burn as the ship's engines powered down.

"The engine is still at critical temperature, Kale, we'd better hurry."

He popped the latch on the spare compartment and quickly helped his mother out of the space.

"Where are we?"

"Out in the wilds. We didn't know where else to go with the military conducting attacks on us and at Wynn's home."

"What about your father?"

"We don't know where he is."

Mirah looked worried, as if the worst may have happened to her husband.

"Mother, I know he's alive, with Wynn. I can sense it."

"Well, what now, have we been followed?"

"I think so. They shot us down somehow, but we never saw them. They have to know our location; it's only a matter of time before they find us. Our best chance is to set out on foot."

"On foot? In the wilds?"

"Wild animals are the least of our worries now."

"Could they track us on foot?" asked Emil.

"I don't know, but all the wildlife out here might just mask us enough to keep them guessing."

The engine compartment continued to smolder more and more, then the whole ship began to burn.

"We'd better get out of here before it explodes," said Emil.

"Let's go."

The trio gathered the gear they had available and headed out cautiously into the cover of the dense jungle foliage.

"SIR, we're picking up some burning wreckage approximately ten miles ahead west by southwest."

"Good, their ship is down, which means they'll be nearby on foot," said Lucin. "I want you to scan for any group of three human size life forms traveling away from us; it will be them. Then I want the transport, with our little *gift*, to swing in front of their heading and drop her one mile ahead in their path."

"Sir, the ship that the king took from the hangar has not been located yet."

"Once we have the boy, it won't matter anymore."

XVIII

GROD could not believe what he was seeing on the display. The image was pulled from one of the skynet satellites by Wynn. He still had access to the data, but the weapons systems were controlled by the symbytes now.

On the display was the site of his home at Nagon-Toth. The entire compound was now nothing more than smoldering rubble and layer upon layer of sand baked to glass. This explained what had happened to the transgate portal back at the detention center. Somehow they had planted a bomb there or sent one through the portal after they left it to rescue Tiet.

His people and his wife were all gone. Only the few of his Horva brothers with him in the ship survived now; and his son, he hoped.

"I'm so sorry, Grod," said Tiet sitting next to him.

He tried to offer consolation to his friend. Grod could not weep. Instead his grief welled into anger so powerful he found himself almost unable to sit still. He looked at his remaining two warriors, Jael and Merab, still sitting near the front of the transport; he would wait to share the demise of their people; wait until they reached the enemy on the ground. Then they would be free to unleash their fury upon these symbyte creatures without reservation.

Grod looked at Wynn through narrow eyes and he placed his hand upon the Horva general's shoulder.

"Soon my friend, soon you will have vengeance," he whispered.

They were the only words of comfort that could have been offered. Wynn was truly his friend and had been since the end of the Baruk war when he knew of the Horva rescue of Tiet and his late brother Kale. And he was right; he would take his vengeance soon upon these creatures. He thought of his son Emil and recovering him safely and it quieted his spirit somewhat.

The wilds were before them now. Tiet pressed the engines hard toward a destination only he could sense; toward his son. He knew the boy was alive; there was no doubt within him.

KALE and the others moved as quickly as possible through the dense vegetation. Emil took the point position and whacked away at the large undergrowth with a kemstick while Kale helped his mother along; she was still a little shaky from being stunned by the soldiers. Every so often they thought they heard the faint sound of engines then it would fade and be gone completely leaving only the sounds of the indigenous wildlife.

All manner of creatures, both deadly and benign, lived in the wilds and the boys knew very well the dangers they might have to face other than the military after them. They thought better than to share those possibilities with Mirah.

Emil was a good twenty feet ahead of them in the foliage which seemed to instantly replace the cut vegetation with more to bar their way.

"Kale! I've found something! Someone!" shouted Emil from up ahead.

They rushed ahead to where Emil was standing. Just beyond, half hidden in the bushes was a little girl of no more than four. She was staring at them with a terrified look on her face as though she might attempt to run at any moment.

"It's alright, Honey," said Mirah as she knelt to try and coax the child from her hiding place.

"Monsters, trying to get me," said the little girl through lips that quivered as though she were freezing out here in the hot jungle air.

"I know, Honey. We won't let any monsters get you. Come here, it's alright, you're safe now," consoled Mirah.

The girl eased herself out of the brush and began to walk toward Mirah. Kale scanned around trying to see if the soldiers were nearby or if he could hear any whining of their engines. The girl reached Mirah and then dodged around her and ran to Kale; jumping into his arms before he knew what was happening.

"Hold me, Mister," begged the girl as she trembled in his arms.

"Well," said Mirah with complete surprise and a little hurt motherly pride. "I guess she prefers you."

"What should I do?"

"Hold her."

Kale sensed something unusual about her but he could not place the feeling.

"What's your name?" asked Mirah.

"Monsters, chasing me; they took my father.... I ran away from the monsters."

"But, what's your name?" asked Kale.

"Don't let the monsters get me, Mister," said the girl trembling as she clung to his clothing.

"I won't let them get you."

"Kale, we need to keep moving," advised Emil.

"You're right."

"I'll take point again," said Emil as he reignited his kemstick and moved ahead of them into the undergrowth.

They followed with Kale still holding the little girl. Her arms were wrapped tight around his neck and her legs around his waist as they made their way behind Emil.

"SIR, our scans show they have taken the girl. The four of them are moving south of our position."

"Very good. Bring us ahead of them one mile...at this clearing here," said Lucin as he punched the info into his display. "We'll lay out our troops here and wait for them. We'll awaken the girl just before they reach the ambush."

"Yes, sir. I'm bringing us to the new coordinates."

GROD sat down next to Tiet as he piloted the stolen transport. Wynn stood behind him.

"Tiet, I have to speak to you," said Grod.

"What is it?"

"I think we have to consider what we're going to do if we can recover the boys."

"What do you mean?"

"Well, considering what we saw trying to get through the city, and if this has been happening in all the other cities…" said Wynn.

"We can't stay on this planet," finished Grod.

"What? But there might be a way to—"

"Tiet, its over," said Wynn.

They were sobering words to his ears and he couldn't reply. He had no words to confront the facts being forced on him now. He had ruled this society, this planet, for fifteen years, and it was all shattering to pieces around him. He had often thought of how far this brotherhood between the Vorn and Horva could go; of what could be achieved and how his rule would only be the beginning of the greatness that would be realized in the future for them.

And yet the undermining of it all had been building like a disease that grows silently unnoticed in the body until it is discovered too late to save the person's life. He had been living a fantasy all this time and it was time to wake up.

"Tiet, we thought we had beaten the Baruk but all this time those creatures have been continuing the war and we are beaten. We're beaten," said Wynn.

"We have to escape this planet," continued Grod.

"How. Where could we go?"

"I have an idea about that," said Grod. "When the Horva acquired the compound at Nagon-Toth from the Vorn military, we also stumbled upon a secret underground compound linked to it by a hidden tunnel from inside the compound. This is where we acquired the transgate portal from, but that's not all that was there."

They listened more intently now.

"There was a prototype transgate, only it was implanted in a ship. We never got around to testing the ship's ability to create and enter a portal, but according to the data we found in the chamber it had been done successfully; there were even a number of test planets and their coordinates left in the ship's computer. I think they might have been trying to prepare for conquering them, but we could escape to one of them and the symbytes would have no way of finding or following us."

Tiet thought about all that had happened in the last hours and his own wife and child still on the run. They were right and he knew it. He had no other ideas to offer in the situation.

"Let's do it. Once we have Mirah and the children we'll make a run for your ship."

Wynn and Grod looked relieved as though they thought he might not be willing to leave; as though he might not be willing to give up on all he had tried to build. The irony for Tiet was that Wynn had been the one who had nearly twisted his arm into accepting the council's proposal to ascend to his father's throne.

"Looks like we're entering the wilds," said Grod.

"I'll begin scanning for their life signatures," said Wynn. "It shouldn't take us long to pick them up and any ships that are in the area."

"Once we have their position," said Tiet. "We'll evacuate them and dust off as quickly as possible."

Wynn eyed Grod whose composure changed quickly at that suggestion, but Tiet was already aware of what the proposal meant for his old Horva friend.

"Grod, I know you want revenge, believe me I would like almost nothing more than to join you in that fight; nothing more that is except to save my wife and our children and hopefully get off of this rock with our lives. You and Wynn talked to me about a hopeless fight and you're right. Now our priority has to be saving them and getting away safely."

Grod looked at him and his anger softened when he thought of saving his son. Emil was all he had left; Tiet was right and he nodded his agreement.

"I've got the wreckage of the *Whiplash* on sensors."

"They crashed?"

"It looks like a controlled landing but the ships just sitting there smoldering. Something must have happened and they've left it to burn."

"Any other ships in the area?"

"I've got three military transports on the ground and…wait a minute…yes, I've got them. Four people are traveling toward the transports; I don't think they realize their heading into a trap."

"Alright then, let's get in there fast; ETA five minutes."

"WE'RE coming into a clearing, Kale!" shouted Emil from the brush ahead of them.

The girl had not let go of him since they found her, but her trembling had stopped. He turned to look at her face as she raised it from his shoulder. Suddenly he felt something; another presence was with them now. The girl's expression was strangely cold and blank, then she moved her hand almost faster than Kale could see and much too fast for him to react with her hanging around his neck. Her hand was over his mouth in a flash as she pulled herself up, putting her knees into his chest and her hand around the back of his neck to leverage her arm into his mouth.

Her strength was unbelievable for a girl her size. He was off balance before he knew it and her weight and effort forced him back to the ground. He could feel something more driving down his throat from her hand, like a slimy tentacle of some sort. He was strangling on the appendage and trying unsuccessfully to beat her off with his fists.

Despite his inability to scream for help, his mother was quick to respond. Mirah was beating and clawing at her, but the girl relentlessly remained fastened to her victim.

"Emil, help him! She's one of them!!"

Kale could see only cold blackness in her doll's eyes. She was killing him, he thought. He noticed Emil coming upon her with his ignited kemstick, but the little monster was faster than expected. Emil swiped at her, but she suddenly disengaged from Kale and rolled off of his body under the weapon's strike and sprang in one move over Emil's head to land on his shoulders.

He was caught off guard and the girl used his surprise to her advantage. She plowed her gnarled hand into his mouth as she pulled his jaw down with her other hand from behind him.

Now Emil was flailing with the girl on his back; her small legs were dug into his hips to brace her self. Emil dropped his weapon and Mirah grabbed it and swung at the girl. She disengaged her second attack under the threat and bounded away from him, landing on the trunk of a large tree nearby. She looked like an animal clinging to the tree.

Kale was on his feet as fast as he could recover with his own kemstick coming alive in his hand. The girl hissed then boldly launched herself at him. His vision was blurred a little as he tried to focus on her and clear his throat from the choking. She bounced off of the ground under his first strike then tumbled in the air over his head. His second strike guided by his kinetic senses struck the girl in mid air as she came down behind him. It was a clean strike; she didn't move again.

"Are you boys okay?" asked Mirah. "Let me get a bioscan."

"We don't have time," said Kale, "The soldiers are near—I can feel it. We've got to keep moving."

The group tried to compose themselves quickly and moved on their previous path, leaving the girl behind. They came into the clearing that Emil had spoken of and almost immediately Kale could sense the soldiers waiting for them on the other side of the open area.

"Wait."

"What's wrong?"

"I think we're walking into a trap here. They're waiting for us on the other side of the clearing. Let's move back into cover."

They turned to recover their position back in the brush. Immediately blaster fire erupted on their position. Emil noticed that the blasts were meant to stun only, as they bounced around the trees without charring the timber.

Soldiers began to move out of their cover into the clearing and close the space between them. There were at least fifty or sixty heading for them while laying down a steady rain of stunning laser fire. Emil and Kale blocked many of the stun blasts that were coming at their position as they retreated further into the cover of the vegetation.

Then they were hit from the rear by more laser fire. More soldiers could be seen closing on them from the trees.

"I'll take the rear!" said Kale, "Guard my mother!"

They were back to back around Mirah deflecting the stun blasts of the symbyte soldiers. Kale decided more action was needed. Soon the soldiers would be upon them. He moved away from his mother and Emil and took to the trees. A kinetic bubble, generated by his mind, formed around Mirah as he took off away from her.

He moved from branch to branch and tree to tree and quickly found his way above the soldiers. Kale swooped down into the enemy forces and began to bring his sticks into play against them. He hacked into the soldiers, taking down as many as possible as he deftly moved among them.

Their attack from the rear quickly began to disorganize as he slipped in and out of their ranks. Many of their own men were being taken down by crossfire in the confusion.

Emil was not having as much success in his efforts. The soldiers were almost completely across the clearing now and the fire was too concentrated for him to block it all. Several blasts got by his defense and brought him down hard.

The kinetic bubble was still in place around Mirah as the soldiers took the opportunity of Emil's unconsciousness and moved in on her. They blasted away in vain at the bubble, but Mirah could not move from the position to run either.

"WE'RE coming up on their position!"

Tiet brought the transport into a descent on the clearing just beyond the raging battle his family was involved in below.

"I've got two transports rising out of the trees ahead!" said Tiet.

"I'm on it; locking on targets."

Wynn brought the transport's missiles online as the targets began to clear the tops of the trees. He fired nearly every rocket the ship was carrying at the enemy transports.

As soon as they had cleared the treetops, the ships turned toward them to fire and were greeted by almost twenty high-powered rockets. The transports shattered to pieces before they could fire a shot and fell back to the ground much faster than they had risen.

Tiet continued his descent and landed the craft very roughly as he bolted for the door. Wynn and Grod quickly followed with Jael and Merab close behind. They all ran into the battle.

The symbyte soldiers now turned to fight them as they ran into the fray. Tiet and Wynn began to maneuver through the symbytes; cutting them down at every turn of their swords. Tiet could see Kale far off among a second group of soldiers, battling with them furiously; his dual sticks whirling about him like circles of death dealing light.

When he came upon Mirah she was under attack by several soldiers trying to penetrate a kinetic bubble being maintained by Kale's mind. Tiet quickly dispatched them and somewhere in the fight Kale sensed him there with his mother and released her from her protective imprisonment.

She immediately moved to Tiet's protection and he headed for the transport with her. Kale and Tiet spoke in mental sensations through the space between them and Kale disengaged the fight and took to the trees after his parents as they headed for the ship.

Grod already had Emil's unconscious body in his powerful arms and was heading back to the transport after them, as Wynn and the two Horva soldiers laid down cover fire and defense for them.

The main group made it to the transport safely, though still under fire, as Kale bounded through the treetops over the symbytes and came down into the clearing en route for the transport. Tiet was already lifting off with Kale in his mind, knowing that he could make the jump to safety without any problem, but something happened as he ran for the ship. Tiet could sense a complete loss of control in Kale's mind and waves of pain taking over his body. He looked back through the open troop deployment door to the field below in time to see his son fall.

No shot had hit him, but he was losing consciousness quickly. Kale could see the transport just ahead and above him, but he could not make his body respond to his desire to lift himself up to it. As his eyes closed he caught a faint glimpse of Wynn touching down next to him on the ground.

Tiet brought the blaster cannons to bear on the soldiers emerging from the trees as Wynn lifted Kale's body to his shoulder and made the leap under mental power to the transport.

"I've got him, Tiet! Let's go!"

He punched the engine throttle controls and the ship surged away from the battle. The computer on board signaled a warning. One of the Horva soldiers slipped into the chair and read the display's information.

"I'm showing an enemy ship following us from ten miles back, sir."

"Grod, are the coordinates plotted in the navigation system?"

"Yes, but that ship will know where the bunker is and lead the others there if we go now."

It won't matter as long as that ship can do what you say it can; we're leaving this rock."

LUCIN slammed his fist on the control panel, shutting off the negative report from the ground forces. The boy had gotten away, but he had still been infected by the girl.

It was very draining on his limited power to maintain collective control on so many human hosts. Controlling the whole population was necessary, but he needed the boy's powerful mind to control the entire body as one organism.

"Can we catch the ship?" asked Lucin.

"We're keeping up, sir, but they're flying the same thing we are. We can't overtake them until they stop somewhere."

"Can you pinpoint where they might be headed?"

"They're heading on a course that will bring them near the area of Nagon-Toth."

"That's it. They're heading to Grod's compound. They don't realize it's gone. Send all available ships and troops to Nagon-Toth."

"Yes, sir."

The boy was of the utmost importance, but he was fighting the takeover of his mind and body; Lucin could feel it. He hadn't thought of the possibility that the boy might be able to resist him. It hadn't been a problem before when the Three had been assimilated to control the Baruk, but the boy was much more powerful than they had been; all the better for his purposes.

WYNN piloted the ship while Tiet stayed at Kale's side as Mirah examined him. He was still unconscious. Mirah passed a hand-held medical scanner slowly over his body. The information fed to a portable display she had setting on the floor of the ship next to his head.

"What is it Mirah, what's wrong with him?" asked Tiet anxiously.

Tears welled in her eyes as she continued to pass the scanner. Any professionalism as a doctor was gone now as she saw the information pouring onto the display. This was happening to her baby; her only child.

"Mirah?"

"It's one of those things, like we found inside the bodies of the Baruk. It's taking over his neural pathways; winding its way around his brainstem and infiltrating his spine.

"Can you stop it?"

"I don't know anything I could do to remove it without killing him," she said through sobs.

"What about Emil?"

"That's just it. His scans aren't showing the same level of infiltration. Somehow his body is keeping it at bay; fighting the takeover and keeping it confined near the entry site. It might be something about being a Horva; I just can't pinpoint it right now with this limited equipment."

Grod was listening intently as Mirah spoke of his son. Emil was still unconscious but it appeared to be completely related to the stun blasts he had received in the battle.

Tiet knelt near his son and focused on him mentally, shutting out everything else. He could sense his pain now and more than the physical pain he could sense his mental anguish. The symbyte organism was fighting for control of his body; trying to push Kale's own mind out. He could hear his thoughts, as he cried out in the darkness of his unconscious mind.

Kale, I'm here.

Father?!

Kale, you must fight the symbyte's control.

It speaks to me, Father; I don't know how to stop it.

Concentrate, Son, you're more powerful than it is; use your power to fight its takeover of your body. You've got to focus and take control back before it can gain anymore ground.

I'll try…it's hurting me!

Fight it, Kale!!

It hurts!!

Kale's body began to spasm on the floor of the compartment. Mirah quickly looked for something in her medical kit to sedate him and suppress the spasms. She pulled a hypo from the bag and went for her son's arm. Tiet grabbed her and stopped the effort. "Wait, Mirah."

I'm trying, Father! It hurts, but I'm fighting it; are you still there?

I'm here, Son. I'll never leave you.

His body continued the spasming as Mirah watched helplessly wanting to intervene with her medical training, but knowing that something more mystical was happening between Tiet and Kale; something she had never quite been able to comprehend.

His trembling then began to quiet and his body became still. Within a few moments, with Mirah terribly concerned and recommencing her scanning, Kale began to breathe normally and his heart rate normalized. Then his eyes opened to everyone's relief.

Mirah fell on him kissing his cheek, as he turned to look at his father. Kale reached for Tiet's hand and grasped it tightly.

"Thanks," said Kale weakly.

Tiet only squeezed his son's hand tighter.

"What's going on?"

"It's still with me, Mother. I can't kill it." He looked at Tiet again. "I can't kill it."

Tiet squeezed his hand again. "We'll figure out something, Son, don't worry."

"Where are we going?"

"We're going to escape the planet; Grod has a way. Just rest, for now."

Kale laid his head back on the rolled up jacket that was serving as a pillow, while Mirah continued to conduct scans of the organism inhabiting his body. She knew it would be up to her to find a way of removing it; if there even was a way to remove it.

XIX

GROD paced the cabin compartment of the transport as they approached the area of Nagon-Toth. He had not informed his two remaining soldiers of the fate of their home or their families. Once they passed over a few more ridges the compound would be in sight.

He looked out the window through the front of the ship and saw a column of black smoke rising up beyond the farthest ridge ahead. His heart sank at the thought of his own wife and all of the families that had perished. His rage was kindled again, and he wanted nothing more at the moment than to be face to face with as many of those creatures as he might be able to put his lethal grip upon.

Grod looked at Emil, still unconscious, but apparently doing fine even with the symbyte in his body and Grod's emotions settled again on what was best for his future. He had to think responsibly about saving his son from the infestation of this planet. Then he looked again at his men and decided now was the time to let them in on the fate of their brethren.

"Jael, Merab…"

"Yes, sir," they said.

"I have something to tell you and it won't be easy for you to hear."

His men looked at him puzzled at what he was about to say to them. Wynn watched the exchange from the navigator/weapons console chair. He could see Grod trying to control his own anger and frustration as he told them what had happened to their fellow Horva and their wives and children.

He felt bad for him as a leader having to break that kind of news to his men. He could see the rage crossing over the faces of the soldiers as the realization of what had happened gripped them. They looked forward through the windshield of the ship and he followed their gaze to see the huge plume of black smoke rising above the area ahead where Nagon-Toth was supposed to be.

Jael rose to his feet and walked to the bulkhead across the compartment; he couldn't stand to hear anymore of it. Grod lowered his head as he sat before Merab who was still looking at the column of smoke in disbelief. Jael slammed a fist into the wall of the transport so hard Wynn was sure he must have broken several bones in his hand, but he did not cry out for pain.

"I want them dead!" said Merab from his seat.

"I know, Merab, but—"

"DEAD!!" he shouted.

Grod just looked at him. What could he say? He felt the same way and the only way he was controlling his own rage was his responsibility to his son, but their children were dead; they had nothing left.

Wynn continued to watch the two men as they fought to keep their control within the confines of the transport. The walls were closing in on them now as their rage grew.

Wynn found it a little difficult to empathize; he had never married. He was used to being alone and had grown to like it. The closest he had ever been to having a family was mentoring Tiet and continuing his training after the death of Orin Vale.

Then he thought about Kale lying back on the compartment floor with a symbyte fighting for control of his body and mind and it hit him. Kale had been his pupil with his father from the time he could walk and he loved him like a son. His reaction to almost losing him back at the clearing among the symbyte soldiers had been to immediately jump out of the transport, risking his own life, without a second thought, to save the boy. Kale was stable for the moment, but Wynn could understand now how much more terrible it must be for these men.

The transport finally sailed beyond the Korsov ridge and into view of Nagon-Toth. The entire basin was charred from the blast. The remains of the compound were nothing more than charred shrapnel and fiery debris on the basin floor. All of the Horva men were pressed to side viewing windows as they passed over the site.

The devastation was unbelievable. Wynn conducted a life scan quietly at his console even though he was sure what the result would be. The computer sounded an alert: "No life readouts within specified parameters."

Grod and his men turned at the voice. Wynn was embarrassed that the men had heard it. They all looked at him helplessly. The scan only punctuated the aching in their hearts at the sight of the smoldering ruins and lost family members.

Tiet began to bring the ship into a descent toward the impact crater beyond the sight of the compound. He recognized it as the same place where Kale's trials had been conducted. He looked back to Grod, "Is that it?"

He nodded back. "The entrance to the underground compound is in the southern wall of the crater. We'll land and get inside quickly."

"If the symbytes are tracking us…"

"They have to be," said Wynn.

"Then it won't take them long to get their forces here," said Tiet. "How fast can you get the ship ready to depart?"

"Prep for the ship and the transgate will take twenty minutes; the ship has never been out of the bunker. I also need a little time to set the detonation system for the bunker; I'm not leaving this planet without taking out as many of those things as I can."

"But, we'll have to wait for them to get into the bunker to do that," protested Mirah.

"Grod—" Tiet started and then thought better of protesting.

Grod stared into his eyes and he knew that the Horva general would not be persuaded otherwise. He glanced over at Wynn and could see a look of understanding on his face. It would be alright; a little close for comfort, but they would survive.

LUCIN pored over the data coming in from his forces as they made their way to the Nagon-Toth area. He had originally planned on assimilating the king, but the boy had youth to his credit and he had all but overwhelmed the two older Barudii during his trials.

Putting an Angelic seed into humans was not ideal; they were strong willed and difficult to control. But if such noble spiritual beings like his self were to be cursed to this disgusting physical prison, then mankind would suffer.

Why had God separated him from the other angels that rebelled? It wasn't fair, to be singled out; when they had at least been given forms that transitioned between physical and spiritual realms. They had rejected him after; even though he had been the greatest and brightest. God had done it; imprisoned him in this disgusting, putrid form for leading the others in the rebellion. He would have revenge; propagate his seed. Lucin would rise again.

One hundred squads of soldiers were currently en route to the destroyed Horva compound. There would be no escape for them now. He saw their coordinates to be near Nagon-Toth at the impact crater where the boy had conducted his trials. It didn't make sense; they were easy targets down inside the crater.

Lucin had quickly become accustomed to the human mind and one thing he had learned about a Barudii warrior was that he would not knowingly put himself in such a situation without a plan of action. The Barudii were very cunning warriors indeed; they had to realize that they were being tracked; the only conclusion was that they were planning some sort of trap.

TIET helped his son out of the transport and through the hidden door in the crater wall. Grod went ahead of the group powering up the lighting systems and leading them through the winding tunnel as they descended deep below the surface.

Merab and Jael remained at the transport ship; they had to set the first defense. Merab keyed through the command sequences in the transport's computer and set the fuel cells for a command detonation. He set the command frequency as Jael set the detonator frequency on his display. They completed the sequence adjustments and ran out of the transport to assume positions on the crater wall near the underground bunkers entrance.

The Horva soldiers carried large tripod mounted rapid fire blasters and set them up at their respective positions. They had plenty of rock for cover and would hopefully be able to take out a large number of the symbytes before retreating into the bunker themselves. The warriors were each looking forward to a lot of payback today, but now it was time to sit and wait.

When the rest of the group finally descended to the lowest level, Grod keyed in a code on the wall pad. The large metal doors unlocked themselves, like a huge vault, and the treasure inside was finally revealed to their eyes. Tiet and the others gazed into the large chamber beyond.

"My friends, I give you the *Equinox*," said Grod somewhat grandiosely.

The entire hangar bay lit up around the magnificent ship. It was a cruiser class ship by appearance, large enough for general housing quarters for twenty people and deep space travel.

"We don't have time for a formal tour, but if you will all get on board I'll prep the engines and the gate and we'll be on our way."

Tiet helped Kale into the ship with Mirah following close behind, while Wynn helped a recently conscious Emil into a harness behind the main cockpit area. Both of the boys looked like they were barely able to stay awake as their bodies fought against the parasites. Mirah stayed close to them, monitoring their vitals and the organisms struggling for control of their bodies. She could see a distinct difference between her son and Emil.

Something about his Horva physiology was causing the symbyte within to shrink in size. His body was fighting it and winning, but Kale was struggling just to keep the organism at bay by mental power alone.

Grod worked at the helm controls, bringing the engines online while Wynn and Tiet went after supplies and weapons that Grod had instructed them to retrieve. The engines came to life obediently and Grod soon passed by on his way back to the transgate compartment.

Once inside he followed the manual's instructions that appeared on the display and proceeded to prep the gate for the jump sequence. He set the target coordinates for the planet Kosiva. The planet itself was one visited before by the Vorn military scientists whom had either built or stolen the transgate technology.

It was reported on file as a hospitable planet with a peaceful, friendly and intelligent race. The Vorn military regime had apparently been surveying for future conquests; fortunately, they weren't around to fulfill those plans.

After the prep sequence was set and counting down toward jump readiness, Grod left the ship to set the bunker's self destruct control sequence so that he could trigger a timed delay from the ship's transmitter.

Wynn and Tiet made quick work of the supplies that Grod had requested and the bunker had an ample supply of weapons; and the best of all for the Barudii warriors was a cache of old Castillian weapons including several Barudii blades and kemsticks. They scooped them up quickly and loaded them onto the ship.

MERAB'S handheld scanner began to sound a warning. Ships were approaching. He took a moment to send a hand signal to Jael forty feet across the wall at his own position.

A swarm of troop transports sailed over the crater rim and descended to the crater floor near the stolen ship their group had used to get here. They remained crouched in their positions as the symbyte troops began to file out of their ships and surround the transport.

They scanned the ship in vain; the hulls materials were designed specifically to block such intrusions into the military vehicles. The soldiers began to approach the transport carefully and gained access quickly into the main compartment.

LUCIN looked on from his own transport as his troops made their way inside.

"Commander, did you find the boy?" asked Lucin over the com-link.

Suddenly the transport exploded in front of him in a massive concussion wave and fireball. It shattered the windshield in his transport, killing the pilot.

Lucin emerged quickly from his damaged transport's main troop compartment to find many of his symbyte soldiers lying dead on the ground around the blast site. Others were filing out of their own transport ships, weapons at the ready as a wave of pulse laser fire began to rain down upon them all.

Jael and Merab began to cut down as many of the enemy soldiers as they could with massive amounts of rapid pulse blaster fire from their respective perches in the crater wall.

The symbytes soon returned their fire and the rock around them began to crumble as hundreds of symbytes soldiers began to advance upon their positions. Realizing they couldn't do anymore out in the open, the two Horva quickly retreated under fire to the bunker entrance in plain view of the enemy. As they passed through the rock door they broke into a sprint downward toward the lower level that housed the *Equinox*; the symbytes followed quickly as expected.

"I want all the levels searched!" shouted Lucin, as the soldiers filed through the entrance, "Find the boy at all costs and kill the others!"

The bunker contained ten levels in all, housing various military and scientific technologies, along with living quarters. The symbyte soldiers dispersed at each level while the next group of symbytes proceeded to each successive level to continue the search.

Lucin proceeded downward toward the base level with a squad of his own. He tried to sense where the boy might be as he attempted to communicate with the organism within him. He was getting closer, he knew it; only a little further and the boy would be with them finally.

JAEL and Merab came running through the hangar bay's only door and proceeded up the loading ramp to the *Equinox*. They tossed their smoking guns to the compartment floor as they entered the flight chamber where the others were already strapped in waiting for them.

"Let's go! They're coming in right behind us!" shouted Merab as they found available flight chairs and strapped themselves in.

Grod activated the landing thrusters and brought the ship upward a little, hovering above the bay floor as he locked the final coordinates into the helm and started the transgate sequence.

A flood of symbyte soldiers came running into the bay with their weapons blazing. Pulse laser fire pounded into the hull with little effect as the soldiers tried to surround the vessel hovering above them.

A wall of light pierced the bay ahead of the ship. Grod tapped the command sequence for the bunker on the ship's transmitter panel.

"No!! Stop them!!" shouted Lucin as the large ship suddenly lurched forward into the transgate jump field. Another flash and the ship and its portal were gone from the hangar bay, leaving Lucin and his troops alone.

Lucin sank to his knees and pounded his fists into the pavement. Now what? He had lost the boy. How would he make the host bodies of one mind and body without a mentally powerful host?

As Lucin pondered the question, he suddenly noticed a voice coming over the intercom. It was counting, "three, two, one."

The symbyte soldiers within the bunker never knew what had hit them. The reactor core powering the underground facility erupted with such ferocity that most of the crater wall above collapsed inward upon the hundreds of symbyte soldiers and their transport ships that covered the crater floor. A portion of their military was destroyed in the last trap of the Barudii and Horva on planet Castai.

IT was a mild sunny day on Kosiva's Guniran province the day that his father, Wynn and General Grod left for negotiations with the Guniran council. Kale sat in the grass outside of the ship thinking about recent events as a cool breeze provided relief from the sunlight.

The Kosivans were a peaceful people, and highly intelligent though they purposely minimized overt technology in their lifestyle. The arrival of the *Equinox* on their planet had alarmed the population somewhat.

They weren't sure if the Castillians were to be trusted and they were familiar with the Vorn military which had visited them in the past. The Vorn had evidently left the impression of a coming invasion, but had not come back since their visit over thirty years ago.

The Council of Gunira province was now ready, after a month, to consider an alliance with the group on board the *Equinox* and his father and the others were to be gone into the main city for at least two days. Only his mother, Emil, Merab and Jael remained behind with him and the ship.

It had not been a good month for Kale. The symbyte within his body was constantly speaking in his mind; still trying to take over. He often had horrific dreams of murdering everyone on board the ship at the symbyte's command. Kale didn't sleep well anymore. He feared he might succumb to its influence while unconscious and actually perform the awful deed.

It had been a difficult decision for him to make, but he couldn't risk hurting his family and friends; he had to leave them to save them. His mother, as brilliant a doctor and scientist as she was, still had no answer as to how to remove or destroy the organism terrorizing him from within. And his body, unlike Emil's, was not able to fight it off. He could feel it getting stronger even while he struggled to maintain control.

His mother, Emil and the two Horva soldiers had gone to survey an area just north of the camp where the Guniran council had recently approved for the group to begin building a permanent facility for housing and other needs. The Gunirans would be providing the necessary materials, technology and labor as long as the talks today went as well as expected.

He was alone with the ship, claiming he didn't feel like making the trip today, and in his present condition they believed him. Kale breathed in another deep breath of the fresh air and stood up carrying a letter he had composed to his father and mother. He made his way back into the ship and headed back to the transgate control room.

He had spent the last week and a half, since making his decision to leave, studying the operations of the transgate by way of the ship's computer. He had found a suitable location, another planet that the Vorn military had apparently rejected because of the hostile inhabitants that controlled the planet. It would be the last place his family would look to find him. And if he ran into trouble it wouldn't be a peaceful people that suffered his wrath if he went out of control.

Kale laid the letter on the transgate console and tapped in his own preset jump sequence. Once the gate was ready, he activated it. A wall of light snapped into place in the room ahead of the console. The gate could jump the entire ship or a small group depending on the need.

He picked up his travel bag from the floor next to the console and hoisted the backpack of supplies up on his shoulder. He wore his Castillian army uniform loaded with weapons that would give him an advantage in the hostile environment, and in the other hand he carried more supplies. He tapped another key on the display that would begin a scrambling sequence on his jump point once he passed through the portal.

This was it. He looked around the room once more then whispered his goodbyes to his family and friends. He turned and walked through the portal into the world beyond. The transgate obeyed his preprogrammed command sequence and the portal snapped the jump gate closed after him—he was gone, without any way to return, but at least his family would be safe.

ABOUT THE AUTHOR

Rev. James Somers is the Assitant Pastor of Martindale Baptist church in Tennessee and also works as a Surgical Technologist, specializing in Neuro-Spine surgery...so you know he's smart! He is married and has five children...all boys. In addition to all of this, he plays the guitar, bass and drums.

The Chronicles of Soone: Heir to the King is his first published novel. Other writing credits include a short story, The Meeting, featured in The Writers Post Journal.

For more about James, feel free to visit his website at:
www.jamessomersonline.com.

His blog can be read at www.jamessomers.blogspot.com and can be reached at: tietsoone@yahoo.com

ALSO FROM
BREAKNECK BOOKS

Printed in the United States
65365LVS00006B/129